Res

The Rise of Letje

(The Commorancy — Book 4)

Al K. Line

Alkline.co.uk

Sign up for The Newsletter for news of the latest releases as well as flash sales at Alkline.co.uk

Commorancy: *a dwelling place or ordinary residence of a person. This residence is usually temporary and it is vacated after a given time.*

New Occupant

A new Queen sat upon her throne — she was not happy.

Letje, twenty two and dramatically changed since her first visit to The Commorancy, sat regally in The Room For Punishment and looked down on those before her. Her white ceremonial robes rustled as she shifted in irritation. The prisoners were dressed in plainer matching garb, their shaved heads bowed — their lives held in the slender fingers of the female oligarch.

The young dictator was far from pleased. She chose to show it.

Five years had passed since Letje had inherited The Commorancy, nowhere near enough time to fully understand its complexities. For that she would need many more years — which was fine; she had all the time in the world as far as she could tell.

On a small stand to her right, nestled by a red velvet cushion, sat a tortoise: Constantine Alexander III.

Friend, companion, the one constant in her life since the age of six. But this was no longer a simple tortoise, inside the carapace was the life essence of her father Yabis — still known as Constantine to save confusion.

To Letje's left stood a girl with silver hair, now fifteen years old: Arcene. A wild girl when Letje first encountered her, moving through her teenage years had not tempered either her carefree spirit or her curiosity.

Relaxing on the steps of the dais was a slender man of indeterminate age with dreadlocks so long they trailed around his body and down the steps to the floor below: Fasolt. Father of the now dead leader of The Eventuals: Varik. Once partner in the attack on The Commorancy he had been reborn when thrown into the sea, then done what he could to stop his son treading a path he felt he had steered him on. It was to no avail, and his son died because of it. He was naked apart from a small loincloth and a leather satchel slung over his shoulder — he looked bored.

On Letje's shoulder sat Bird. Already the scar tissue from countless landings and takeoffs had built up to a thickness that meant Letje no longer felt her friend's comings and goings. Talons as sharp as steel and twice as deadly were now a welcome sight.

Letje's forehead was still a little too broad, so she kept her hair long to cover it, and her lips may have been a touch too thick, her nose a little too angular. But she in no way tampered with her appearance as was often the case with those lucky enough to be Awoken. Soon after she had entered The Commorancy as the new ruler she had fully Awoken, meaning such body chemistry modifications were simple enough once you knew how. She had, however, begun the process of halting the aging of her body; cells would constantly renew and be as good as the last, keeping her forever a grown woman of twenty two but no older.

The dais was exactly as it had been when Marcus had sat on the throne in the very same Room — simple, yet designed to convey precisely the right amount of fear and awe. Bound to the plain shaker style chairs on the floor were two men, they were about to meet their deaths one way or another. Most took the path offered: seppuku — Commorancy style.

Five years, thought Letje. *It feels like a lifetime...*

Head in a Box

"Something's not right," said Letje, stopping dead in her tracks before turning back to where the confrontation took place.

"What is it? We should be going Letje. My son's Eventuals may be subdued, and I can't sense a threat, but it's best to be sure. My son..." Fasolt hung his head. He didn't know what to feel, but at the moment it was mostly a sense of blame — it had all been down to him. He had warped his child, been cruel, uncaring, dishing out countless acts of random violence to him, and now the result of the actions of the man he once was meant his son was laying in a field in the center of a ravaged city with his face stripped of flesh, his eyeballs eaten by eagles and the very future of humanity almost lost.

All because of him.

"It's not all your fault Fasolt, he could have changed, made things right. He didn't want to."

"It doesn't make it any easier though. Fasolt's head hung low, not because of the weight of his hair. "You, you can see my thoughts now? You are truly Awoken?"

"Yes," said Letje. "I can see so much. It hurts."

"It will for a while but it gets easier, or, well, you learn to accept it at any rate. Time for mourning later though, what do you sense? What's wrong?"

"The head. It's the head." Letje was frowning deeply, trying to figure out what it was about the head. She was struggling with too much, everything was happening all at once. Not only could she sense the beginnings of true Awakening, but the new responsibilities she had were already weighing heavily, not to mention the events just occurred.

She ran.

"Hold on to Arcene," she shouted, as she sprinted back toward the scene of battle, arms and legs pumping like well greased pistons. Something was coming back to her, a glimpse of ink that was only now registering on her overwhelmed mind.

They were still there, thousands of Eventuals, milling around, unsure of what to do, who to follow, how to act. Letje slowed, assuming a calm exterior while her emotions roiled inside her. She heard the fluttering of wings and whispered her thanks to Bird as he alighted on her shoulder — he knew her need and was happy to oblige.

A determined young woman with Bird perched on her shoulder, already self-pronounced leader of The

Commorancy, was obviously a force to be reckoned with. She marched up to the head of Marcus Wolfe and once more grabbed it by the hair. Sweat trickled down her back, sending shivers through her entire body, as Letje slowed to a casual stroll and swung the head in a gentle arc, as if blessing her congregation with every steady swing. She whistled tunelessly as she walked away.

Bird took to the wing, promising he would catch up with her soon, showing glimpses through The Noise of his family and his reasons for his treachery toward Varik. Letje broke into a gentle lope to distance herself once more from the confused Eventuals and only felt safe once back with Fasolt and Arcene.

"It's his head," pointed out Arcene, jabbing at it in case Letje had forgotten.

"I know," said Letje. "I just picked it up Arcene."

"Oh," said Arcene, rather dejected at obviously being little help. "What for?" Arcene brightened at the clever question. Fasolt stared eagerly at Letje, waiting for the answer.

"Let's get somewhere a little safer and then we can find out, okay?"

~~~

They went back to the house in the city — there was no way they would be able to travel further. Letje was half dead on her feet, too overwhelmed by it all to think past closing a door on the madness and sitting down. The head, she had to look at the head.

"Arcene! Stop poking it, it's gross." Letje pulled Arcene's inquisitive hands away from Marcus' head.

"It's only a head, he won't mind." Truth was Arcene was trying to overcome her fear the only way she knew how: confronting it head on, literally.

"So," said Fasolt, "what are we supposed to do now?"

They were sat at the table with Marcus' head in the center, his face peaceful as if he was happy to be finally in The Void.

"I saw something... in his mouth. I think it was a message, I'm not sure." Letje was trying to think back to what she had seen as Marcus' head rolled toward her and winked. A split second before that he had mouthed words meant for her alone, but it wasn't the words, it was the blue ink on his tongue. She hadn't even noticed it at the time.

"In his mouth?" Fasolt stared at the closed lips of Marcus, wondering what it could be.

"Yes. We need to open his mouth, look at his tongue."

Arcene was silent, squirming in her chair as if scrunching up would make her invisible. "Don't worry," said Letje, "I'm not going to make you do it."

"I'll do it," said Fasolt.

He leaned forward and pulled the head closer, leaving a visceral trail across the table. Then, as respectfully as possible, prized open the jaw. All three peered inside Marcus' mouth and sure enough there was some form of a tattoo on his tongue.

What does it say? asked Letje's father, who had been quiet since Marcus' death, allowing his daughter to slowly gain her composure and accept her new life without any imposition on his part. He felt he would be little use, occupying the body of a tortoise did have serious drawbacks after all.

I don't know, I can't read it, it's tiny.

Let me look, I may be some use for this.

Letje picked up her father and moved him close to Marcus' now locked open mouth. Yabis, with a little help from Constantine, the tortoise he occupied, craned his neck forward and pushed his head right into the open void. Yabis had been working hard to be the best possible tortoise that he could, so had been changing the body chemistry of his host as much as possible. His eyesight was one of the first things to be improved as before that it was relatively weak.

"What you doin'?" Arcene stared at Letje like she had gone mad.

"Daddy said he might be able to read it better, so he's having a look." Suddenly the complete insanity of the situation struck Letje. If an outsider were to be watching they would think she had seriously lost her mind — she was stuffing the head of a tortoise into the mouth of a severed head!

Okay, you can put me down now, said Yabis through The Noise.

Letje placed Constantine down gently.

Well?

It said 'Don't throw away. Give to son.'

"What does he mean by that?" said Fasolt out loud.

"What? What? It's not fair, what did it say on the tongue?"

"Ssh," warned Letje, "Give me a minute."

Are you sure Daddy? Absolutely sure that's exactly what it said?

I'm sure.

Okay, thanks. Let me tell Arcene before she pops.

"Arcene, it said 'Don't throw away. Give to son.' That's it."

"Do we have to cut the tongue out then?" Arcene squirmed in her chair. Letje was unsure if because it was gross or because the young girl wanted to actually see it happen.

Letje turned to Fasolt. "I think it means the whole head, do you?"

"Yes, that sounds more likely than to just keep a tongue. And I suppose it means we have to take it to his son. We can do it on the way, right?"

"Right. Now, how do you go about keeping a head from rotting and stinking while we travel all that way? Not to mention that I doubt he will be very pleased to see us now Marcus is dead and we are giving him a present of his head."

"We can put it in with Constantine," said Arcene chirpily.

Letje, do not dare put that head in with me.

Don't worry Daddy, I have an idea.

A Parting Gift

"We, um, have something for you," said Letje to Oliver, feeling ridiculous, extending her hands, offering up the large cool box.

Oliver stood quietly, staring. "He's dead isn't he? Both of him? I felt it, felt him pass."

"We only know about the Marcus that we met, and yes, he is dead. But I got the feeling the other one died, if he was really real? It all seemed a little far-fetched, and vague."

"Yes, well, it doesn't matter any more. I felt my father die, whether there were one or two of him, what he believed, at least at times, was there were two of him, that's what counts."

"Did you meet them both then?" asked Arcene, tact not a word she had ever come across.

"What? No, not at the same time. Although often his behavior meant there were obviously two of him, plus it was impossible to get changed that quickly and reappear otherwise. It doesn't matter, he's dead. And I was young, I don't remember it that well anyway."

"Hmm," mumbled Letje, sure there was an undertone of evasiveness.

"The box, the box." Arcene nudged Letje sharply in the ribs, excited to see what would happen next.

Letje patiently stared at Arcene until she calmed herself. "He... um, that is to say... Okay, let me try again. Here goes. Varik cut his head off before he too died, and I saw something, in his mouth. There was a tattoo, it said to not throw away the head and to give it to you. So here we are." Letje held out the container once more. This time Oliver took it.

He sighed deeply. "Even from beyond the grave he drags me back into his Commorancy business. But okay, I accept the head." He turned to go back inside, apparently in no mood for further conversation, or for guests.

"Hey, wait a minute. Don't you think we're owed an explanation?" Fasolt wasn't about to leave without understanding what was happening, it could be important — for all of them.

"Fine, I suppose you better come in. I believe I too am owed an explanation: for how my father died yet you three are alive and well." It was an accusation, but not one of them felt guilty — they had done their best. Not even failed in the end. Marcus had chosen.

~~~

"Sorry to be so blunt," said Fasolt, "but why would Marcus want you to have his head?"

Letje and Arcene leaned in close as Oliver began to speak. "Okay, I guess you deserve to know, and thanks for telling me what happened to him. We may have been estranged, but I did love him dearly. His life was simply too bizarre for me, far too crazy. You be careful Letje, be sure this is what you want. Once you take on something like The Commorancy it consumes you. It won't be easy to change your mind."

"I know, but I have my friends to help me out. I won't be alone."

"Good, that will help a little I suppose. Now, the head..."

~~~

After walking for miles the silence was finally broken by Arcene. "Right, everybody stop. I can't believe you haven't said anything yet. You aren't really believing that guy are you? Nobody would do that to their father's head would they?"

"That's why nobody has said anything, little one," replied Fasolt, who had been steadfastly trying to ignore the words of Marcus' son concerning instructions he had been left if the head did manage to make it back to him somehow.

"Marcus sure was strange, wasn't he?" Arcene remembered the day he told them what it was like to be him. She had thought of him almost as a god since then. Now she truly believed he must have been — only a god could be that mad.

"He sure was," said Letje. "I really hope Oliver doesn't get it done too quickly, it's going to be pretty weird having a stuffed head of Marcus in a glass box staring at me every time I go into The Orientation Room." Letje shuddered at the thought.

"Well, he said it would take a few months, he wants to do a good job. But really, who picks stuffing the heads of animals, or whole animals, and now his dad, as a hobby. Crazy. But then, it did used to be quite popular long ago."

"Well I've never heard of it before. What did he call it? Tacky Dermy?"

"Taxidermy," corrected Fasolt. "And Letje? You can always put a cloth over him or something, maybe turn him around."

"Can I? Can I Fasolt? I don't think he would like that one bit, would he?"

"No, I doubt very much that he would be impressed at all if you did that. But, you know, he's dead, isn't he?"

They carried on walking. There was a long way to go before they reached The Commorancy, and there was a final obstacle they had to confront — one that nobody was looking forward to after Letje had described it to Fasolt and Arcene.

Just Call Me Letje

Well, Marcus really is gone, for good now, thought Letje, as they spent yet another night in yet another isolated farmhouse. At least this one had functioning furniture and they had a nice roaring fire going, but it was the exception to the norm. Ever since they had left The Commorancy living had been mostly rough, and the threat of constant danger set her nerves on edge.

Too much had happened too soon.

People had come and gone from her life at a pace that felt truly hectic for someone who basically never encountered other human beings up until no longer than a few months previously. And Sy, the man she was going to call husband? Dead. Others too, or else gone, living their lives elsewhere now they had found their place in the world. Umeko with her husband, Stanley with that perfect house and garden with the lake that had been waiting for him to make it complete.

Why couldn't she have something like that? A place that called to her and would make her truly happy? Would she ever get that? She doubted it. The Commorancy wouldn't be like that, she knew. Look what it did to Marcus. Or did he do that to himself?

None of it mattered in the end, she would do it, become what she had to be. Meet her destiny head on and become... What? What would she become?

Even thinking about it scared her.

Bird nuzzled her ear gently, giving comfort before he took flight to go to his family. He could communicate with her and she knew that once his chick had fledged then he would move his family to The Commorancy, but for now he would have to stay with them at the source of Varik's religion of The Eventuals: The Sacellum. Letje understood, family was all important, but she looked forward to Bird living at her own new home, a place that now terrified and excited her in equal measure.

It wasn't merely the pressure that scared her, and that was huge, nor was it the unknown. It was what was happening to her that was making everything so much harder.

She was special.

This was something she understood now. Marcus and the others had said as much, hinted at potentials that were locked up inside her — well, now they were beginning to show themselves, and it was both unnerving and exhilarating.

She had a mini-Awakening when her father revealed himself to her, but it was the moment that

Marcus sacrificed himself to Varik and his head rolled toward her that she truly Awoke, became something more than she imagined possible. Everything opened up to her in ways that made the old her seem like nothing but a wisp of a person. Now the world was peeled back to reveal layer after countless impossible layer.

It was infinite in its complexity and she understood that the transformations going on inside were making her unique in a way similar to how Marcus had been. Something more, something beyond what most others became when they Awoke to their true potential, the gift that was the legacy of The Lethargy, the revelations imparted to a few people on the planet that had the potential to lead humanity beyond its current state and onward into something else. Something different.

Advanced.

Letje wasn't really sure. It didn't matter, there was a long way to go yet. Centuries, maybe more. Millennia? It didn't bear thinking about, such a life was truly terrifying and would surely lead to madness.

She had such a life to look forward to if she chose it, yet there was a choice. There was always a choice.

Growing up, Letje had thought of herself as a rather ordinary girl, albeit lucky enough to be Whole, but she no longer believed this to be the case. When Sy was amazed that she healed so quickly from an injury she thought it was normal, now she wondered what else she thought happened to everyone else when really it didn't at all? Almost everything now, she knew, as her real Awakening forced her to see the world with fresh insightful eyes.

Innocence was lost. Her childhood was over.

Letje was a woman now.

She had to be, no child could cope with the things she had seen, what she had to do.

Everything was new and strange, she wasn't sure how to handle it all.

Letje thought back to just a few weeks ago. Was that really all it was? Back when Arcene had asked Marcus what it was like to be him, and he had done his best to answer.

She understood now, the immensity of it enveloped her.

Already Letje felt her Awakening change for ever the way she saw the world. It was like cataracts were removed, allowing her to see clearly for the first time. The world revealed was infinite in its beauty and complexity. Life began to open to her in ways she could never find words to describe. Intricate, convoluted ways that made a mockery of any pre-Lethargy explanation for how the world worked.

She saw the way that everything relied on everything else, could even see the way a blade of grass was as important as a field. Letje witnessed firsthand the truth of what it was to be alive and part of an ecosystem that was impossibly complex yet totally meaningless in its scale at the same time.

There were horrifying glimpses of The Noise and The Void in their entirety, showing quite how irrelevant her life and that of the whole planet was in comparison to the vastness of the whole. It was only the slightest of insights as to what was possible once she developed and truly understood her Awakening, but already she knew more than most who had ever Awoken. Hers was no ordinary extended awareness, for her, as it had been for Marcus and a few others, absolutely anything was possible.

Anything.

She felt the responsibility try to crush her under its weight, for with such infinite potential came the knowledge that this was no common gift, this was what humanity may have someday hoped to aspire to if The Lethargy hadn't gone so horribly wrong. She understood now that it had been a cleansing of sorts, and those that had survived should have remained Whole, then Awoken. It hadn't worked out like that at all. The same way it had gone wrong for countless other civilizations over millions of years — only a few ever made it out the other side and became all that they could be.

Now it was her destiny to stem the flow of consciousness that wept into The Void and brought humanity closer to extinction every single day.

Letje felt a welcome puncturing of the skin as Bird settled on her shoulder.

"And I'm only seventeen," whispered Letje to her new friend.

Bird said nothing, just stared at her through eyes that had watched the pointless games of man for over three hundred years now.

Death Cometh

Letje looked like a bucket of blood had been poured over her head, Arcene wasn't looking much better, and Fasolt was as red as if he'd returned to the side of The Eventuals and taken The Ink.

The shanty town was deathly quiet, a fog had descended making whispers thick in the air. The dampness began to chill those that forgot to control their temperature via The Noise and poor Arcene began to shiver through the thin material she had worn the past few days as a short spell of unseasonably warm weather returned before winter took hold.

As they rounded the headland and the pitiful collection of makeshift homes came into sight there was no doubt that it was going to be even worse a return visit. Letje had given as much detail to her companions as she possibly could, but nothing could have prepared them, or her, for what they were confronted with. The wails of the maimed and dying met them even before the smell, then for a brief thankful spell the fog dulled the sounds and the sight was hidden from view.

Nothing could stop the stench though — it was a lot worse than Letje remembered. As they got closer the lingering after-effects of cruelty could be felt through The Noise, and Letje understood that The Eventuals had passed through just as she had done — they had wreaked bloody vengeance on those that had done nothing more wrong than once cared.

Those that lived and died in the pitiful place had once upon a time wanted nothing more than to be a part of The Commorancy, lost out in the haze, hidden by the sea mists that carried freezing droplets of fine spray and chilled to the bone those unable to control their temperature or lucky enough to have plenty of protection from the weather. Most that scavenged a life here had succumbed to The Lethargy or lost themselves in a dream-haze of wishing for salvation through acceptance to The Commorancy, their previous lives forgotten. All that remained was a mystical pull from the forces that had been at work for hundreds of years in The Commorancy.

People were drawn to the place, at first often unknowing as to the reason why. Then the lure of being so close took hold, and those that found themselves fighting over sheets of tin or planks of wood got lost in their desperation, finishing their pitiful lives in extreme unsanitary conditions of abject neglect.

That was in the past.

Now things were really bad. At least most had been put out of their misery, but The Eventuals had obviously been unconcerned about ensuring the purge they had instigated had been seen through to its bitter end — the streets were littered with not only the dead but the horribly mutilated and dying too.

As Letje and Fasolt made their way through the tortuous winding alleys and inexplicable switchbacks that were the only way to the top, they took turns either holding Arcene's hand or carrying her to shield her from the worst of the butchery, but eventually it was no use; Arcene bore witness to the worst that humans could do to others.

Beginning their trailing of Marcus and his group when they first made it to the mainland, Varik had directed his Eventuals to commence their pursuit from where they had disembarked. They had obviously taken great delight in slashing their way through the debilitated people they encountered.

The acolytes were hyped into a frenzy, and although normally Varik would not concern himself with killing those already being eaten away by The Lethargy, he felt it opportune to not only eliminate those that continued the blasphemy of life, but were obviously still in thrall of The Commorancy. It would be good for his church if they were allowed to run rampant, the more manic and geared up for fighting they were then the better chance there was that Marcus and his evacuees would be caught and dealt with.

It hadn't gone according to plan.

The Eventuals had merely sliced and diced their way down the steep hill, affronted by the stench and the depravities of those they encountered. It was an indignity to have to deal with such lowlifes and they had not taken care to deal with their quarry effectively.

Now it was left to Letje and Fasolt to clear up their mess.

It began right at the bottom of the hill they were about to climb.

~~~

"What are we going to do? Look at them all. Half of them are still alive — just."

"We must do what is right Letje, we must send them to The Void." Fasolt found it impossible to believe he was once a part of such inhumane acts, long ago even the instigator. To think his son could behave in such a way almost made him glad he was finally dead — almost.

"I've never killed anybody before, I don't think I can do it." Letje had seen more than enough bloodshed since first coming into contact with Marcus, but she had never been the one actually dealing out death. Now she was going to have little choice if they were to make it back onto the island — they couldn't leave the people to die in such ignominy.

"Do it via The Noise. Shut them down and send them to emptiness, it is the right thing to do." Fasolt turned to a man sitting on the ground in front of them, his arm a festering mess, his mind a confusion of hunger, despair and longing for an Awakening that would never be his.

"I can't, I don't know how. Not yet. Will you show me?" Letje would rather be able to do such a thing than to physically end their lives, but her lessons with Marcus had not been directed at such acts of violence.

"It will take some time Letje, and maybe it is not such a fine gift to have anyway." Fasolt withdrew from the mind of the man on the ground. Feeling empathy for people for the first time meant that it would be no easy task to enter their minds, feel their pain, then send them to The Void. Something he had never even thought about before now touched him deeply. He didn't think he would be able to cope with so many degraded mental states and do what had to be done. He pulled his knife instead and before the gangrenous man on the ground knew anything more about it his life was over, blood pumping from the fatal wound at his neck.

"Come, we will do this together. Arcene, you must not look, this is no way for a child to experience life."

"Okay Fasolt, I won't." Arcene clung to Letje, showing her age more than ever.

Letje stared down at her, the uncharacteristic silence and agreement to do as she was told a sure sign that Arcene was very scared, yet trying her best not to show her fear either.

They began their walk of death.

Most people were long dead, but many had been injured and left to die slowly. Physically unable to maintain shelters, scavenge effectively for food or scant supplies, meant that the once emaciated were now downright skeletal. To begin with many had been cared for by those only in the early grips of The Lethargy, but as time went on their patients were abandoned so the relatively still able-bodied could try to survive themselves.

Young and old littered the streets like nothing more than trash, gnawing on anything they could get their hands on, or simply waiting to die. The wounded were killed as efficiently as possible, Letje and Fasolt sending them to The Void with a swift stab or slice of their daggers.

Letje felt sick to her stomach, yet at the same time knew that she was doing the right thing. You couldn't leave people in pain to die of starvation, could you? But what about those merely with The Lethargy? Surely they shouldn't be left to wallow in their hopeless lives? They would not know themselves soon enough, many mostly lost to nothingness already. But was it her place? Was it the place of anybody to end the lives of those that would die?

Boundaries became blurred, she no longer knew what was right and what was wrong.

Who decided?

Who had the right to take it upon themselves to choose the time of death for somebody else?

It was an impossible situation, so Letje and Fasolt dispatched only those that were wounded or who were obviously totally incapable of caring for themselves and would be dead soon enough from starvation.

~~~

They sat at the entrance to the station, each one of them covered in the blood of human beings killed by Letje and Fasolt. Arcene's arms were stained dark from where she held tight to hands that shook because of the lives taken. There were smears all over her face where she had wiped away the tears, replaced with something worse. Her silver hair was tinted pink where she had pulled at it, dragging it over her face to block the mercy killings.

Fasolt was death personified, a naked, skinny man with haunted eyes.

Letje simply felt numb, oblivious to the gore of those she had killed, the numbers no longer meaning anything. It was already becoming nothing but a dream — somebody else had acted, not her, not her.

"It is done," said Fasolt.

"Yes, it is. Finally." Letje released her tight grip on Arcene's hand and smeared a bloody line across her forehead as she obsessively brushed her matted hair aside. She began to shake uncontrollably and her temperature began to plummet dramatically.

"Fasolt?"

"Yes Letje?"

"I think something's wrong, I feel funny."

Fasolt looked into her eyes, noting the onset of shock and spoke to her via The Noise, showing her how to raise her temperature, to shut down the parts of her mind that would drag her into oblivion if she didn't. Letje did as instructed, more of herself opening up through her newly Awoken state, until she got control back of herself, her body and mind.

"I hate The Eventuals. I really hate them Fasolt. Look what they have done. What they had us do."

"I know. And I am sorry, it is my fault, all my fault." Fasolt knew he could never begin to be forgiven for the acts of his son, a man who had once been a child and treated so badly that his view of the world became so warped that he wanted nothing more than to eradicate people from the planet in their entirety — nothing short of extinction would have made Varik happy. Now he was dead, just like so many others were. So many.

"I'm sorry," whispered Fasolt to Letje, to those he had mercy-killed, and to his son and to Marcus. Was that right? He wasn't really sure, he wasn't sure about much at the moment, apart from that he was probably the guiltiest man left alive on the planet.

The fog had lifted, showing the burned and smashed hovels, the bodies, and the few still alive roaming the putrid streets below. The sun mocked the death by peeking out from behind a cloud for an instant, shining its cool light low on the ocean, shimmering orange before the grayness returned and the air once again grew cool.

"Come, we should go. Show me how you got to the mainland, and maybe we can get clean before we go any further?"

"There were facilities in the tunnel, I'm sure," said Letje, trying to remember what she had seen in between blacking out — it felt like a lifetime ago when her father first revealed himself as the train came to a halt and the chase began.

You've been quiet.

I don't know what to say my dear. Apart from sorry.

It's not your fault Daddy, you didn't do anything wrong.

I know, but still, you are my daughter. You did the right thing though Letje, now you must forget about it.

I don't know that I ever will Daddy, such death, such hurt.

I know. This is the world we live in Letje. It is beautiful and it is terrible at the same time. Think of the good, forget the bad if you can.

I'll try.

Abracadabra

Letje, Arcene and Fasolt walked up the ridiculously large steps to The Commorancy's entrance. Her father was being carried carefully by Arcene, who had promised on her life that she would never ever drop him. Bird sat on Letje's shoulder, the fast healing slices to her skin already building up into a thick crisscross of scar tissue that would see her shoulder numb to feeling soon enough.

This was it, the return to The Commorancy as the new caretaker, owner, or ruler, Letje wasn't quite sure. Maybe all three? Maybe more?

Letje put all thought of the journey back to what she supposed she should now refer to as home out of her mind — she needed mental as well as physical distance from the ordeal for a while. So much had happened to her in the few short weeks since Marcus had died and Bird had eliminated Varik that she was still finding it hard to adjust.

Even something as simple as no longer needing to worry about clothing was still alien to her. Like Fasolt, she had corrected her body chemistry to keep herself at the ideal temperature, meaning clothes were now for modesty and pure indulgence rather than anything else. She had done it as Bird was very unhappy at not coming into contact with bare skin, so now she wore a tight black vest, exposing her arms and shoulders so her friend could connect to her more closely.

Her skin had always healed fast if she was injured, but with new-found skills since her true Awakening her body opened up to her in ways she hadn't imagined. The one thing she didn't do, however, was anything to stem the injuries caused by Bird. Much like Varik, she had decided that if Bird was to perch on her shoulder and touch her skin, then the scar tissue caused by his huge keratin talons would be a sign of her friendship and commitment. A gesture. One that had already seen her left shoulder become disfigured in only a few weeks. Now it was cut, ripped and healed countless times, the blood no longer flowing as often as his claws repeatedly opened up already scar tissue heavy skin.

Still, she rubbed at her arms as if the wind she felt was actually giving her goose-bumps, a reaction of habit rather than feeling.

The wind had built up as winter took hold of the United Kingdom, and out on the island, surrounded by the sea on all sides, strong eddies whirled, blowing the hair of them all wildly. Letje's, brown and long, apart from the fringe that reached a fraction below her eyebrows, flapped wildly about her face, the same as young Arcene's. Her silver locks twisted and turned and she repeatedly kept spitting out loose strands as they tried to find safety in her small mouth.

But this was nothing compared to the dangerous locks of Fasolt. His yards-long dreadlocks were picked up and snapped about in the air like living weapons, thick coils that could knock you unconscious or leave burns on your skin if you happened to be in their way. He repeatedly tried to contain them, but the strong wind kept pulling them away from him and he was getting some seriously uncomfortable looks from the two girls.

"Can't you put them in a bag or something?" asked Arcene, hurrying up the steps, shouting back at him as she ducked to avoid being smacked on the head by a coil of hair as thick as her wrist.

"I'm sorry little one, the wind keeps stealing my hair away from me. I will try to be careful."

Arcene scowled at him, then ran up the last few steps to join Letje outside the imposing entrance of their new home. The Commorancy.

The wind died down to nothing, not even a gentle breeze.

Letje heard Arcene join her, then Fasolt. "It's like Marcus can even control the weather from beyond the grave," said Letje, staring about suspiciously.

"Must be some kind of a force-field or something," noted Fasolt.

"Force-field? Did they even have them back before The Lethargy?" asked Letje.

"Well, no, at least I don't think so anyway." Fasolt dragged in his hair as he spoke, wrapping it in huge bundles on top of his head, throwing the rest over his shoulder.

"So how could Marcus have one? I thought that he basically built The Commorancy from technology available back then?"

"But who knows what secrets he uncovered? With nobody to stop him I would imagine there are many things that most people never heard of. Anyway, you've been inside, did it seem normal to you?"

Letje couldn't help but smile. "Haha, no, it was anything but normal. And the stories of what the others told me, well, their Rooms sounded like impossible things, crazy Rooms where all sorts of impossible things happened. And Sy said..." Letje trailed off, the thought of his death still bringing up too many confused emotions for her.

"Can I have a Room, can I? Can I?" shouted out an excited Arcene, jigging about and stepping forward to test if the front door was locked or not.

Letje reached out with lightning reflexes and grabbed Arcene's arm a split second before she touched the door.

"Ow, waddya doin'? I just wanna see if it's open or not." Arcene rubbed her arm and stared grumpily at Letje.

"Sorry Arcene, but you have to be careful. Marcus said under no circumstances to try to get in without using the key, and not to touch the door unless it was unlocked. It could be dangerous — probably is." Letje paused for a second, thinking. "This goes for everything inside as well. Until we know exactly how things work then don't go trying to open doors, pull levers or push buttons, okay?"

"Mmf," came an angry reply.

"What? What was that? I can't hear you," said Letje, cupping her ear with her hand.

"I said okay, alright. Jeez."

"Good, now shall we go inside?"

"Yes, yes. C'mon, open it, open it."

Letje pulled the cord from around her neck, the key dangling unobtrusively on the end. She stepped forward to the impossibly huge door, above which the words THE COMMORANCY were carved in letters higher than a human being. It was grandness on an epic scale.

Letje, careful not to touch the door itself, slotted the key into the tiny keyhole and turned.

Snick.

They waited.

Thump. Thump thump thump.

Kreeen.

The door opened inward. Letje stared at it suspiciously, the *kreeen* very much sounding like somebody doing an impression of a door opening on rusty hinges. *It wouldn't surprise me,* thought Letje. Thinking back to the way the door to The Orientation Room went *whoosh*.

They stepped inside.

~~~

"I believe Marcus must have been quite mad," said Fasolt, as the door slammed shut behind them.

Letje nodded in agreement, wincing slightly as Bird took flight, soaring high up into the cavernous interior. He perched high up on an ornate beam, carved with intricate abstract patterns. Letje wondered where it had all come from.

"Arcene. Arcene! Don't run off, stay close until we know where we're going. If you get lost in here you may never find us again. And don't touch anything." Arcene skipped about happily, peeking into alcoves, pulling aside thick drapes, jumping up on tip-toe to peer closely at all kinds of bizarre objects set into the walls or on strange pieces of furniture.

None of it was anywhere near as interesting as the vast collection of bizarre and mostly unfathomably dangerous looking contraptions that were placed all around the huge foyer, a Room that Letje no doubt had been titled in Marcus' usual idiosyncratic way.

Probably something like The Foyer Room For Failed Contraptions, or something like that, mused Letje, looking from one strange thing to another.

Letje supposed she should begin at the beginning, so turned back to the door and followed along the wall to the right, trying to take things in with a clear head, to get her bearings and begin to make sense of what was to be her home for... who knew how long? For ever?

Fasolt followed her gaze and walked up to a small brass plaque screwed neatly to the bare stone wall. "The Foyer Room For Pointless Machines," read Fasolt, peering at the perfectly neat etched script. "Well, that's kind of apt I suppose, assuming the machines are pointless, of course."

Letje smiled at the name, liking it, memories of Marcus and his obsession with clothes and somehow managing to capitalize words as he spoke them flashing through her head, only to be suddenly replaced with an image of herself holding his head high in the air, staring down thousands of Eventuals as Bird and his mate ripped the flesh off of Varik's face.

"Ugh. Come on, let's see what's next. Arcene, do not touch that lever." Arcene paused, hand about to descend on a tantalizingly inviting pale blue lever with a shiny gold knob on the top. "Not even a little bit," warned Letje, knowing her young friend only to well.

"Fine," sulked Arcene, lowering her arm. "I hope you're not going to be like this all the time. Boring." She skipped off to poke at the next machine, all cogs and chains with some kind of seat made out of something that looked like an upside down umbrella made of very sharp knives.

"It's art," said Fasolt, as they walked past the towering menaces, many so high they almost touched the rafters.

Bird flapped noisily from one perch to the next, calling to them with a loud *screeee* from further down the vast hall. It echoed on and on, reverberating around The Commorancy. Once home to Marcus Wolfe, oligarch supreme, now dead, its new owners unknowing of exactly how many people currently resided in their Rooms — Awakening to their true potentials or at this very moment wondering if they would ever get out with their lives.

"Where's the kitchen?" shouted Arcene, running after Bird and then stopping to peer at a three meter high statue of fat-nosed creature that let out a loud 'Boo' as she put a hand out to touch the dusty fur.

Letje had the feeling that she was gong to need a lie down, and soon.

Big Innit'

"Well, how's it going?" Letje smiled down at Arcene, sat on the floor in Room0, otherwise known as The Orientation Room.

Arcene straightened herself, backbones cricking as she looked up from the massive leather-bound book that weighed too much to sit it in her lap. "How's it going?" she scowled at Letje, then gave The Book such a foul look it would have burst into flames to escape her wrath if it had any sense at all. "It's going the same way it's been going since I started reading these damn books three years ago, that's how it's going."

Letje smiled, all too aware of the impossible task of ever coming to a true understanding of The Commorancy. The Book, as it was called, was far from merely a single tome. There were seventeen of them, each one larger than the last, thousands and thousands of wafer-thin pages with every rule, regulation and way of doing things carefully noted down, each job listed, daily chores directed. How things worked, what to do, what not to do, what Rooms were where, what Rooms never did what they were supposed to, how to perform Orientation, how to oil the gears in The Room For The Moving Of Rooms, and even how to deal with those that found themselves tied to a chair with razor-sharp wire in The Room For Punishment.

It was all laid out, everything to do with The Commorancy from how the plants were watered, how the whole thing worked, to what to do when you really couldn't face doing the necessary research on another potential occupant of one of The Rooms — it mostly involved either going down dark holes and screaming, or hanging high in the air and praying you didn't fall to your death.

Letje thought back to the first days of her new life. It seemed like lifetimes ago now, not only a few years. How things had changed, how she had changed, and she was still unsure whether or not it had been the best gift a person had ever received or her absolute worst nightmare.

~~~

"Where's the map?" asked Arcene, peering over Letje's shoulder at The Book. It had been sat in pride of place in The Orientation Room, on a plain bleached oak desk that apparently could be swapped for any number of other desks, as the whole Room could be changed to suit any whim or fancy that took you. Marcus usually changed it to match his clothes. How it worked Letje had no idea as of yet, but The Book promised to hold all the answers, if the first pages were to be believed.

Letje flicked through the huge book, there were no pictures, no maps. "There isn't one. Just instructions, rules, guides and what to do and what not to do. Oh, and there are a few more after this one." Letje pointed to the book-lined wall and sighed.

"That's going to take you years," pointed out Arcene gleefully.

"Don't get too happy about it. Soon enough you'll have to read them too if you're going to stay here. I'm not doing all the work on my own." Letje's smile widened as Arcene's faded. Then Arcene's face lit up again.

"Ha, I can't read, so there."

"Well, that's the first job then, isn't it?"

"I will teach you," said Fasolt, "it won't take long."

The three people peered down at the imposing stenciled brown leather cover as Letje slammed the book shut with a thud, curiosity mingled with apprehension — as yet they simply didn't know what to expect. Constantine sat on the desk idly munching a lettuce leaf, pleased that for once his tortoise form meant he wouldn't have to get involved.

"Well, I guess we should start at the beginning," said Letje. "Let's see what Marcus had to say, shall we?" There were nods of agreement and eager faces as Letje opened the book once again and three pairs of inquiring eyes read from the first page.

This is the last page of The Book, although, obviously, if you are reading this then for you it is the first page. There was little point writing an introduction until I knew what this Book would contain, and unfortunately for you it has ended up containing rather a lot. But all of it needs reading, The Commorancy is a complicated beast, and has grown more complex over the years. As I sit here, writing this introduction, I find it almost impossible to fathom quite how it got to be quite as large and significant as it has, but what else is there?

Letje, this is no easy task you undertake, and if you do ever decide that this life is not for you then it is of the utmost importance that you know without any shadow of a doubt that there is a suitable replacement. And if that is the case then be sure to rip out this page and replace it with your own introduction. Yes, I know it is you reading this, there is nobody else who could take on such a responsibility and hope to make my work carry on functioning as successfully as it has. People need hope and they need something to believe in, but more than that they need a place to Awaken to their true selves, and although there is much for you to learn I know that if you are reading this then you will have Awoken yourself. Ever since I first met you I knew that you were the one, somebody extremely special, just as I was. But enough of this chatter, let's get down to business shall we?

This Book, or collection of books, holds the complete guide to the way The Commorancy must be run. You may find much of it bizarre, convoluted and rather eccentric, and I hold my hand up to rather enjoying the quirky nature of some of the methods, but it is all here for a purpose. There must be rituals, there must be tales and legends, and there must be a deeply embedded mythology for the remnants of humanity to believe in. It goes beyond mere hope, The Commorancy is all there is for many people, the one thing between despair and a chance of salvation.

The Eventuals will have been mostly dealt with, I have no doubt, but it doesn't mean that there won't be problems, interferences, maybe even a new leader and a resurgence, but I doubt it, and I'm sure you are more than capable of dealing with any problems that arise, especially now that you find yourself in such good company. Say hello to everyone for me.

Well, I won't bore you any longer, there is much to learn, much to do, and thank you for doing this Letje, I know how hard it is.

Oh, and this is Marcus writing this, the one that stayed behind, so I guess I don't really know you as well as the other Marcus, although I feel like I do.

Marcus Wolfe.

"There really were two of him, weren't there?" asked Arcene, still not quite believing such a thing was possible.

"I guess so. But if it was the other Marcus that wrote this then it means that he knew... Oh, I can't think about it, it all gets too confusing."

"So, what shall we do first then?" asked Arcene, hopping about excitedly, itching to explore the countless Rooms she had heard so much about.

"Maybe find a Room each for our bedrooms? That sounds about perfect right now."

"Oh," said Arcene, deflated. "I thought that maybe we could share, you know, for the company."

Letje was going to have to be careful how she acted, she realized, it was all too easy to forget quite how young and innocent Arcene actually was under the brave facade she tried to maintain. "Of course, that's what I meant," smiled Letje.

The Dangerous Room

"Well, this doesn't look like it's anything I will be using any time soon. How the hell did he even get up there?" Letje stared up the post, it must have been a third of a mile high. Atop it there appeared to be some kind of small clear platform. What on earth he had built such a thing for she had no idea. Marcus also seemed to have a real thing for dramatic lighting. She had already found a rope that disappeared upward into darkness; she assumed it went as high as the platform.

And the rock face, lit with countless directional lights to show up every tiny nook and cranny, that was something she definitely didn't think she would ever be climbing.

~~~

Things changed.

Letje began to understand.

Initially, as she wandered around The Commorancy, some of the Rooms seemed downright daft, others too strange to even contemplate. She had found Rooms where meticulous records were kept, ledgers so thick it would take years to read. And that was only for lists of Rooms with their names, how they worked, countless minutiae, and on and on it went. She called this Room The Very Dangerous Room, re-naming it close to Marcus' naming, but not quite. It really was very dangerous.

But that was five years ago, things were very different now, and Letje had become accustomed to The Commorancy. It was like a friend, one you were constantly discovering new things about. She came to love The Very Dangerous Room, and she used it on a very regular basis.

It's Bionical

"Arcene, what on earth are you doing?"

"Dum. Dum. Dum."

Fssst.

"What? I found it, can I keep it? Look." Arcene crouched down then jumped into the air.

"Be careful!"

"Ow. Ow, ow, ow. My head." Arcene lifted an arm and scratched, or at least tried to scratch, her head. The thick gloves with rods and cables wrapping over her hand made such delicate actions rather difficult. "I need more practice I think. But how cool is this anyway? There are loads more, lots of different ones. Wanna go?"

"You need to be careful with what you find, you can't just go around putting... well, whatever that is, on. What if it was some kind of torture device? Is looks like one. What is it?"

"It's bionical, that's what the Room was called anyway." Arcene frowned in concentration for a moment. "Bionic, that's it. It was in The Bionics Room.

Lots of things, you can put some on. I found this one that was for young girls, must be for it to fit me."

Letje walked over to Arcene and studied the strange contraption she had attached to her body. She had on some kind of large backpack with thick struts running from it down her legs, attached to a pair of very strange looking shoes. Countless other bits and pieces ran around her thighs, over her knees — everywhere. The upper body section ran around her chest, over her arms to her fingers and right up to her neck. There were various cables and all manner of extremely complicated joints that were obviously there to allow complete flexibility.

Letje couldn't help herself, "How does it work then?"

"Not sure really, but I don't actually do anything. The Bionical does it all. I think about moving and it starts whirring and then my legs are moving but without me actually walking. Same with the arms. Brilliant eh? Look, I'm going totally limp, ready?"

Letje reached out in horror, not wanting Arcene to fall flat on her face with so much weight attached to her. She needn't have worried. There was a strange *fssst* and the contraption seemed to take on a life of its own. The legs locked straight, the arms bent slightly at the fake elbow, and Arcene's back went rigid.

"See, told you," said Arcene, smiling like she had definitely proved a very important point.

"Wow. You be careful though, how does it do it?"

"Dunno, but it's really cool. It feels funny but I've been practicing for an hour and you get used to it. But there are loads of buttons, and I've only tried a few. Look, there are all these on the front as well." Arcene pointed to the breastplate, full of various colored buttons, each with a tiny symbol on it. Letje peered closely at the breastplate, reading the writing running along the top of the matte black material.

"BiCorps Inc. MonkSol Prototype M376."

"What's it mean?"

"Who knows? I'm just glad you haven't pressed any more buttons though. It could do anything. Good job there's a cover on the buttons." Letje stared at the clear plastic, noting the tiny keyhole near the bottom that kept it secure. Whatever the machine was, Arcene could get into all kinds of trouble, especially as it was some kind of a prototype.

"Oh that. I found the key but you don't need it anyway, look." Arcene moved a pneumatic assisted arm and flipped open the clear lid. "See," she said proudly, "it's not locked."

"Please, be caref—"

Psst, choom. Psst.

"Uh-oh, I don't think I should have done that." Arcene stared at Letje, moving her finger from the yellow button she had 'accidentally' pressed. Mechanical arms unfolded from the backpack and swiveled around to the front. A tinny voice came from somewhere on the breastplate, a mechanical voice that sounded completely bored.

Monkey Soldier Prototype M376 is now armed and live. Person detected, please state friend or foe.

"What did you do? What did you press?"

"I'm sorry, I'm sorry. I pressed the yellow one, look."

"Don't press it again! Oh my god, it's a soldier, or something to turn monkeys into soldiers anyway. Arcene, get it off, now." Letje ran to the back to see how to unstrap the thing from Arcene, but she turned before Letje could even manage more than a cursory glance at the contraption.

"What are you doing? I need to get you out."

"It wasn't me, the bionical turned on its own. Um, I don't think it likes you Letje." Arcene's eyes widened as her arms raised and the mechanical arms pointed straight at Letje — there were mean looking weapons in the strange grip of the fake arms.

Please state if this is friend or foe, failure to comply will result in termination of the unverified entity.

"What do I do? What do I do? I don't like it Letje, turn it off, turn it off." Arcene began to cry as the arms extended further. Letje backed away into the corner.

Arcene followed her.

"Tell it I'm a friend. Say friend. Just keep calm."

"Right, okay. Friend. Letje is a friend. Is it working?"

"I'm not sure." Letje stared in horror as a thick pistol rose, a red laser bead pointing squarely between her eyes that she could feel even though she couldn't see.

Repeat please. Friend or foe?

"Friend. Friend, friend friend."

Thank you. Standing down.

Letje drew a deep breath and Arcene had the good grace to look embarrassed. "I don't like this Letje, I want to take it off now. I think bionicals are a bad thing, they're no fun at all."

"It's okay, we'll get it off. How did you put it on?"

"Well, there was the thing standing there and I walked into a sort of big box where it was standing and walked around the back then stepped forward and it sort of wrapped around. Then I did up this bit here at the waist," said Arcene, pointing at a thick buckle. "Then I sort of... I'm not sure. I guess I clicked things and strapped things and eventually I found how it fit together. Maybe if I press this one? See, it's got a little picture of the suit on, maybe it undoes itself."

Letje could hardly believe it when Arcene pressed a black button this time. It was easy to forget she was a ten year old and not quite up to speed with what was sensible or not. Too late, Letje yelled, "Don't press another button."

It was no good, the machine started moving again, but at least this time there were no weapons produced.

Fosh. Fosh, fosh fosh. Fosh fosh fosh fosh.

"Letje, help, it's moving, it's getting faster. I don't know how to stop it."

The contraption with Arcene trapped inside picked up speed and marched out of the door, getting faster, and faster, and faster still.

"Don't worry, I'm right behind you. But do not, under any circumstances, press any more buttons."

Arcene was already far down the hallway, but Letje just about made out a pitiful, "Okay, but please stop it, I don't want to play anymore."

~~~

Letje was out of breath as she came to a dead stop banging into the rear of Arcene in her crazed contraption. It was banging repeatedly into the door jamb of The Bionics Room. Arcene was wailing pitifully for the thing to stop, but it was no use, it had a life of its own.

"Okay, I'm here now. Has it done anything else?"

"No, it just keeps banging into the wall and saying 'unable to connect with docking station', but I don't know what that is. Do something!" screamed Arcene.

"Okay, it must want to go back where you got it from or something. That's probably the button you pressed. You haven't pressed another one have you?"

"No, I can't. My arms are pinned, I think it's slowing down. My legs feel funny Letje, and it's hurting my chest too, it's getting tighter. Help me. Please."

Letje thought for a moment, wondering how best to approach the crazed thing, then it came to her. She barged into its left hand side and it took a step to the right to steady itself. It made a strange high-pitched *beep, beep, beeeeep*, then marched stiffly but very slowly into the Room. With no time to look around at the madness that surrounded her, Letje ran forward to where it was heading, toward a closed large glass tank built into the far wall. There were others too, lots of them.

"Is this where it came from?"

"Yes, I got it from there."

"Right, how do you open the door? Quick, before it reaches it."

"The big orange button on the side, I pressed that."

Letje pressed the button and the clear door slid aside the same time as the machine reached it. It was now going painfully slow, but managed to get inside. A series of clamps came out of the walls and connected with the backpack as the floor spun and Arcene was now facing forward looking at Letje.

Docking complete. Recharging fuel cells now. Disengaging.

"Phew!"

Snick. Snick, snick, snick.

Arcene fell backwards away from the machine, landing on the floor with a bump just as it was hoisted off the ground. Arcene got up fast and ran out of the tank. She slammed her hand onto the orange button and the clear door closed behind her.

"You little monkey," sighed Letje. "Are you alright?"

Arcene smiled mischievously, holding out a hand to Letje. "What's a monkey? What do you think the other things do?"

"I think it's best we don't find out. Please stop going into Rooms and getting into so much trouble, it's too stressful."

"Well, it's your fault anyway," pouted Arcene. "You're the one that gave me and Fasolt permission so we can see how to open the doors and let our handprints work when we put them in the shiny bits that show up. So there."

"Yes, well, I think we may just have to change that if you can't behave, hadn't we? Don't you know how dangerous it is to play with things you don't know about?"

"Spoilsport." Arcene poked her tongue out at Letje, but it was obvious the young girl had got a real scare. Letje really would have to see about how to change permissions for Arcene so she couldn't simply open any door she wanted to. This hadn't been the first time she had got into trouble playing with things she shouldn't have, and Letje was sure it wouldn't be the last.

"Come on, let's go have lunch," said Letje, ruffling Arcene's hair.

"Yippee, can I use the Michael Wave? It's so cool that you get your food hot so quick, it beats waiting for a fire to get going any day."

"Fine, but promise you won't put any more raw eggs in there, it took me days to clean that up."

"Promise," said Arcene, saluting smartly and skipping off out the door.

I'll be glad when she's a bit older. This is exhausting, never mind all the Commorancy work that needs to be done.

Letje took one last look into the Room full of bizarre mechanized humanoid machines then closed the door behind her.

Another One?

"The Appendix Book For The Book," read Letje, not quite believing Marcus had really titled the index such a mouthful. "Marcus really did like to give things their full titles didn't he?"

Letje, no need to talk out loud, I keep telling you, said Constantine/Yabis.

"I know Daddy, but sometimes I really like to talk out loud to you rather than through The Noise. You know, like we used to?"

I understand, I only wish I could do the same. But never mind, at least we can have a conversation, that's the main thing, right?

"Absolutely. Now, let's see if Marcus left an entry for self-doubt. I really don't think I'm up for running The Commorancy, it's too huge, too complicated. How am I supposed to deal with all the people? I don't even know what to do, what to say. I'm seventeen and some of these people are going to be hundreds of years old when they come out, they'll think I'm only a silly little child." Letje had been getting more and more overwhelmed and panicked in the few weeks since she had arrived, her initial reading of The Book making it more and more apparent that The Commorancy was even more complex than she had thought.

There was a lot expected of her, and a lot she didn't understand in the slightest even after reading Marcus' entries on it. She still had no idea how quantum levitation worked. However much she read about the Meissner effect, and magnetic flux pinning, it simply wouldn't make any sense. Just because she read how certain Rooms or whole buildings managed to effortlessly move about in ridiculously complex and seemingly random pattens based on the now long-dead technology didn't make her understand it any easier. She couldn't fathom where Marcus had learned so much.

Stay calm, you'll be fine, we will work it out together. Oh, and all that? Just think of it as magnets and special tracks.

"Daddy, no offense or anything, but you are a tortoise you know? You won't be much help when it comes to moving furniture or making Rooms for guests." Letje tried not to pout in a teenage sulk, reminding herself she was expected to be an adult now.

No, she was an adult, and a very powerful woman who saw the amassed Eventuals bow on their knees as she held aloft the head of Marcus with blood dripping down her arm and Bird sat... She shook, trying to forget, trying to focus back on the matter at hand. How was she going to run such a complex place?

Point taken my dear, now let's see what we can find out.

Letje flicked through the pages of The Appendix until she found what she was looking for. There were multiple Books and pages listed for self-doubt, so even looking it up was going to be a chore in itself.

It's okay, you get the books down and I'll read them to you.

"Thanks. But this is crazy. Marcus had three hundred years to write this 'Book', how can I possibly understand it all enough to make this work?"

You simply start at the beginning and read, you'll get there in the end.

Letje sighed. She was getting a serious headache even thinking about more reading. She felt like it was almost all she had done since she arrived. "Yeah, and maybe in three hundred years I will get to the end of it," she muttered, dragging huge leather bound books off the shelves and plonking them down harder than necessary on the well polished desk. "And that's another thing, how did he find the time to clean? There must be something in one of these books about that. Everything's all shiny, it would take you all your time just to go around with a cloth and wax and keep everything looking nice. There must be a cheat somehow." Letje flicked her head to move her hair from her eyes and grabbed pen and pad. "Right, I'm going to start a list of things I want to look up. At least that way I can learn what I think I need to as we go on, and gradually read The Book from the beginning as I have the time."

That's the spirit. Now, open a Book to the first mention of self-doubt, and let's see what Marcus had to say about it. He must have felt just as overwhelmed as you do, and lots of times. He didn't have anyone helping him did he?

"He had himself, but I'm not even thinking about that, it gives me the creeps. I keep expecting him to pop his head around a corner and say he is the original Marcus or something." Letje shuddered, dreading the day she came across a Room where Marcus had somehow managed to make a copy of himself, thinking she would enter a space and find inanimate clones of Marcus lining a wall, waiting to be activated somehow and resume control of The Commorancy. She balked at the thought, unable to stop thinking about how he could have done such a thing. Or was he simply mad? Was there never another one of him at all? No, there had to be, otherwise how could he have done what he did?

Letje? Letje, you're daydreaming again, come on, let's get this done then we can move on once you know you aren't the only one doubting their abilities.

"Sorry, I was just thinking."

No time for thinking, let's get reading.

Letje looked at The Appendix again to check the page number and opened the first Book, finding a chapter in which Marcus talked about his self-doubt concerning running The Commorancy a few short months after he began accepting guests. She propped the Book up on the stand and sat Constantine on his plush red cushion. She had found it the first day and her father said it felt lovely even through his thick tortoise skin.

He began to read. And read, and read, and read.

"That's enough," said Letje, slamming the seventh book shut and rubbing the top of her head furiously, tangling her long hair and looking like she had just now got out of bed. "I think my brain is actually going to explode all over the carpet if I hear another word."

See, said her father, *at least we know now that he had his doubts too. I guess he had a lot of them, and wrote a lot of them down. His guide to The Commorancy is more half confessional, part guide and part diary, it really is going to take forever to get through it all. But no matter, now you know, he was uncertain about lots of things, but he did it anyway and grew more confident the more guests he welcomed, the more Rooms he designed for them, and the more people that left having Awoken and gone back out into the world. You can do that, easy.*

Letje smiled at her father, grateful for the encouragement. "I can, can't I? I'm Letje, oligarch of The Commorancy, the only hope for humanity. I can do it." Letje frowned, she hadn't convinced herself one bit that she was up to the task, but maybe if she repeated it enough times it would sound true at some point.

~~~

Marcus' entries had been intriguing to say the least, and when Letje had time to think about what her father had read out to her she found that it did actually help quite a lot.

It was clear from what she had read of The Book so far, and certainly from the chapters containing references to self-doubt, that Marcus had been an incredibly powerful man, impossibly so, but he still had serious concerns about what he was doing. From the way he had used those with The Lethargy against their will, to concerns over using some very cutting edge and dangerous technology, to strange hints at hidden things where whole pages and random paragraphs had been scrawled out to hide what he obviously didn't want anyone, even her, to know.

As The Commorancy evolved over the years so Marcus got more and more lost in his own fanciful world, and his eccentricities were not lost on him. He sometimes reveled in them, other times seriously doubted his own sanity and his ability to do anything to help others. But he kept on, slowly gaining an understanding of the fact that nobody was perfect and a part of being human was to have flaws and be grown up enough to admit it.

Contained within the chapters Letje's father read to her via The Noise were hints and glimpses behind the facade of both the man and the myth. Those entries written in the quiet times, when thoughts spiraled out of control, showed quite how fallible he truly was. Yet he had written it all down for others to read, so they too would understand that it was perfectly normal to be unsure of their abilities to run such a complex machine, which The Commorancy was at its heart — so much was automated once you found out how to get things going.

Above all else Letje understood that her fears were not unique, Marcus had them too, but carried on regardless, sure in the knowledge it was all worth it if people could be helped, saved from missing out on what The Lethargy had brought with it for a lucky few: the chance to Awaken.

Otaku 2.0

Arcene had heard of Letje's adventures before they met up at her home, and was always intrigued by what she had been told about Calvin. His life-story had been related by Marcus to Letje, and from Letje to Arcene. She couldn't help but be curious. Arcene had grown up to be a girl that never had the ability to read comic books, play computer games or get lost in the magical worlds that can be opened to a child that reads.

When she very first met Letje and was shown comics, or what Letje referred to as graphic novels, she had been eager to not only look at the pictures but to understand the story contained within the pages. Well, at the age of thirteen she was now proud of her ability to read well, even if it had been infuriating to have to be spoken to like a little child and put in hours of practice most days to slowly unravel the mysteries contained within the squiggles.

Combined with her surprising — to her and everyone else — and amazingly quick grasp of anything to do with numbers and data organization, it made her pester Letje even more about Calvin and his obsession with fantasy worlds and computer technology — she wanted to be an Otaku too.

After months of nagging and a search of the archives, Letje finally relented and allowed Arcene to occupy Calvin's old Room. It was still exactly as he had left it.

Arcene went to be an Otaku for two months.

Commorancy Rules applied.

~~~

"Don't forget The Rules, okay?" said Letje sternly, already worrying about Arcene's safety. She was extremely impetuous and following Commorancy Rules for her Room meant there was danger if she broke them.

"I won't. C'mon, c'mon, I wanna see inside." Arcene was hopping about from one foot to another as she always did when she got excited.

"Well, I've seen it and I don't know what all the fuss is about. I still don't know why you would want to mess with such things."

"Duh, because it's cool, that's why. You're lucky, you got to read and look at comics all the time when you were younger, and you had a computer. You even said yourself that you watched movies when you found them. Well I didn't do any of that, don't do any of that, as I never got the chance, but now I can, so I want to. I wanna watch old movies and read weird books and play all kinds of games and do stuff that all kids of my age used to do before The Lethargy, and Calvin was alive right when The Lethargy began so his Room is going to be the best one to experience all that in."

"Okay, okay, fine. You have told me all that before you know? You wouldn't be here otherwise. Just don't leave until your time is up, and no trying to come back out of this door, you know The Rules."

Arcene sighed deeply. "I know. Now, gimme, gimme. Where's my key?"

Letje produced a dull looking key from her pocket and handed it over to Arcene. Arcene went to put it into the keyhole immediately, hands shaking with excitement.

"Um, what do we say?"

"Huh? Oh, thank you Letje."

"You're welcome. See you in a couple of months. Be good," warned Letje.

"I will. And thanks. Love you lots." With that Arcene was gone, the door clanging shut behind her before Letje could say another word.

"Love you too," said Letje to the closed door, before she wandered off nervously. As she made her way back to The Orientation Room she wondered if it had been the right decision. Arcene was such a manic child that having to stay put in one Room for months was going to either see her change considerably or else she would be a nightmare and would be screaming for release after a couple of days.

Although Arcene didn't know it, Letje had disabled the usual devices at the entry and exit doors so Arcene could leave whenever she wanted. She wondered if Arcene would try to get out. Hopefully not, as she knew The Rules and knew that if she tried the handles she would be killed — such simple yet deadly deterrents were there for a reason when Marcus implemented them. The tradition had continued, even though life was more precious than ever before.

Or maybe she'll emerge all grown up and her spontaneity will be cured somewhat. Letje didn't know if that was a good thing or a bad thing, only time would tell.

~~~

"Oh boy, this is gonna be so great." Arcene ran over to the nearest shelving unit that stretched off into the distance. There must have been ten thousand movies running along the shelves. More. Arcene ran her hand along the cases, picking one out at random then placing it back when she didn't like the look of it. She walked along slowly, reading the names on the cases, head angled sideways, a crick in her neck starting already. "Cowboy Bebop," she read, picking the third collection. Minutes later she was engrossed as she watched Ed and Ein on an adventure that seemed to involve water melons, magic mushrooms, and a man carrying around an empty coffin. Six hours later she emerged from her anime-fest and realized half a day had gone without her even exploring the rest of the Room first.

With mad ideas of living in a spaceship and wondering where she could get an outfit like Faye's — the anime's anti-heroine — from, she took a proper look around what was to be her home for the next two months.

The space was vast, impossibly so. Arcene knew many of the secrets of The Commorancy by now but it never ceased to amaze her quite how incredible it all was. And the stuff, so much of it. Collection after collection of just about everything to do with life before The Lethargy ruined it all, yet her Room was as nothing compared to the quantity of things Marcus had amassed. Through his Book Arcene had come to understand that he saw it as a time capsule as much as anything else; a place to securely store major achievements from human history. It was why architectural salvage had been just as important as social, scientific and even the collecting, cataloging and storing of clothes. It all made up a whole that reflected life before The Lethargy put a halt to man's endeavors. Marcus wanted to be sure that it was all saved for what would hopefully be countless future generations that would be starting again from almost nothing.

Arcene put such thoughts aside and focused on her surroundings — there was a lot to take in.

Not only were there stacks of movies but no end of comics, graphic novels and fantasy books, and that was only the start. The computer games were a revelation. She had played a few since she first arrived at The Commorancy, but the number of games available to her now was truly mind-boggling. From role-playing to straight out shoot-em-ups, she lost herself in countless adventures for weeks on end. She even found Space Invaders, a reminder of the interactive version she had played in that strange Room in the city when Marcus had still been alive.

Days were spent immersed in games, from the most old-fashioned, although still modern to her, to crazy ones where she sat in chairs, strapped herself in and went along for a bonkers interactive ride. They all amazed and astonished her in equal measure.

Arcene had gone through her youngest years in a mire of drudgery and sorrow, there was no technology for her, or any interests at all really away from simply surviving. Such luxuries as idling away time having fun were alien to her. There had always been things to do. Even at The Commorancy it was the same: always busy, always stuff to do or places to go. This was a revelation.

To have the luxury of knowing she didn't have to be anywhere, do anything, have a routine or make sure so and so chore was done — it was liberating. Arcene felt like she was actually having a childhood for the first time — condensed down into no more than a few short months.

Was this what it used to be like for all kids? No responsibilities? Nobody telling you to do things, or having to do things just to survive? No worrying about keeping warm and dry, hoping you would have something to eat the next day? A proper childhood free of worry, no need to put a brave face on and make sure nobody thought of you as just a little girl? Letje had told her stories, ones she herself had been told, about what it used to be like, but they paled in comparison to what Fasolt had told her of times long ago. He had been there, had lived through the last days of civilization before life changed forever.

It all seemed impossible.

Time spent alone in such a Room, surrounded by what were everyday leisure activities for huge numbers of the global population, made her re-evaluate the truth of his tales. He wasn't making it all up, was the conclusion she finally came to.

People really did just sit in rooms and play, for no other reason than for the sheer enjoyment of it — nothing more.

How liberating, how cool was this? Lazing around, reading, playing games, watching anime, picking movies and seeing how people used to dress, the funny way they spoke, the bizarre way they did things. It was like a condensed history lesson of everything that had been lost.

Brilliant!

~~~

Arcene was bored out of her mind.

How could people have lived like this? It was all so completely and utterly pointless. Reading was boring, games ended up all being the same, and what was with all those people in the movies, didn't they have anything better to do? Arcene resented the lives people had in the past. As far as she could tell it was mostly all utterly wasted. Did everyone really actually sit around watching TV and playing games all the time? Didn't they go mad with boredom? It all blurred into one extended movie or game in the end, the differences so small that she couldn't believe people had actively sought out such mindless 'entertainment' at all.

Stupid.

~~~

Arcene slammed the door shut behind her and stared accusingly at the EXIT sign.

"Stupid Room. Ugh."

Breathing deeply Arcene saw Letje approaching down the corridor.

"Well, how was it?"

"Boring, really boring. Anything need doing? Have you coped without me?"

"Well, now that you come to mention it I am having a few problems understanding the data from some applications, those stupid charts don't make any sense at all. Think you could take a look at them?"

"Oh yeah, you betcha. What's for supper?"

First Orientation

Letje was unbelievably nervous, she knew it even though she had rather aggressively altered her chemistry to slow herself down so she wouldn't be a gibbering wreck when she performed her first ever Orientation.

Time had passed so quickly she couldn't believe it. Had it already been over a year since she first turned the key in the front door? So much had happened since then, so much to understand, so much to marvel over, so much to mistrust. It still all seemed like some kind of cosmic joke — The Commorancy was impossibly complex and much of it was impossible to decipher.

Yet it all worked, mostly flawlessly. Yet inescapably the things that went wrong added up to a lot of work plus a lot of head scratching. She didn't know what she would have done if she didn't have Fasolt, and yes, even Arcene to help. The young girl was a real handful and always getting into mischief, but she was settling down a little and Letje was sure that over time she would be just as much a part of things as she was.

Arcene had actually been very helpful already. Getting the Room prepared for their first new arrival had been very difficult, but by following The Rules and the order in which things were to be done they had successfully made the Room ready for what should be their first guest — as long as he passed Orientation successfully. The work that had gone before should mean it was a fairly straightforward affair, but in The Book Marcus had warned that this was not always the case. Sometimes he refused guests for no other reason than they didn't feel right somehow, or he merely didn't like them once he met them in person.

Letje sat behind the desk in The Orientation Room, nervous yet excited at the same time. Picking an outfit had been tough — the extensive clothes collection was limited as most of The Room For Clothes was for Marcus personally. Outfits for guests only took up a tiny but still substantial portion of the whole. She had settled on something that would make an impression, something bold and youthful, yet showing in no uncertain terms that it was her that was now most definitely in charge.

A tight red vest showed off her toned arms, the thick scar tissue on her shoulder warning that she was one tough lady and not to be messed with. Then she had gone rather youthful with a black and white striped skirt and thick brown leather belt. The whole thing was finished off with matching brown biker boots and leggings, and, of course, the Room matched the outfit, or vice-versa. Sat on a soft leather cushion atop the table was her father, or Constantine, well, both really she supposed, they were, after all, inseparable.

Letje leaned back in the comfortable chair, arms folded across her chest, and wondered what the man was thinking as he made his way to what would either be a wonderful future for him, or a bitter disappointment. Not forgetting his possible death if he didn't follow The Rules that had been laid down over three hundred years ago by a man whose head would stare down at him from a glass box on a shelf set in the wall to the left of the chair he would occupy throughout his Orientation.

Letje drifted. She felt tired. This was just the start of it all really, the true beginning of her life as a dictator and absolute oligarch of the greatest achievement by man since... she didn't know enough history to know what beat Marcus' achievements really, and wondered if anything could ever be as complex and as downright bizarre as her new home.

~~~

"You're a bit big aren't you?" said a little girl with silver hair that was prodding his arm and flexing her bicep to see how it compared. She kept hopping from one foot to another and it seemed like she found it impossible to stay still. She took a step back when she lifted his sleeve to better see his muscles and caught sight of the dream-inducing markings.

"Um, it depends what you compare me too I suppose," said Gammadims. "Big compared to you, small compared to a giant."

"Ooh," said the excited young girl, pig-tails flying wildly as she danced around him. "Have you seen one? A giant?"

"Well, no. I don't think there are any."

"Oh," came the disappointed reply. She brightened instantly and seemed to remember what she was doing at the strange entrance. "Hello Sir, I will be your escort today for your Orientation. You are Gammadims aren't you?" she asked suspiciously, bizarrely pulling out a pair of spectacles, placing them on her nose, then peering over the top of them — they didn't have any glass in them.

"Well, yes I am. And thank you for the very nice welcome. And you are?"

"Oh, damn, I forgot. I was supposed to introduce myself first and then do the welcome. Shall we start again?"

"No, that's fine, you did very well I think."

"Really? Cool. C'mon then, waddya waiting for?"

Gammadims watched as the manic little girl went skipping off down the corridor, seemingly inured to the crazy dimensions of the passageway that seemed to widen in a strange mockery of perspective as she beckoned him to follow. She suddenly turned and came running back. "Sorry, forgot. I'm Arcene, it's French. It means silvery, like my hair," she added helpfully.

"That's a very nice name, it suits you."

"It does, doesn't it? Come on, Letje's waiting. It's Orientation time. You nervous?"

Wow, this is one talkative child. Not really the welcome I was expecting, but I guess things are bound to be different now that Marcus has gone.

Most people still Whole and trying to gain acceptance now knew that The Commorancy was under new ownership, and if anything it had made those that could, seek out a way to get access with renewed vigor — part curiosity and part wishful thinking that The Rules for acceptance would be somewhat more lax now there was a new ruler. They weren't.

Gammadims had been trying for years to gain entry and get a Room, and his search for a way in had taken him all over the country on one mad chase after another. Finally he had stumbled upon a way to make an application and for the past six months had been going through a strange and often seemingly random selection process that seemed to want to both evaluate his very soul and make him go stark raving mad at the same time. Still, it had been worth it, he hoped, and when the cryptic message arrived telling him what to do next he had been overjoyed that his long search was seemingly finally over.

"What? Sorry, I was miles away," said Gammadims, coming out of his reverie. The girl, Arcene, was staring at him again. She was one intense child that was for sure.

"I said, your application was quite good, I helped with it. A bit. Soon I'm going to be doing all that kind of stuff, I just need to get better with my writing and my numbers. Which is a real pain. Do you like reading?"

"Eh? Yes, I do, and I like writing too. But I'm not so great with numbers."

"I am, I'm going to be brilliant at them, you wait and see. When you come out from your Room, which is very cool by the way, I've seen it, then I will be all grown up, maybe really old and all crinkly, and I will show you how great I am with my numbers. C'mon, stop dawdling, you shouldn't keep Letje waiting you know? She might get mad, and you wouldn't want that, would you?"

Arcene stared at him intently, as if waiting to see if he would say he really did want to make Letje angry, like she had devised her own cunning test to sniff out his true intentions and was quite proud of it. "No little one, I wouldn't want that at all."

Arcene scowled at him, then with a flurry of flying pig-tails turned and carried on down the perspective-skewed corridor.

Oh Dear!

Arcene left him at a strange door with a large zero etched on it. She skipped off without saying another word and he wondered what he was supposed to do now. Knocking seemed like the appropriate course of action.

So he knocked.

Whoosh.

Gammadims stared suspiciously at the door as it slid into the wall revealing the interior of Room0. The sound seemed off somehow, like the door didn't make it, but that didn't really make any sense.

Inside was a pretty young woman sat behind a black marble table perfectly reflecting the rest of the Room. There was a tortoise and nothing else apart from a chipped mug on the table. He could swear that the tortoise was looking at him suspiciously.

He waited.

Then he waited a bit longer.

Nothing. Was this a test?

"Is this a test?" he finally asked.

"Wassat? Eh?" The woman rubbed her eyes blearily. Letje, that was the new ruler's name.

"Sorry, should I have not come in?" Gammadims couldn't help but stare at her shoulder. So the rumors were true, she really was the new companion of Bird.

"Oh, yes. Sorry, I must have nodded off. It's been a bit of a whirlwind around here lately. Never mind that, I'm sure you don't want to hear about any of it. Gammadims isn't it?"

"Yes, that's me."

"Welcome to The Commorancy, I'm Letje." Letje got up and walked around the desk and held out a hand. Gammadims shook it politely. His hand enveloped hers easily but he couldn't help noticing the powerful grip.

"You're pretty strong," he noted.

"For a woman?"

"Um, no, just strong." Damn, this wasn't going so well.

"Well, I guess I have been working out a lot in The Dangerous Room," said Letje, flexing a bicep, the scars rippling all the way around and down her triceps.

"That sounds... dangerous." Damn again, what was wrong with him?

"Well, it is and it isn't. It's all about The Flow, staying in the moment, never thinking about the death that awaits you if you fall. There is no falling, only you and the rock, the rope, the moment. Please, do take a seat. I assume that you met Arcene?"

"Thanks. Yes, she's... energetic." That was better, good job Gammadims, very diplomatic.

"Haha, or you could say she's a cheeky little monkey and doesn't know when to stop talking. Please, sit," said Letje again.

Gammadims lowered his massive frame into the chair, huge thick forearms resting on the arms, trying to relax himself.

Fa-thud.

"Oh no! I'm so sorry, are you alright? Oh, how terrible. Look at the mess you're in. Let me help you up."

"Oh, ah, ooh, it's alright. Sorry about the chair." Could things get any worse? Talk about embarrassing.

"No, it's my fault. I thought the chair looked nice, it matched, but maybe wicker wasn't such a good idea. You're um, quite big. Strong." Letje held out a hand to help him up and he politely took it. Not that she would be able to budge him one bit, what with him weighing almost three hundred pounds and with muscles the size of—

"There you go, no harm done." Letje dusted off her hands and smiled now he was on his feet again.

"Wow! You really are strong. And I don't mean for a girl. No man would be able to do that. Sorry about the chair again." Gammadims stared down at the splintered mess of wood and wicker, knowing he should have known better. Under normal circumstances he would have said he would probably break it, but he had been flustered and didn't want to be rude. Hadn't even thought about it if he was honest.

"Haha, yeah, I told you, lots of work in The Dangerous Room."

"I sure would like to see that Room, it must be impressive."

"Well, c'mon then. Orientation can wait, and I could do with stretching my legs anyway. See you later Daddy. Let's go."

"Um, right, yeah, okay." Gammadims stared curiously at the tortoise as he followed Letje out of The Orientation Room.

Did she say Daddy?

~~~

"Are you telling me that you go up there?"

"Oh yes, and over there," said Letje, pointing to a pole way off in the distance, the top lost in darkness.

"You climb the pole?"

"No, it's too slippery. I walk across a tightrope from the rocks and then swing down off the platform and go back across another rope until I'm in the middle then climb down one that leads to the ground — almost to the ground anyway."

"Well, no wonder you're so strong then, that's some pretty impressive stuff you do there."

Letje beamed at him, clearly proud of her adventures in The Dangerous Room. "When I first read about this Room I didn't think it would be quite as described, so when I came in it was a bit of a shock. It really is very dangerous, unless you do it right."

"The Flow?"

"The Flow," confirmed Letje.

Gammadims was shown around more of the impossibly huge space, where all manner of strange exercise equipment vied for his attention, all of it way more advanced than he could possibly attempt, his brute strength meaning little when so much of it was a mental game as well as physical.

Soon enough Letje led him back through countless twists and turns to The Orientation Room once again, where, much to his surprise, there was a very robust chair where the broken one had been.

"Bit of an overkill Arcene," muttered Letje under her breath, which he politely ignored. The chair must have weighed half a ton and could have taken a bear rather than a large man, but still, when he sat he had to admit it made him feel confident. At least he wouldn't make a fool of himself and fall to the floor.

Letje settled herself in her chair behind the desk and opened then closed a drawer.

Snick.

"It's yours, your key. Congratulations Gammadims, you passed Orientation."

"I did? Really? I didn't think it had started yet."

"Oh," Letje waved away the notion, "It's different for everybody. Well, it will be, you're my first."

"Really? Wow, you seemed so confident, like you'd been doing it for ages. Please call me Gamm, all my friends do."

"I did? That's great... Gamm. And friends, now that is a rare thing these days. Tell me more."

Damn, being stupid again Gamm. "Well, sorry, figure of speech I suppose. I meant my wife and her brother really, they're the only people I knew."

"Yes, I'm sorry about them. You had some good years though, right?"

"Yes, more than most I guess."

Letje jumped to her feet. "Right, please, take your key, it's yours after all. Let me show you to your Room, it's ready and waiting."

Gamm could hardly contain his excitement. "Okay, well, thanks, I thought it was going to be some kind of tough interview. I have to say I was a little nervous you know?"

Letje smiled at him. She was a bit unnerving if he was honest.

As they exited the door Gamm eyed it suspiciously again.

"The door that goes *whoosh*," pointed out Letje, as it *whooshed* shut behind them.

"I figured as much."

~~~

"Now, Rules. There are Rules. You sure you don't want me to go over them once more? They're very important."

Gamm's head was in the clouds. Here he was, just a short walk from The Orientation Room, now outside his Room. The space, what Letje called The Anteroom Room, contained a mix of furniture, a surprisingly comfortable looking seating area, and seven completely bizarre looking doors. He felt it a good omen that his door was a large battered wooden thing that would allow him to at least enter without having to duck his head.

"No, I think I have them."

"Don't think, you either do or you don't. It's very important, your life important."

"Sorry, wrong turn of phrase. No, I know The Rules, I'll be good." *Damn, what is wrong with you?*

"Hmm. Okay then, one moment please." Letje leaned against the door, her right hand placed above a thick peel of shocking blue paint, her left at an angle a fraction above the tiny keyhole. "Okay, care to unlock the door? Time to meet your Room."

Click.

"Well, thanks for everything, see you... when will I see you?"

"That depends on you. Could be next week, next year or a few hundred years from now. In you go."

With a gentle shove Gamm found himself inside. The door clinked closed behind him. He turned and grabbed for the handle before pulling up short a hair's breadth from the rusty knob. *Damn, that was close. What's wrong with me? Most important Rule, don't ever touch the handle or try to leave by the door you came in. Now, let's have a look at the place.*

As he turned Gamm let out a low whistle.

He must be going mad, this kind of thing wasn't even possible, surely?

Bzzz

A buzzer sounded and a neon pink EXIT sign blinked.

Well, time to go I guess.

An Awoken Gamm went out to meet his future.

It started off in a very disappointing way indeed.

Arcene in Wonderland

Arcene was twelve now, growing up fast.

She still roamed The Commorancy most days, although there were times when she stayed in one place for a few days, lost in some crazed wonder or other. Sometimes it was weeks, and she would have to use the simple flip talker to assure Letje or Fasolt that she was alright and not getting into any more trouble.

Or, and it was the bit she hated the most, she would carry on studying The Book, that stupid book that she hated more than anything. But Letje had insisted, explaining fairly that she shouldn't be the only one that understood at least some of how the convoluted Commorancy worked. So Arcene had learned how to read and wished she never had, as now she also had to read bits of The Book and slowly work her way through it. It would take years, but as Letje had explained, there was no hurry and if Arcene Awoke one day then she would have all the time in the world — literally. If she chose such a life at any rate.

After a few certain 'incidents' Letje had taken away Arcene's privilege of access to all the Rooms, and only after a lot of sulking, a period of extended good behavior, and a promise to be careful were her rights restored some time before her eleventh birthday, a date chosen by Letje so Arcene could feel like a proper girl with a date to celebrate her maturing and growing to be a fine young woman.

Arcene was ecstatic when she was given her freedom once more when she was eleven. The last year had been spent learning to read and write and do math and all other kinds of boring things, so she had been enjoying herself immensely since being allowed to roam again as long as she reported in daily and didn't do anything stupid.

Arcene smiled to herself. She had done loads of stupid stuff and got into all kinds of mischief, it's just nobody knew — she hadn't done anything so dangerous that she had needed anyone else's help, yet.

But right now? Well, she would do her best, but she was feeling like a little girl again and really wouldn't mind somebody coming to get her and even telling her off for going places she really shouldn't have.

She was stuck.

And confused.

Even a little bit scared — just a little.

Had it only been a day? It felt like she had been lost in the madness for a lifetime.

It had started out as such fun too.

~~~

Arcene skipped down the corridor whistling tunelessly, her silver hair in long pigtails bouncing against her shoulders. Her red skirt flapped around her as she made her way, arms out to her sides, spinning her hands as if the air could tell her where to go on such a lovely morning. She had found some matching red plimsolls and a pair of perfectly white knee-high socks, and smiled with pride when Fasolt told her that she was the prettiest thing he had ever seen in his entire life.

Summer was back, and it was glorious.

Warm, she could wear nice dresses, and the air seemed to sparkle with life all over The Commorancy.

And she had her freedom. She rose early, excited to have a day of no chores, no reading, no lessons, no instructions on this or that, just a day to be eleven and be off having adventures.

Safe adventures, Letje had warned. Arcene had promised to be a good girl, knowing that was what Letje wanted to hear. Adults were *so* predictable.

Arcene stopped in her tracks, trying to discover the source of her distraction.

"Huh, what's that? Hello? Hello?" Nothing. Arcene spun in a circle just for the fun of it, wanting to make her dress swirl, then carried on her way.

Psst.

Arcene stopped, frowning in concentration.

Nothing. Off she went again.

Psst. Hey, over here, the voice whispered. This time Arcene was sure about it, it was somebody calling her.

She peered at the wall, did it move? Anything was possible in The Commorancy, that was for sure.

Not there, over here silly.

Arcene turned to the source of the noise, sure it had moved. *That's it, over here. Wanna have some fun?*

It was some kind of a doll, something in a large glass case set into the wall. Sights like that were common enough — Marcus had amassed no end of often useless stuff, Arcene had learned. She walked over to the doll, it looked like a wooden puppet with fading paint. Stenciled on the glass was something about a House of Fun.

"Are you talking to me?" asked Arcene suspiciously. "Dolls can't talk you know?" she stated with conviction.

A red arrow suddenly shot down from the top of the box, pushing the doll down and out of the way. Arcene looked down where the arrow was directing her, and saw that the bottom half of the large box was actually a small green door, again with badly peeling paint. There was a tiny brass handle, almost too tempting to ignore.

"Oh no Mr. Box, I'm being good today. I know only too well that going through that door will get me into trouble. Lots."

Arcene felt proud of herself as she turned to leave, so was shocked to see the little door open and the arm of the wooden puppet that had disappeared shoot out and grab her by the ankle.

"Hey, leggo. Gerrof me you, you stupid doll you. Argh, noooo..." Arcene was pulled forcibly through the small door, and her ankle was released as she was plunged into darkness as the door simultaneously slammed shut behind her, making way too loud a noise for such a small entry, and she hoped, exit.

~~~

Arcene sat huddled in the dark, knees up tight by her chin, waiting for whatever was supposed to happen to happen. The anticipation was killing her.

Was she afraid? Yes, but she couldn't help but be a little bit excited at the same time. She had been on plenty of adventures since they came to The Commorancy and although many had been dangerous, and not all of them had been fun, they had each and every one of them been better than her last memories of the outside world. Blood and cruelty, that's what there was on the outside.

She liked it here. Although she often went out into the grounds to enjoy the fresh air and to have even more adventures, she always somehow felt safe away from the mainland where there were people that would be nice to you, but also those that would do you harm as well.

So she waited, scared but excited too.

Then she waited some more.

Then she was simply bored.

She began to tap her foot with impatience.

Then she sighed, she'd had more than enough. "Is this it then? I'm supposed to sit here and—"

Welcome to the House of Fun, came a laughing voice from right in front of her face. Arcene jumped back and felt something hard against her back, she assumed it was just the wall. Hoped it was. She didn't like this Room. Then something struck her. "Marcus? Is that you?"

Silence.

Arcene waited for something to happen but it remained silent, and dark. It was Marcus' voice though, he must have recorded it on one of his crazy machines, maybe centuries ago. It still made Arcene's head hurt to think about such things. Life was so fleeting in her world so far, people that could live such lives still seemed like an impossibility.

The lights came on, hundreds of them, thousands. Bulbs of all colors hanging from cables and receding into the distance along the low ceiling, so low Arcene could almost touch it with her fingertips as she stood.

Then music, nothing like she had ever heard before. High-pitched and slightly manic, mixed in with what sounded like people shouting for business and something about coconuts — whatever they were. The floor began to move, dragging her away from the tiny door and along what was almost a corridor it was so narrow. It stopped and Arcene was confronted with a small vehicle in front of her with a metal bar across the front of it. Nervously, she peered ahead. All was blackness, the Room had curved inward forming a tunnel, and there were tracks that the vehicle would obviously run along.

Arcene looked back and could just about make out the tiny door, a pinpoint of green.

"I'm getting out of here. This Room is bad." Arcene walked back to where she came from, but found she wasn't making any progress. Looking down she realized the floor was moving again, stopping her getting anywhere.

She ran, hair flapping wildly. The floor sped up until she eventually couldn't keep up and fell flat on her face. Her feet bumped into the back of the vehicle again.

What choice did she have?

With a deep frown and a scowl at the blue vinyl seat she got in. "Fine, but you better not do anything horrible. I'm eleven."

The bar that had been vertical descended and locked her into place, squeezing tight against her chest but not tight enough for it to hurt.

Hold on tight, came the cackling voice of Marcus, a ghost come to play tricks on young girls.

The small vehicle trundled along the tracks, entering the tunnel. It went pitch black.

"Whoa. Ugh, stop, make it stop, make it stop." Arcene felt sick as her stomach leapt into her mouth. She must be upside down. She went faster and faster, and gripped on tight for fear of falling out. She was almost vertical and going faster by the second. Then everything lit up.

She was outside, and in front of her was crazy spiral after crazy spiral, tracks loping and turning and slanting sidewards, lost behind buildings she had never seen before.

This might actually be fun, thought Arcene, as she raced along the track before hitting the first loop-the-loop and quickly changed her mind as her pigtails hung toward the ground while she sat upside down — screaming to an absent Letje, "Come and make it stop. But not until I'm the right way up," she added hoarsely, as she continued around the ride.

Up, down, flung left, flung right, and spinning, always spinning. Arcene was green, but smiling. Once you got used to the unexpected then it was rather fun. You had to go with it and not listen to your belly, that was the secret.

She sped along the track, aiming right for a huge black monolith that reflected it's surroundings. As she hurtled past she came so close that she could run her hand along the perfectly smooth surface before she was whisked away at breakneck speed and found herself dropping hundreds of feet as the ride took her down along the ground and then came to a jarring halt in a large courtyard.

"Well, that wasn't so bad after a—"

A circular line appeared around the cab and short sections of track as Arcene was turned ninety degrees, then the ground opened up and she was falling through space. *I guess I wasn't on the ground then,* she had time to think, before there was a dull thud and she was once again traveling at speed, this time back up the way she had come down.

Another spin and she was facing the way she had come.

"Cool, back home then?"

The ride began again, but in reverse, speed faster than ever, Arcene enjoying it more because she knew it wasn't trying to kill her, just give her a bit of fun.

Something was wrong, there were loud *thunks* and *clacks* as she sped along the tracks, weird noises that made no sense. Looking forward the explanation was obvious — sections of the track were rearranging, sliding into different positions on huge extended struts that kept them secured to the ground.

Hurtling toward the black shiny tower Arcene didn't just brush close to the surface this time, the tracks went up to the side then dramatically stopped.

Nothing.

Dead space. Emptiness.

The bar lifted, Arcene felt vulnerable and aware of the height now the tracks were no longer there.

A door in the tower opened. Arcene climbed out carefully and stepped gratefully into the bright interior.

It wasn't at all what she was expecting.

How could it be?

She was only a child.

Maternal Instinct

"And then as I stepped into the black tower thing the door closed behind me and just before it did then tracks were there again and took the little vehicle with the bar away, probably back to where I started the ride I guess," mused Arcene, as she took a breath from recounting her story to Letje.

"That's no excuse at all, you should have used your flip talker, it's what it's for," said Letje, trying to piece together the tale so far from Arcene's rambling and hastily told story. Once Arcene was excited it was often hard to keep up with what she was saying. She became manic and her arms would dance wildly as she explained what had happened and why she simply had to go into this Room or that Room, or try to make Letje understand the importance of pressing buttons and pulling levers if you happened to find one. It was what they were for, was an explanation Letje had heard on countless occasions.

There had been a lot of tellings-off, but Arcene seemed inured to any sense of danger to herself at all.

"It wouldn't work," protested Arcene, "and anyway, I was going too fast."

"After the ride stopped I meant, not that you should have been there in the first place."

"But I told you, the arm grabbed me and pulled me into the Room, I didn't go in on my own. Promise."

"Okay," sighed Letje. "What happened next that meant you were away for a whole two days and not once thought to use your talker to tell me where you were?" Letje had been out of her mind with worry. After a few nerve-wracking days near the start of their occupancy Arcene had been surprisingly good at letting her or Fasolt know if she was going to stay away for long, so this had made them both very worried for Arcene.

"Well, I didn't know where I was even if I did call, but, well, Letje it was just too sad. I was too sad, and I lost track of the time, honest." Arcene begin to cry, not dramatic tears of a child making her point, but true tears, slow and steady and carrying a despair no young girl should ever have to bear on such immature shoulders.

Letje leaned forward in her chair, a brown leather 1950's Barcelona original that matched the thick leather trousers and accent button-down jacket she had picked for the day's work in The Orientation Room. She had things to do, a guest to get ready to interview over the coming weeks. She still hadn't got used to it and she didn't think the guests would either. Not that anyone ever knew what to expect back when it was Marcus who would be performing the Orientation if they passed their assessments.

"Okay, sorry. What happened?"

"Marcus was so sad you know? So very sad. I feel bad for him, even after we did have to carry his head around."

Both of them stared at the alcove where the preserved head of ex-oligarch Marcus Wolfe watched over them — for eternity.

With a shudder Arcene and Letje turned back to each other.

"Poor Marcus," said Arcene. "I think he made that ride just to cheer himself up before he went into the Room I was in, you know, so it wouldn't be so hard. But maybe he forgot all about it, about that Room. It didn't look like it had been used in..." Arcene stopped to think of a suitably long amount of time, "well, ages anyway. A hundred years at least, I bet."

Arcene began fidgeting with her pigtails, which, like the rest of her, were filthy. Her socks were splattered with mud, as were her plimsolls and dress, and with one sock up, one riding low, she reminded Letje of the wretched thief she had met in what seemed like a different life.

"Well? What happened! Come on, we need to get you into a bath and clean, and I bet you're hungry, aren't you?" Letje knew the promise of food more than a wash would speed things along.

"It was full of things, pictures, stuff like that. And there were books, not like The Book, little ones with just stories of what he did each day. It went on for years. I stopped reading them in the end, I was getting too upset. I just wanted to have a day doing young girl things."

Arcene went on to explain what it was she had read. Letje pointed out that it sounded like they were diaries. Arcene had picked one at random and sat on the comfortable sofa in the Room she found herself, a Room devoid of any cunning. It was a place for remembering events from Marcus' life that he didn't, couldn't, dwell on for long.

Arcene had discovered The Ten Year Room, a Room Marcus had re-appropriated well into his stay, and the roller coaster had been diverted so he could begin his reminisces with one of the happier memories he had of his second and only love, a woman he had spent ten years with out in the world before she finally was lost to Creeping Lethargy and once again he took up his lonely vigil in The Commorancy. They had traveled the world, explained Arcene, going to loads of countries, going somewhere called Disneyland and getting rides working again, and had Letje ever heard of Mickey Mouse? Was it really a giant talking mouse?

Letje hurried Arcene along, saying she would answer such questions later, after she was clean, so

Arcene explained best she could what else she had discovered.

There were photos of Marcus and a woman looking happy, smiling at the camera, with backgrounds of all description. Huge metal pyramid towers, mountains that seemed to be lost in clouds, massive stone buildings and lots of just them, looking happy, smiling.

But as she walked around the Room the photos got more depressing. Marcus' smile seemed forced and the woman was often not looking at the camera. "That was The Lethargy," supposed Arcene.

And the journals, or diaries, got sadder too. Arcene hadn't read them all, but had been lost for a day in the Room reading them at random. The last few were of a journey into mountains somewhere foreign Arcene couldn't remember, and Marcus had written about how lonely he felt now, and that loving somebody was horrible as they were taken away from you but that he wouldn't change having the chance to love for the second time even if he could.

And then he had left the woman, who no longer recognized him, and who he had been with for ten years, and he had returned home and his last entry was that he was sure he would go quite mad, knowing that he could never allow himself to risk having another love, and that he was better off alone now as loving and losing twice was about as much as he could bear.

"That's so sad," said Letje, interested in hearing more about Marcus' life, maybe understanding him a little better.

"I know, right? And that's why I didn't use the talker. I was too sad and I really did lose track of time. And then I walked down some stairs and I was outside and I didn't know where I was and it took me ages to find out and then it began to rain and I got my dress all dirty and I was hungry and knew you would be mad at me and—"

"Ssh, it's alright. I'm just glad you are safe. Come on, let's get you clean and then we can make something nice to eat. Okay?"

"Okay," sniffled Arcene, wiping her eyes and perking up at the thought of some food. "Poor Marcus." Arcene walked over to the glass cube containing his head and patted the top of it.

"Come on," said Letje.

"Coming," said Arcene, already thinking about what they could have for their supper.

Charts Away

"Well, I can't see any reason not to give him a Room," said Arcene, turning away from the monitors and taking off her glasses, now complete with glass. "If you look at the number of his ancestors on his mother's side that became Awoken then there is a very good chance that he is going to be very important in the future." Arcene spun in the chair back to the screen, and called over her shoulder to Letje, "Look, if you compare the data here, to the data here, then there is no doubt that he is a great candidate. Plus look at how well he did with the questionnaires, it's off the charts."

"Arcene, you know I can't make any sense out of any of that, all those lines are just squiggles to me, nothing more. And what's that?"

"What?"

"That, at the top? What does it say? Wiggle chart? Did you make that up?" accused Letje. "Wiggle chart!"

Arcene sighed. "No Letje, I did not just make that up, a wiggle chart is a very good indicator of just how well suited potential guests are when it comes to charting their psychological profile from questionnaire seventeen. You should know that, it's in The Book you know." Arcene pulled her glasses down onto her nose and stared accusingly at Letje. It was now one of her favorite poses.

"Hey, I've been busy alright? And that's what you're for anyway. It's your job, not mine."

"Just as well isn't it? Otherwise I bet we wouldn't have had a single guest in five years."

Letje smiled, and backed out of the Room quietly. "Yes Arcene, sorry Arcene. Thank you Arcene. See you at supper?"

"Hmm?" Arcene was already lost in deep concentration again, tapping her mouse, eyes flicking from one monitor to another, double checking her graphs, charts and Venn diagrams to ensure that she hadn't missed anything. There had been a few mistakes since guests had been taken, mostly down to Letje, and since she had found her surprising talent for all things mathematical so far she was at a hundred percent success rate, something she was extremely proud of.

"I said see you at supper?"

"Supper? Oh, goodie. Is it ready? I'm starving."

"No, it's not ready, it's half past two and we haven't long had lunch. Later, see you later?"

"Oh," said a dejected Arcene. "Yep, see you later."

Letje closed the door behind her. *Some things never change. Where does she put all that food?*

~~~

The five years since The Commorancy had been handed over to Letje had seen an incredible number of changes for both her and Arcene. Each had waded through the many volumes that made up The Book, and although there were still gaps in their knowledge, and a number of really rather boring parts to still read, they had both finally got a real grasp on how to make a success of The Commorancy.

Once Arcene had been taught to read and write they were both as surprised as each other to discover that Arcene was actually a bit of a mathematical wonder-child. She simply had an amazing head for figures. Nobody would have thought it, least of all Arcene, but she enjoyed the order out of the chaos. It was at total odds with the rest of her personality — that thrived on bedlam, disorder, and seemingly inexplicable acts that always resulted in danger and disarray of one kind or another. She was, when all was said and done, an anarchic child.

But numbers? She loved them.

Maybe it was because she came so late to such things, or maybe it was the fact that she finally felt secure now she had a home and family. Whatever the reason, Arcene reveled in all things number related.

It had all begun in the Room that Letje had just vacated. Arcene had sidled up to her at the age of twelve or so and asked why she was crying. Letje had shouted at her that there was something wrong with the stupid computer and that it wasn't doing what it was supposed to. She had spent the whole morning trying to understand the charts and to gather up her data and none of it matched, something screwy was going on somewhere.

After Arcene had finished sulking about being shouted at and Letje had apologized, Arcene had shouted out "Stop," just as Letje was about to delete a pie-chart she was glaring at suspiciously. Grabbing the mouse off Letje and clicking around the various open windows Arcene had sorted, categorized and collated the data into a cohesive whole before Letje could have even finished reading the results from a single page.

"Ta-dah. There, done," beamed Arcene, standing up and getting ready to skip off for an afternoon of adventure.

"Wait. What?" Letje clicked around the pages and looked at the results of Arcene's flurry of work then sat back, amazed. "How did you do that? I've been trying to sort it all out the whole morning, it took you, what, thirty seconds?"

Arcene mumbled something about stupid adults and with a sigh only twelve year old girls can perfect turned back to the monitors and began to explain. "Look, you were doing it all wrong. Instead of trying to get the bobble chart to..." Letje couldn't keep up and from then on Arcene was given more and more responsibility with the technical side of running The Commorancy.

She became administrator, data verifier and collator, ran countless background checks on potential guests, updated things in The Room Of Responsibility, and numerous other tasks that left Letje's head spinning and in a total mess.

As Arcene grew to reach fifteen she grumbled less and less about being an unpaid slave and grew into her role with an intensity that was scary to watch. You interrupted her at your own risk.

Arcene was proud of her gift and never did a day go by that she didn't secretly thank Letje, and Marcus, for the life that she now had. When she thought back to the nine — or was it eight? — year old that Letje had first encountered it was hard to believe it had really been her. What if she had gone through her whole life without learning to read, write or understand numbers? It made her shudder to think about such a future.

Now she had a role in life, a home and a family.

Things were perfect. Almost.

~~~

After Letje had closed the door behind her Arcene leaned back in her chair and her back clicked. She needed to spend less time sat down, get more exercise. But that wasn't her main concern at the moment — the state of the planet, that was what worried her. Well, not the planet, that wasn't the right word. People, that was what had her worried. Or, more to the point, the lack of them.

If her data was correct, and she certainly believed that it was, then time was running out, and fast.

There weren't enough people, not by a long way. Unless some kind of miracle happened then according to everything that Arcene had spent the last six months discovering, organizing, double then triple-checking and then checking once again, there was every likelihood that there would be less than a handful of people left alive in the world in three or four generations at most.

Four generations? That's like the blink of an eye. A generation was less than twenty years now, more like sixteen or seventeen as those that could bear children were doing so at a younger and younger age — to try to bring life into the world before they too succumbed to The Lethargy like nearly everybody had or would.

Arcene had no idea things were quite as desperate as they were, and wasn't looking forward to having to tell Letje and Fasolt the bad news either.

Well, may as well get it over with, she thought. *This evening, at supper, I'll give them the news. Maybe they can come up with a plan.*

Arcene got back to work. It was more important than ever that anybody suitable was allowed entry to The Commorancy. People had to be given a chance, they simply had to.

Loss of Appetite

"...so unless either of you have a very cunning plan then that's it — the end. Nobody left; no new guests, no babies, no weird cults like that one where they all lived in tunnels and thought that—"

"Arcene, can we stick to the topic."

"Oh, yeah, sorry. As I was saying, unless you can think of something then we're all doomed, it's over. The. End. Hey, what did you put in the sauce, it tastes... different?" Arcene stuffed a sauce soaked slab of beef into her mouth and stabbed her fork into another one; it rapidly followed its predecessor.

"Arcene, I have known you for five years now and your appetite never ceases to amaze me. Even knowing such bad news you can still eat?" said Fasolt, shaking his head in wonder, dreadlocks threatening to tumble from his head and destroy the carefully laid table.

"Hey, a gal's gotta eat, right? Letje? You not eating that?"

"What? Eh? No, I've lost my appetite."

"Goody." Arcene scraped Letje's supper onto her own plate and tucked in with gusto.

For minutes the only sound was the clinking of Arcene's plate as she devoured her own meal and Letje's. After a final lick of her knife and a surreptitious licking of her plate, even though she had been told countless times what bad manners it was, she sat back contentedly and patted her belly. Fasolt and Letje were both mutely staring at her, amazed.

"What? Something wrong?"

Letje couldn't help herself. "You just told us that basically it could be over for us all and then you carry on like normal, stuffing your face and looking like it doesn't matter."

"That's not true. I've been working hard all day so I was hungry, doesn't mean I don't care. I suppose I assumed you two would come up with a plan or something. Don't forget, I'm fifteen. Letje, you're older than me, and Fasolt, well, you're ancient. No offense."

"None taken," said Fasolt, smiling despite the seriousness of the situation.

Letje turned to him, nose all scrunched up. "Not you too? This is serious!"

"I know, I know. What are we going to do?" Fasolt twirled a dreadlock absentmindedly, hoping Letje had an insight he didn't.

"I wonder what Marcus would have done?" mused Letje.

"You don't get it, do you?" exploded Arcene. "He must have known, he ran this place. He used the computers, did all the things I've been doing. He picked the guests, went through their information and collated all the data. Heck, he has, had, well they're still running so... never mind, there are cameras all over the country, information on every person that entered The Commorancy. Facts, figures and countless graphs, charts and projections concerning past, present and future population densities so there is absolutely no way Marcus didn't know exactly what kind of a problem we are facing. Not unless he was as bad as Letje at using computers, which he wasn't." Arcene poked her tongue out at Letje, then scoured the table-top searching hopefully.

"Any dessert?"

"No," mumbled Letje, then poked her own tongue back out at Arcene.

"Right, well if Marcus knew about it then he must have had a plan. Yes? Stands to reason doesn't it?" Nobody answered. "Well?"

"Maybe he knew and that's why he, you know..." Arcene made a chopping motion with her hands.

"Arcene!"

"Sorry. Bad taste, I know."

"Very."

Arcene brightened. "Hey, I have it, I know how to solve the population problem."

"You do? How?"

"Letje just has to have lots and lots of babies."

"Very funny," said Letje, smiling despite herself.

~~~

The Room For Evening Drinking had become a regular hangout in the evenings for all three of them, along with Constantine, who Letje still found hard to address as anything but Daddy. Even he had little in the way of advice to offer after the revelations of earlier that evening, and had decided to drown his sorrows with a very watered down drink of wine.

"Arcene, can you go over it again? I still don't quite understand it. Is it really so dire? Is it such an emergency?"

"It is and it isn't. It's not like we have to rush out and solve the problem right now, but the fact is that ever since The Lethargy the population has been in decline, and it keeps on getting worse and worse. It's to be expected for a few generations after such devastation, people in shock, not knowing what to do, all that kind of stuff. But then people should have started to increase in numbers again, except they didn't."

"Why? What does the data say?"

"It's simple. Most people are too scared. Who wants to have a child knowing the chances are very high that you are going to have to watch it die a slow death in a year or two if you are lucky? I know for a fact

I wouldn't dream of having kids unless I knew that I was Awoken and could be sure my child wouldn't get The Lethargy, especially when they were young. Would you?"

"No, absolutely not. But I understand the point. I already know I can have children and they will be Whole, so all I need is a nice man."

"There you go then. And that's the problem too, isn't it? Judging by the records the country is in a sorry situation. Everyone is all spread out, living on their own or in small groups, and nobody is getting to meet anyone any more."

"This is true," said Fasolt. "People are staying put because they can't travel easily, and if you combine that with so many living alone, or being too scared to talk to people they do see, then it's no wonder things are getting so bad."

"So, what's the answer then?"

"We need to go and see Stanley, Umeko too, see if they can't help."

"Why do you think they could help, little one?" asked Fasolt.

"Arcene?"

"Well, it stands to reason doesn't it? I know I didn't meet them but you did kind of tell the story rather a lot Letje, about how Marcus kept saying it was the best possible future, the way people, um, died and others were at exactly the right place at the right time. Umeko meeting that man? Her husband? You said Marcus said that was why things happened, so that you would all be on that road the exact time he was, so Umeko could meet him. Same with Stanley wasn't it? He had to be at that place when he was; all destiny, fate, that kind of thing." She waved her hand dismissively, as if it was all obvious.

Letje stared at Arcene suspiciously.

"What? It's a good idea, isn't it?"

"It is, a brilliant idea. I'm simply wondering where the other Arcene is, the one that gets into trouble and goes off and comes back days later after having discovered dangerous Rooms and let out of control machines loose in the corridors that threaten to explode The Commorancy."

"I'm all grown up aren't I?" said Arcene beaming, glowing with satisfaction at her idea. She was also very pleased that she hadn't told Letje or Fasolt about the rather unfortunate 'incident' yesterday where she might, just might have accidentally made half an acre of the lawn outside The Room Just For Having A Name disappear and be replaced with a pit full of three meter long spikes made out of what looked like sharpened pencils. It wasn't really her fault though, why would you put a big red button in the middle of a Room unless it was there to be pushed? Still, no point telling about it now. Or ever.

"So, who's going then? I can't, I have things to do here," said a rather furtive looking Fasolt.

"What things?" asked Letje suspiciously.

"Oh, you know, things. Important things. And actually, is that the time? I must be off, got to finish some work for the day. See you later."

"Hey, you don't even wear a wat—" Fasolt was gone.

"Well, that was weird," said Arcene, watching Fasolt close the door behind him. "And when is he going to start wearing clothes? I know he covers up his bits, but still, I keep getting glimpses of them every time he sits down or stands up. Ugh."

"Get over it, I think it's too late for him to go back to wearing clothes now. But look, I think he just doesn't want to go back outside yet. After living so long I think he's worried about losing himself again, like he did before. The Commorancy makes him feel safe, like we do, right?"

"Yeah, I love it."

"And Fasolt's hundreds of years old, and was a bad man. He doesn't want to risk being like that again, so wants to stay here, not go outside where bad things happen and you have to do bad things even though it's the right thing to do."

"Ah, you mean 'deathy' things, right?"

"Yes, 'deathy' things Arcene."

"Well, guess it's just down to you then Letje. I'm busy too, I still have lots of background checks to do on the candidate before I know if he's suitable for Orientation. So, gotta go, thanks for supper, I'll clear up later."

"Hey, hang on a minute. You're not fooling anyone. You and Fasolt are as bad as each other, but at least he's got a proper excuse. You told me earlier you had basically finished collecting info on him and tha—"

"Sorry. What? Kinda busy, see ya later." Arcene closed the door behind her, still making lame excuses as she rushed down the corridor.

Guess it's down to me then, thought Letje, wondering what the quickest way would be to go and visit Umeko, Kirstie and Stanley. Not forgetting the children, the more precious than ever children. Now that she thought about it maybe it would be quite nice to see them again, and to get away for a while, have some time on her own away from the responsibilities that weighed ever heavier on her still young shoulders. Maybe Bird would go with her, keep her company?

"Well...

...how was it? How are they? Are they going to help?"

"I don't want to talk about it. I'm going to bed, I need to lie down."

Arcene and Fasolt had rushed to greet Letje at the front door, probably one of the least used doors in the whole of The Commorancy. This wasn't what they had been expecting at all.

Letje? Letje, what happened? Yabis had decided to stay behind. Now that Arcene was older he trusted her enough to not drop him, and she had done a mostly good job in Letje's absence.

Later, okay?

Letje rushed past, cursing the size of everything as she sped up, finally just running until she was alone once more.

Alone. Soon everyone would be alone.

~~~

"I'm sorry about earlier, I just couldn't face talking about it. It was awful, not what I expected at all. I was feeling happy about seeing everyone again, maybe seeing Umeko's baby, or babies, thinking maybe they could help show people how to Awaken and make sure you had Whole children. And Stanley, he was such a nice man, and he had such plans for his home. He wanted people there, wanted to help set things right."

"Hang on, you said 'was', he 'was' such a nice man? You mean 'is', right?"

"No, no I don't." Letje broke down in tears. It was as if she was crying for everything bad that had ever happened in the world.

Arcene and Fasolt looked at each other, both nodding to Letje for the other to do something to help. Finally it was Constantine/Yabis that spoke. Although Arcene was not actually Awoken, her close proximity to him for so long allowed her to mostly hear what he said via The Noise now. *Letje, my dear? Please tell us, it will make you feel better, I promise.*

Give me a minute, then I will.

A few minutes later Letje described her journey and what she had encountered.

They were in the huge kitchen, a place they frequented often, usually as it was the only place Arcene would stay put for any length of time apart from The Room For Doing Things With Computers, and it was one of the only normal Rooms in The Commorancy anyway. In fact, it was the one Room Letje had insisted early on not even have a name — no 'Room For The Kitchen', nothing like that. Just 'the kitchen' — she insisted. The huge open fire crackled with warmth, bringing a glow to Letje's face that had been dangerously pale when she had staggered in earlier asking for coffee and apologizing for her behavior the afternoon before.

"I was so excited, thinking that surely Umeko and Kirstie would love to be able to help ensure more babies were born and all the work of The Commorancy hadn't been for nothing. We couldn't let the legacy of The Eventuals actually win, which is what it would be like if people just became extinct."

"And what was the hot air balloon like, was it fun?" Arcene had been totally jealous when she realized Letje had been secretly practicing with it and was going to take it to the mainland.

"No, it was totally scary." Letje managed a weak smile, not wanting to even think about the ridiculously dangerous flying contraption that saw her almost killed on numerous occasions. Whoever invented such a thing was an idiot there was no doubt about it.

Letje moved her seat away from the fire, and greedily finished her second cup of coffee. "Okay, I'm just going to say it. They're dead. All dead."

"Who? Umeko's babies? Her husband?"

"No, all of them. Babies, husbands, wives, Kirstie, Umeko, Stanley. Dead. All dead."

Fasolt took Letje's place by the fire, enjoying the feeling even though he didn't need the heat. "But how? Why? They can't be, surely. It was Marcus' plan, what he saw in the future, what the future had to be. How can he have been wrong? Are you sure? How do you know that they are dead?"

Letje took a deep breath, using her Awoken knowledge to calm herself, take back control. She couldn't believe she had lost it so easily the day before — she should be above such childish behavior by now. But it was part of being human, so she had nothing to apologize for did she? No, she didn't.

Feeling resolute and calm, she began again. "Okay, let me tell it properly. Something has gone very wrong somewhere, and we need to understand how if we are to figure out what is going on. I don't think there is anybody left at all. Nobody."

Arcene stared at Fasolt, mouthing silently if he thought Letje had gone a bit funny, twirling a finger by her head and rolling her eyes in case he didn't understand her.

"No Arcene, I'm not mad. Everyone's dead. I couldn't find anybody; there's nobody out there. Either we are dead ourselves and in some kind of purgatory, or we are the only ones alive and everyone else has gone. Left or something, I don't know."

Fasolt felt a tingle run up his spine, as if what Letje was saying were true. It felt true. His extended lifetime meant he knew to trust such feelings — they were always right. Come to think of it, when was the last time he went deep into The Noise, communed or looked through the eyes of creatures away from The Commorancy? Had anything to do at all with things away from his new home? It had been a long time. Maybe something really had happened? He would find out soon enough, do his own investigation after Letje told her tale. His thoughts were interrupted...

"...I'm sure of it."

"Sure of what? Sorry, I missed that."

Letje gulped from a fresh cup of coffee. "I said we are in the wrong future, something's happened. We are in the wrong timeline. It's the only explanation. Marcus wouldn't have been wrong, so the only other explanation is that somehow we have slipped into a different future, not the one we should be in."

"Well, that's a bit of a jump to a conclusion isn't it?" said Fasolt, dread falling like a blanket that wrapped you in a nightmare and wouldn't let you free, tightening the more you struggled for release.

"It's the only answer. Marcus always said that when you have eliminated all other possibilities then what you were left with was the truth; no matter how bizarre it may seem."

"He certainly knew all about the bizarre that's for sure," offered up Arcene, certain that there had to be a simple explanation and Letje was just confused by whatever had happened to her on the mainland. Maybe she had a bang to the head or something?

"Okay, start at the beginning please, and don't leave anything out." Fasolt leaned back in his chair, crossed his arms over his naked belly, causing Arcene to scowl at him, and Letje began her story once more.

Not all Futures are Created Equal

"I'll skip the journey in that damn hot air balloon, but don't ever go in one, they're death traps. But one thing is for sure, you get a good view. And that was the problem."

"The view? That was the problem?"

"Yes, it was beautiful. But I didn't see anybody. Not that I expected to see loads of people or anything, but traveling should mean you would see at least a person or two, or fires, smoke coming from chimneys. There was nothing. It was like everyone was gone. Everyone."

"They can't all be gone, how could they be?"

"I don't know, I'm just telling you what I saw, more like what I didn't see. Anyway, the hot air balloon got too unstable, and way too wobbly, so I landed it, kind of crashed it anyway, and then traveled on foot until I found a bicycle. Then it got really weird." Letje swiped across her hair, thinking back to how many times

Marcus had told her to get her bangs cut. She couldn't help but smile.

Me too, I think I told you to cut it more than once Letje.

Are you looking into my head Daddy?

Sorry, just wanted to check you are... you know, not bonkers or anything.

Well, listen to the story and then make up your mind. No peeking into my head, warned Letje.

Sorry.

You should be.

"C'mon, get on with it." Arcene had stood up and was jigging from side to side, keen to hear what happened next.

"Well, it all just felt empty. Like something was missing. Stuff was just not right. I felt alone, properly alone. You know when you just get that feeling? That there is nobody about? I had that, all the time. The country is like it's empty or something, everyone gone, taken by The Lethargy I suppose. Arcene, you yourself said it was getting bad, that people would mostly be gone in maybe just a few generations from now, well what if you were wrong and it's even worse than you thought? What if basically everybody is dead or dying?"

"I'm not wrong, the numbers are right," said Arcene, crossing her arms across her chest.

"Well, okay, but there must be some kind of an explanation then. I am telling you that I didn't see a single person or feel a single person. There should have been something coming from The Noise, even if only a hint of people — I got nothing."

Fasolt had been quiet, listening and delving deep into the source of so much Awoken power. Letje wasn't exaggerating — it was as if somebody had finished work for the day, turned the lights off and closed up shop. It was different, quiet and empty. "Letje is right, there is something going on. In The Noise? It's like the people have disappeared, gone. But it's not empty, it's almost like there is a replacement emptiness for where things should have been, as if the timeline is fighting back. It doesn't like the emptiness. I didn't know as I haven't been going into The Noise in such a way as to notice."

"Exactly, and neither have I. Why would you? Unless you wanted to talk to somebody privately or sense where they were, or do something nasty then you don't go searching for people really, do you? We've just been in here getting on with things so there hasn't been any need. But I'm telling you, we are in the wrong timeline, we're all alone here. There's nobody out there any more. It's just us."

"You guys, can you please stop with all this. People don't suddenly disappear do they? Something else must be going on. We can't all suddenly jump timelines and everything be different. If we aren't in the future that we should be in, at least according to Marcus anyway, then we are all in the one that has happened somehow."

Arcene waved a hand dismissively. "I don't believe in all that anyway, what happens simply happens, but people don't vanish so there must be something else going on. Okay, wait here, I'll prove to you there are still people out there."

Arcene ran for the door and shouted over her shoulder, "Be back in a mo."

"Letje, while Arcene is out of the way, are you being serious about this? The timeline? The people?"

"Fasolt, I am. You know better than I do how the smallest actions can change the future. Marcus did too. It's why he made very specific decisions once The Contamination began, so events unfolded in the right way for the right future to happen. Something's gone wrong. He didn't say anything about people dying so soon. It didn't seem like that was his plan at all. Otherwise why would he have bothered in the first place?"

"Unless..."

"Unless what?"

"Well, what exactly did he see? You don't know, nobody does. He just steered you in a certain direction, but he didn't know everything. He never saw me in the futures so it wasn't like his knowledge was absolute or anything. And anyway, maybe this was a part of what he saw, maybe everything that happened five years ago was leading up to something else, something like this? I must admit that weaving through the countless possible futures and picking the right path is beyond me. Marcus had a very special gift for that, so who knows how far ahead he saw? Maybe whatever is happening now is a result of his death, your occupation of The Commorancy, and don't forget all that stopping and starting of time he and Varik did when they fought. Neither of them had done that before — stopped things for the rest of us and allowed themselves to move freely between the gaps. Some things should be left alone, and that is definitely one of them. I am not a person to tamper with the likes of time, are you?"

"No, definitely not. Okay, maybe this was supposed to happen, but what if it wasn't? What if it was? What does that mean, that everyone's gone? We're alone now, forever? What would be the point then?"

"You forget yourself Letje Sandoe. You are the ruler of The Commorancy and it is filled with countless people in their Rooms learning how to be the best they can possibly be. Nothing is over, not everyone is dead."

Arcene burst through the door, slamming it open and denting the wall. "Everyone's dead. Gone. Letje was right, we're doomed!"

"Harith is gone, that guy who I was just about to finish processing. He was ideal for a Room, but he's not there."

"How do you know this little one?"

"Fasolt, I'm not little any more," sulked Arcene.

"Please, can we do this another time?" said Letje, wondering if she would ever get to tell her story.

"Sorry."

"Sorry."

"Good. Right, Arcene, how do you know he's gone?"

"Because he didn't finish his last questionnaire, that's why. I can see it through our Web, it's just there, half done since two days ago. There's no way he would stop like that, this guy has been trying to gain entry since we first got here. Longer. Talk about keen, he wouldn't dream of stopping like that."

"Ah, little one, um, Arcene," said Fasolt hurriedly, wilting under the gaze of the fifteen year old even though he was older than her by three centuries. "Arcene, he may just be feeling a little unwell, couldn't finish for a few days."

"No, you don't get it. This guy has never been ill a day in his life. His family going back generations have all been Whole, some almost Awoken, and he's pretty obsessed with becoming fully Awoken himself — he finishes everything he gets sent almost immediately. He's gone I tell you. Letje, let's have it, tell us what happened. This is getting weird, and I for one don't like it one bit. Ugh, creepy."

"See? I told you, I told you both. Something is going on, we're out of the loop, drifting in space and time all alone and I really think we may be in some form of The Void or something."

"Let me stop you right there," said Fasolt. "I am over three hundred years old, have been reborn and given a second chance at a good life, but I was a bad man before, for centuries. I have been deeper into The Noise than you could ever imagine, seen things and done things that would give you nightmares for the rest of your life, controlled ten thousand Lethargic in The Commorancy; controlled them while I was out to sea in the dark bowels of a ship, and I have done much worse. I will tell you this now, we are not in The Void or any form of it. If we were then we would most definitely not be having this conversation. The Void is nothing, what everything is eventually, but it is also everything, and we are not there."

"Well, thanks for nothing Fasolt. Everything and nothing? Real helpful old man."

"Enough! Can I please tell you what happened now? You two are not making things any better you know?"

Letje finally got to tell her story.

And so it Came to Pass

Letje told of her crash landing and subsequent travels through the countryside toward the home of Umeko and her husband. There had been sporadic contact so Letje knew there was now a young child of three and Kirstie's baby had grown to be a right little handful.

They were happy, all of them. The children played, the home had grown, with Ryce repairing machinery and plowing a few acres — enough to keep the extended family fed now that the crops were in their second season.

They were happy. Blissfully so.

Letje arrived to find nothing. They were gone. The place was as if everyone had suddenly given up, succumbed to The Lethargy and were unable to continue running the home. Nothing was out of place though, so it wasn't like they had stayed while they all finally succumbed. Letje had seen enough of The Lethargy with her own family to know that if they had been slowly fading away then everything else would have degraded along with them. This was different, like they had left to die someplace else. Away from their happy home.

The freshly farmed fields were full of crops, ripe for the picking. Soon they would go over and be no use for food. That was certainly out of character and it did not bode well at all for the future of her friends. That's what they were, weren't they? Even if she had known them only for a brief spell they had been on a rather epic adventure together for the short time they were in each others company.

Now they were gone.

Vanished.

As if they had been in the wrong time and had simply been transplanted to where they should have been all along.

Letje described the eerie emptiness of the countryside surrounding the house — it all felt so quiet. She really did feel like the last person on earth. Reluctantly, she had gone into the house uninvited; something was wrong and she had every intention of finding out just what it was.

Empty.

It was all gone — any sign of life had been eradicated. Nobody lived in the house any longer, there was nothing but the creaking of the floors and the sounds of trees scratching at the house, waiting to reclaim the territory the building sat upon in silence.

"What about their stuff, was it still there?" Arcene was getting creeped out, people couldn't really disappear could they?

"I don't know, how can you tell? Everything was neat and tidy so it wasn't like they had been slowly dying from The Lethargy, but I don't know if anything was missing or not. Anyway, I kind of got spooked and thought that maybe they had just gone off somewhere, gone to visit somebody, gone for provisions or something. But the more I thought about it the more that didn't make sense either. Then I found a dog."

"A doggie? Was it alright?" whispered Arcene. She loved dogs so much and it brought back memories of a horrible time in her life that she really didn't want to drag up from the past.

"No, no it wasn't. I um, I..." Letje glanced at Fasolt who shook his head.

"Look, I don't need to go into details, but it was a sure sign that nobody had been at the place for a good long time, probably months."

"Thanks for sparing me the details," said Arcene. "But what the hell is going on?"

Letje shook her head. "I don't know, it all sounds crazy. I—"

"It's not true though, is it? That everyone is gone? We have guests don't we? We have people coming for Orientation? How many have you given a Room too? Lots, yes? And Arcene, you are dealing with all the technical things, so you must be processing countless people at the moment?"

"Well, um, it's not really like that, no. I had this guy, Harith, but he's disappeared. Apart from that we haven't really had many applications for a while. Everything kind of slowed down about a year ago."

Letje confirmed it. "We both assumed it was sort of a new ownership thing. You know, people were brought up hearing of Marcus and his Rooms, now there's some young girl running things. We thought people were sort of put off and it would take a while for us to get their trust back, enough for them to want a Room. I assumed people wouldn't really believe that they could get the same thing they did when Marcus was alive."

"Well, how many have there been in the last year then?" said Fasolt.

Letje turned to Arcene.

Arcene mumbled something that nobody heard.

"What? Speak up."

"Three. There have been three applications, alright. Happy now? And only Harith was anywhere near suitable, the others were total write-offs from the start, so I didn't pursue them at all."

Letje was shocked. "I didn't realize it had been quite that quiet."

"Well, it has," said Arcene sulkily. "Nobody wants to come here any more."

Fasolt sat up in his chair. "Or, something really has happened out there and they aren't able to try for some reason. That would make more sense. The Commorancy is all there is for most people, they won't all suddenly stop coming because Letje is in charge. If anything it would make people more curious. I know it would if I were Whole and wanted something more out of life."

Arcene thought about it for a while. "Hmm, you might be right. We had loads of applications the first four years, right Letje? I know I didn't take over for a couple of years, doing the technical stuff, but you managed didn't you? You did lots of Orientations? People wanted in, right?"

"Gosh, I'm trying to think, but yes. I didn't do anything for a few months, not until I'd read enough of The Book, but then it all got pretty hectic. I was juggling so much work, but we had regular applications, and I did loads of Orientations. But you have to understand something, the numbers were never huge. And that wasn't just down to us being new. I looked over Marcus' records, you did too right Arcene?"

"Yep, I was a bit shocked I have to tell you."

"Go on," said Fasolt.

"Look, Marcus ran The Commorancy for what, three hundred years or so? We all assumed it was limited to the seven Rooms until he told us different. We know now there are thousands, thousands and thousands, almost ten thousand by my reckoning. Sounds about right Arcene?"

"Sort of, although he didn't ever use them all, and some are better than others. It was never at full occupancy even though the way Marcus spoke he thought it was. But you know about that better than me Letje, you knew him longer."

Letje thought back to what he had told her of The Rooms. Hindsight made it clear that Marcus was far from living only in his present. "It's hard to tell exactly, a lot of the records are rather jumbled. I still don't understand the whole two of him thing, whether it was true or not, but it was obvious he was living two lives either way, real or only in his head. The occupancy rate wasn't what he believed it to be, it couldn't possibly have been anyway, not even if there were two of him. I worked out how many there really were, and it took months, but we had to know where people were and when they were ready to come out. What a nightmare that was."

"Yeah, and then I went over your numbers and you were totally wrong," said Arcene smugly.

"Okay, no need to be rude."

Arcene smirked but touched Letje's shoulder affectionately. Letje continued. "Anyway, the total number was about two thousand, give or take a few, I can't remember exactly as some people were leaving as we were arriving. But the thing is that this place has been going for so long, and some guests stayed so long and some are still here after centuries, that the numbers kind of all add up slowly without there actually being that many coming in any one generation, let alone year or month or week. If you think about it, even with two thousand people currently here, it only works out at seven people a year over three hundred years. Now I know that isn't how it works, but it means that there isn't a constant barrage of people every day, even every week."

Arcene interrupted. "Yeah, and don't forget that lots of people came near the beginning. Stands to reason doesn't it? For the first few generations, even for a hundred years after The Lethargy, there were a lot more people than there are now, a lot more. So there were a lot more applicants. And some are still here. It's crazy. What are they doing in their Rooms? But anyway, there are a few thousand now. We have, Letje has, done a number of Orientations, but it's the build-up over time that gives the numbers. Everyone apart from us assumed, still does, if there is anyone, that there are seven Rooms. It's top secret how long people really end up staying, otherwise nobody would ever apply as they would be dead before they got their turn."

Letje continued the point. "Anyway, as I was saying, it was surprising how few applications there actually were every month until we looked, Arcene looked, closely at the figures and realized that what Marcus had said wasn't true. He was lost so much to the past and the future, and his double life, that his count was just plain wrong, by thousands. He was remembering people that had left I think, not those still here."

Fasolt's head was spinning. "So what you ladies are telling me is that nobody is really applying any more? Correct? But they were before, but not as often as I may have thought? Correct?"

Letje and Arcene both agreed.

Fasolt was ramrod straight in his chair now, hair draping over the table, creeping dangerously close to the fire. "Letje, I think you better finish off your story please. If even the somewhat sporadic applications have died down over the past year then I'm afraid things might be even worse than I first suspected. Carry on." Fasolt closed his eyes to better listen to everything Letje had left to say.

Letje picked up the story once again, trying to focus whilst taking in what Arcene had said about the total lack of applicants and the fact that Harith, their only recent applicant, had seemingly disappeared from the face of the planet. What on earth was going on?

~~~

Letje had traveled on foot, drawing a total blank at the place she had watched Umeko get married five years ago. Now you would never believe that anyone had lived there for some time, let alone that there were children, husbands and friends too. She thought of the poor dog that was half starved and she had put out of its misery. It was too far gone to bring back to health, that was more than obvious once she connected with it through The Noise.

She left that out of the story for Arcene's sake, knowing how raw the memory of what had been done to dogs was when she had been held against her will before she had exacted her terrible revenge on her kidnappers. She had reluctantly gone back for the balloon, and once again took to the skies, following their old trail to the home they had found that was deeply connected to Stanley.

She landed close by and tethered the terrible contraption, vowing never to set foot in one again if she managed to make it back to The Commorancy after, she prayed more than anything, she got to see Stanley and maybe the company he had assured them all would find their way to his new home soon enough.

"But nothing, it was empty, same as everywhere else. Just nothing. I wandered down to the large lake first. I had this silly idea in my head that I would walk down through the grass and there would be Stanley, sat on a rock, fishing rod in one hand, a drink of something strong in the other, a fire lit behind him ready to cook what he caught. You know, the way he loved to spend a day?"

"Never met him, I have no idea," said Fasolt.

"Me neither. I only know what you told about him," said Arcene.

"Oh, yeah. Sorry, I forgot. Well, that was what he loved to do, more than anything. But he wasn't there, I knew deep down he wouldn't be. But still, it surprised me at the same time. I wanted him there so bad, wanted there to be people. I wandered back up to the house, hoping that I would find him hard at work inside maybe, doing decorating, maybe even chatting with people, or tending the garden, something like that. I was kind of in a panic by this point, getting a bit manic.

"The front door was open, which I took as a good sign. You know, that somebody was home and would be out at any second on some chore or something. I shouted, nobody came. So I went in. Ugh, I need more coffee, any left?"

"I'll make some more. Fasolt?"

"That would be lovely little one." Fasolt got a scowl for his choice of words and snickered into his hair so Arcene couldn't see. She was funny when she got annoyed with the names he called her.

When the coffee was made and Letje had taken a few sips she continued with what little there was left of her story. Not really wanting to ever finish it though, as then it would mean she would have to try to figure out what was going on and if it truly meant the end of everything. She felt like she could be going mad, and understood, probably for the first time, the weight of responsibility Marcus had taken upon himself for all those years. How could he have the weight of humanity's survival on his shoulders for three hundred years and not go absolutely insane?

She had her answer didn't she? His head was in a box in The Orientation Room; that was what she had to look forward to if she was lucky.

"Hey feather head, wakey wakey." Arcene nudged Letje, then tapped her on the head with her middle finger until Letje managed to rouse from her meandering thoughts.

"Oh, gosh, sorry. I was thinking about Marcus. No wonder he was... um, a little bit eccentric. All this responsibility is a lot to take in you know? I really wish he'd built a Room For Morning Drinking."

"Which is exactly why he didn't," chimed in Arcene and Fasolt at the same time. It had become a running joke over the years. Countless times either Letje or Fasolt had opined the fact there were no Rooms For Drinking In the Day. Something Marcus himself had commented on in quite a number of volumes of The Book.

"Haha, got me. Well, Stanley's home was empty. You have to understand that when we found it, as Marcus knew we would, the place was alive with energy. It practically screamed out welcome to Stanley. He was the missing piece of its near perfection. What did they call it? Good Vibrations, that was it. All of that was gone. It just felt like a run-down house with a flooded lake and a garden that had gone out of control.

The energy had gone, dissipated into The Void like Stanley himself."

"Dissy what? I wish you two would stop using stupid big words," moaned Arcene, hating to be reminded that she still had some schooling left to complete. "Anyway, you don't know that Stanley is dead, he might have just gone on a trip."

"No, he wasn't there and he wouldn't leave. It's hard to explain but it was Stanley's home, he belonged there. He was gone though. Poof. Vanished like he had never been a person at all. The house was just empty. You could see that some work had begun, the same in the gardens, but not much, not more than he could probably have done in a year or so if he had been alone there for that time. He's dead."

Letje gulped the remains of her coffee, now almost cold. She grimaced — she hated cold coffee — then excused herself. She really needed to shower and try to clear her head a little.

"Well, little silver haired lady, I think we need to come up with a plan, don't you?"

Arcene scowled at Fasolt, although secretly she enjoyed the jibes. It was family after all, her family. "Okay old man, let's hear your plan then."

"Oh," said a deflated Fasolt. "I was hoping that you had one."

What a Shower

Letje's head was a mess. The last few days had been one long nightmare that she saw no end to now that she was home. If it wasn't fearing for her own life, having to fly that really, really stupid machine — she wished she'd had the nerve to take the helicopter — then it had been the sense of downright wrongness when she thought about the total lack of people.

Could it really be that they were somehow out of sync with their own present? Or that they were stuck in some kind of a loop, everything on hold and in stasis because of the extreme forces that both Marcus and Varik had brought into play all those years ago battling each other in a London park? None of it seemed like a valid or even logical explanation, but she simply couldn't think of a reasonable answer to the disappearance of people so totally.

If she wasn't fairly sure of her own sanity then she would find it rather easy to believe that they had just simply never existed in the first place — just a glimpse of a life that never really came to fruition. It was like a re-emergence of the feelings she had when she was younger — that she was the only person alive on the planet and as soon as she turned her back from people then they ceased to exist. They were there just so she didn't feel as alone as she really was.

Such feelings pressed in hard and it was tough to shake them. Her new life was so bizarre, The Commorancy was so bizarre, that it was quite easy to believe almost anything.

Take where she was right now for example. If she tried to explain it to someone who knew nothing of The Commorancy then they would assume she was totally off her rocker, wouldn't they? The Commorancy did strange things to you and there was no doubt — just look at the crazy way Rooms were customized for their guests — it was mind boggling in its complexity.

Marcus may have been vastly intelligent but he had definitely got carried away in his construction. His Rules, and The Rituals that she had carried on in his stead, had obviously got more and more bizarre the more ensconced he was in his position as oligarch of just about all there was between the extinction of the British population and it's survival, however tenuous that may have been — and obviously still was.

Well, whatever else was going on, she was having the absolute best shower. Ever.

Letje knew she was going to need more than just the shower in the en-suite that she reluctantly shared way too often with Arcene. It had been five years since they first moved in and although Arcene had moved into her own room a few years ago Letje still often awoke to find the younger girl snuggled up with her. She may have been a brave little girl, but so much had been taken away from her as a child that she reveled in finally having a family, no matter how dysfunctional.

So Letje had walked out across the huge expanse of lawn in one small corner of The Commorancy and entered The Room For Big Showers, and what a Room it was.

Twenty meters a side, and twenty meters high, it was a perfect glass cube that was nigh on invisible from the outside. If you squinted and turned your head 'just so' then you could maybe get a glimpse of there being something there, but it was hard to tell. It blended in so perfectly, was maybe see-through, maybe reflecting perfectly its surroundings, or had some chameleon-like coating, that to all intents and purposes it was invisible.

Which was just as well as if anyone could have seen inside then they would have been confronted with countless views of a very naked twenty two year old Letje. She could view herself from every possible angle and it was definitely not a Room for those with any kind of body issues.

Arcene had used it once and ran out screaming as she had never seen her bum before and was appalled to discover that she had a dimple on each cheek and she swore blind that she had a bit of cellulite too, and that wasn't fair as she was only twelve and who cared anyway and was there a cream for it and what was the point in seeing your own bum anyway and Letje better not make fun of her bum or she would not be happy.

Letje smiled at the memory and wondered if Arcene had seen her bum again in the three years since that incident.

She examined herself closely in the countless angled reflections, finally clear of the dust and dirt of her trip away from The Commorancy. She felt so much better now she was clean — as if she had washed away some of the madness along with the detritus of travel.

She was rather satisfied with her figure, now that of a fully grown woman. She had a swimmers build, broad athletic shoulders and a firm but still curvy chest. Strong thighs swept up to full hips and a taut waist, and she prided herself on never having adjusted her body chemistry specifically to keep herself in trim, although with her fully Awoken state it would have been as easy as turning on the shower she now stood under.

The only imperfection was the mass of scar tissue that had now formed a solid lump right across her left shoulder. It crept up toward her neck, along her scapula and criss-crossed it's way ever so slightly down her chest. Letje saw it as a thing of beauty, just as Varik had once done. It was a mark of friendship, of sacrifice for being the friend of a creature that found her company welcome.

Letje put her hand to the mess of knots, feeling each lump and bump, tracing the lines of the gashes that recorded the history of her friendship with the giant eagle in blood. Letje always healed rapidly so most of the scars were pale, only the freshest, from only a day ago, were still livid pink and even they were already fading. The number of cuts and puncture wounds now numbered in the thousands, most built on top of the other, making even her fast-healing body struggle to cope. With scar tissue repeatedly opened as Bird landed or took flight they were now hard, tough like his talons, better than any leather shoulder sheath and less bothersome.

Feeling in the shoulder was now almost non-existent. Bird's repeated puncturing of the skin and the old healed scars meant most nerves were now long dead. Just like Varik, Letje made no attempt to heal them through physical manipulation of her own body — it was a mark of pride and trust in a creature that was the most powerful bird on the planet. It could kill her in a second if it so wished, and Bird and his white-striped mate had done just that to his old ex-friend when Varik had interfered with his life — resulting in the death of one of their chicks.

Letje finished soaping the shoulder; it was important to keep it spotlessly clean. She rinsed off the rest of her body and couldn't help but wonder again at the miracle that was the Room she found herself in quite often these days.

The Room For Big Showers was indulgently luxurious just to get clean, yet it was one of the emptiest Rooms she had encountered. She always took her own towel inside, and the only other things were her small number of cleaning products that were stored in an oblong pillar that was made out of the same impossibly invisible material. She had to leave the door ajar on it or she spent most of her time trying to find it.

There were no temperature adjustments, no dials or knobs to change water pressure or even a shower head. You stepped in, leaving your clothes by the door on the hooks — again, invisible unless you knew where they were — and then when you were ready you simply clapped once and the shower began. More like it rained really, always at the perfect temperature. Thousands of tiny holes in the twenty meter high ceiling sent down perfectly temperature controlled droplets directly onto your body. It didn't matter where you were, the Room sensed the temperature of a human being and only sent the water directly at the person so there was no wastage, yet there was a decadent luxury in being able to wander around a twenty meter Room and continue with your shower.

Letje still found it strange to be able to look out and see the perfect grass and the bizarre architecture, knowing that nobody could see inside, not that there ever really were any peeping toms anyway.

Lost in thought Letje spent close to an hour soaping herself then rinsing repeatedly. The trip had been so soul-crushingly depressing that it was the only way to wash away some of the feelings that had been boiling up inside her since she first got the eerie feeling that the rest of the world had somehow gotten up and disappeared into The Void.

There had to be an answer, there just had to be.

Clap, clap.

The dryers blew warm air across her body and Letje smiled as her hair blew wildly while the strong jets did their job. When they stopped she padded across the perfectly dry and impossibly always clean floor and got dressed.

Time to figure this out. Where had everybody gone?

Strange Encounters

Fasolt had spent a considerable amount of time exploring The Commorancy, and the more he saw the more he realized just how much most people underestimated Marcus — him too. The impossibly complex systems in place to keep such a home running, let alone the construction and the planning that must have gone into it in the first place, were nothing less than superhuman.

It wasn't just that the buildings were impressive, or the technology — all of that had been on the cutting edge when he and Marcus were young men, it was the way it was all organized together, to make the place seem so magical. Marcus must have had the ability to search out much of the information used in the technological parts of The Commorancy via The Noise. There was no way one man could have known so much; he must have simply been able to discover where to go looking for the knowledge.

It also became more than apparent that Marcus had pilfered on a grand scale. From whole buildings to advanced computer systems, cutting edge design elements and a lot of very advanced, and dangerous weaponry made up only a small part of the whole. Sourcing, moving, implementing and designing such a home would have been the life's work of countless individuals back before The Lethargy, so how Marcus had managed to construct it by using only controlled Lethargic was beyond him.

Day after day then year after year, Fasolt wandered the corridors, Rooms, and outdoor spaces of The Commorancy and each day he found something that surprised him. It may have been the way electrical equipment and atom-thin circuitry weaved their way through almost the entire series of structures or the downright seemingly impossible Rooms where things appeared to work as if by magic. It all confounded Fasolt until he simply assumed that the world he had left behind must have been a lot more progressive than he had thought.

That, or Marcus had become incredibly intelligent and had designed a lot of the systems himself, but Fasolt just couldn't see how one man's knowledge could have been so extensive.

Exploring The Commorancy was a revelation really, and the fact that it had taken years and he hadn't even finished meant that Marcus really had been a true genius. Nowhere had he been able to find out how long the building had taken, but hints of additions and changes to work did lead him to believe that it was constructed mostly in the first decade after The Lethargy, then continuing sporadically for a few more decades. Marcus' son had certainly said that his father was always busy with building or some form of Commorancy construction right up to when he had left. Fasolt assumed a lot of that work involved getting the more advanced technology as well as the defenses running properly.

Some of it was never finished, especially the biological weapons that were so deadly to those that would try to attack The Commorancy from on the ground. Fasolt had learned an incredible amount by studying the work contained in a few very carefully entered buildings — what Marcus had done to certain insect and plant species would have earned him both praise and maybe a lifelong prison sentence back in pre-Lethargy days.

Now Fasolt too had a lot of the knowledge that Marcus once had, and there was no doubt that Letje, even Arcene, had taken the time to understand a lot of what had been accumulated. It was simply that none of them had chosen to share all their findings with the others. Which was probably a good thing really, days were busy enough without continually talking about Commorancy issues and the past of Marcus Wolfe, ex-oligarch, now dead and in a box.

That was the one thing that really did perplex Fasolt the most, keeping him from his slumber on countless nights. Why had Marcus done it all? It seemed over the top in every way and there was little rhyme or reason to a lot of what had been done as far as he could tell. Yet he knew there was an overall logic to it, a hidden flow that connected the countless parts to the whole. He understood it was part repository for mankind's achievements, as well as a place to store seed, even eggs and semen of countless animals that may or may not be extinct now but could be at some point in time. A lot had been taken from vaults throughout the country, and other countries, brought to The Commorancy so there was somebody to look over it, ensure it stayed viable for thousands of years. How this had been achieved he had no idea.

No, what bothered him the most was the talk of two of him.

If this were so then where was the other one?

Hiding in The Commorancy? Watching them all? He certainly hoped not.

Fasolt still had flashbacks to the man he had once been, the terrible Contamination he himself had unleashed on what was now his home, and he couldn't believe how cold and uncaring a person he had been. He had sat in the bowels of a ship out on the sea and controlled the minds of ten thousand Lethargic. He shuddered at the thought. So many deaths were on his head, and he was a large part of why Marcus eventually did what he had done. Yet he had been forgiven so readily, even Letje and Arcene forgave him, understanding he was not that man any longer.

He wished he had been able to stop his own son from dealing the death blow, but it was not to be — another death that was his fault and his alone.

Yet on he went, day after day, year after year. Learning new things, enjoying being alive, reveling in finally having friends. He couldn't help smiling at that. A man of his age and his only friends in the world were Arcene and Letje. Although come to think of it Letje was one of the most powerful people alive, so maybe he wasn't doing so bad.

Fasolt stayed away from doing anything extravagant, but the truth was that he was incredibly powerful — with hundreds of years of learning how to master The Noise to his name he was a force to be reckoned with if anybody dared try to interfere with his life or that of his friends. To all intents and purposes it was Fasolt that was now the most powerful man alive and he wondered if somehow it hadn't been a part of Marcus' machinations all along to have him be the new guardian for Letje. He often had a nagging suspicion he had been manipulated in some way, saved when he hit the sea as if it was a part of Marcus' plan all along.

Had he been part of a long term game-plan without even knowing it?

He suspected this had been exactly what had happened, but how far back Marcus' manipulations reached he had no idea. Could it have been years?

Anything was possible.

~~~

One day Fasolt was sat on a lichen covered rock overlooking the sea that surrounded his new home, just enjoying the warm sun, the clear blue day and the fresh salt-tinged air. He was lost in a dream-haze of purely being. He wasn't thinking or not thinking, wasn't doing or not doing, he was just in The Now. Not happy or sad, not thinking ahead or to the past, totally in the present, letting it envelop him in its continual Now.

His hair hung over the sides of the rock, trailing to the ground as if wishing to commune with the scrub. He was mostly naked as always, and as clean as a freshly bathed baby. He was as pure as one too, empty, just being, almost at one with The Void, just removed enough so that he could come back to himself in an instant rather than be lost forever.

Look after them Fasolt.

Then it was gone.

It was but a single sentence but as Fasolt focused and opened his eyes after listening to it he realized that the early afternoon had turned to dusk — he had been listening for the better part of an afternoon.

The slow and ponderous voice from the deep was almost too alien for communication to filter through effectively, but there was no doubt that it was Marcus, or what had once been Marcus that had spoken to him from the watery depths.

Fasolt smiled, and answered. *I will, don't you worry. Happy dreaming.*

Fasolt walked back to The Commorancy, now more sure than ever that Marcus really was a powerful man.

Grab a Chair

"Anything?" asked Letje, pulling up a chair and sitting next to Arcene.

"Nope, nothing. It's getting seriously creepy now, like everyone has just vanished. Whoosh."

Letje leaned forward and peered at the screens, there were too many to count so she didn't even bother, but these were their eyes to the outside world.

Neither of them had paid much attention to The Room For Seeing What Was Happening 2, it was there just to keep tabs on those that agreed to stay in touch after they left The Commorancy or for any of those applying for a Room, if surveillance equipment could be easily arranged. There were also strategically placed cameras all over the country in the old cities to keep watch over the comings and goings of the scattered remnants of civilization, not that they often had anything to report.

Now all there appeared to be was an absence of human activity. It was as if the United Kingdom had simply been wiped clean of people, a fresh slate for the plants and animals.

"You don't think Varik, well, The Eventuals anyway, have finally got rid of everyone do you? What if it's just us now?" Arcene looked to Letje for answers, knowing that she didn't have any.

"It can't be. Surely we would have heard something, this is different, like people were never even here. This is seriously beginning to spook me out."

"Have you found anything yet?" asked Fasolt, as he walked into the Room and peered over their shoulders at the screens.

Arcene spoke without turning. "Nope, everyone's been eaten by ghosts."

"This is not good, not good at all," mused Fasolt, leaning closer, hair dropping over Arcene.

"Hey, watch it mister," warned Arcene. She turned to look at him. "What have you been doing?" she asked suspiciously. "You look like you've seen something cool."

Fasolt was smiling, he thought only inwardly, but apparently not. "Oh, nothing, let's just say I've been having a nice day staring out to sea."

"Hmm," said Arcene, turning back to the screens, flipping switches, rotating cameras via a small cream colored ball sunk half into the desk in front of her.

"Look, we need to do something. Where is everyone? How are we going to find out what's going on?" Letje wished she had spent more time searching for clues when she had gone to find Umeko, Kirstie and Stanley, but the shock of them having vanished sent her scurrying back home as fast as she could, convincing herself they must have died somehow, somewhere.

"We are going to have to go and look for them, that's the only way to find out what's happening. People can't just disappear, they can't vanish." Fasolt was getting increasingly nervous, things were happening that he had no knowledge of, no hint of in The Noise, and that wasn't right, not for a man like him.

"What about The Eventuals?" asked Letje, "You think it could be them?"

"After all this time? I don't think so. Varik's church collapsed in on itself right after he died," said Fasolt, unable to stop a lump in his throat. "We haven't heard a thing from them in years; they were ruined without their leader. They just went their own ways mostly, apart from a few zealots, and, well, you know what happened to them."

"Yeah," said Arcene, "You got all deathy on them and sent them to The Void, didn't you?"

"Don't say it like I'm a monster, we agreed, it was for the best. They would have killed people, innocent people."

"I know, just sayin' is all. Anyway, look, here's The Sacellum, not much going on there, is there? Well, nothing at all actually. Not sure when I last checked, but there used to be a few Inked hanging around not knowing what to do, now there's nothing."

Arcene was right, since the death of Varik the church had fallen dramatically, with only the most die-hard clinging to their beliefs in the face of obvious defeat. Some had remained at The Sacellum, or made their way there hoping for sanctuary, but it was a desolate place. Without Varik running the religion it fell away to nothing quickly. He didn't become a martyr, a legend that his followers looked up to. No, with so many witnessing his defeat and death, and the way Letje Awoke and became the new favorite of Bird, his powers vanished with his life. All that was left was sullen regret or disappointment in a man they had believed to be all-powerful. Proved wrong, the faith was in ruins.

After five years there were few left that followed the religion — most apathetically returned to depressing lives unsure what to do with themselves and waiting for The End to come, or brooding over their defeat, never summoning up the necessary strength to rebuild the church and make it the force it once was.

Arcene made some adjustments to the myriad knobs and buttons, sliders and roller-balls in front of her until a bank of screens flickered then showed views of The Sacellum from numerous vantage points. Most were quite distant, but a few discreet spy cameras had been placed fairly close to Varik's old lair and center of his church.

"It's empty, unless everyone is holed up inside and hiding." Letje watched, hoping to find signs of life, even if it would be Eventuals. Nobody entered, nobody left, there was no movement but the rippling of the grass and the swaying of branches. All was silent.

Fasolt pushed upright, gathering his hair in. "There should be at least a few people wandering around there, even now. It was a powerful religion, some still cling to it, such forces don't disappear entirely in only five years. There should be people. We need to go there, it's somewhere to start, where the largest grouping of people would have been apart from The Commorancy."

"Let's not be hasty, look at the place," said Arcene, "it's creepy."

"It's meant to be," said Letje. "Power through architecture, making people feel inferior to a higher power, that's the point of it."

"Well, I don't like it."

"Me either," said Fasolt, still amazed after all these years. Amazed his son had built such a place, been the leader of a religion that he manufactured and convinced so many desperate people was the true path for humanity — extinction, utter extinction of a whole race.

One Step Backward

Letje was used to the silence of The Commorancy but being in The Sacellum made her appreciate quite how much background noise there actually was, apart from when she was in the anechoic hole, of course.

As they wandered the halls of Varik's old home, what he had named The Sacellum once the daunting church was built and opened for his flock, the silence was so intense Letje wanted to scream just to break the wall of absolute quiet.

At least Bird was with her, but he seemed to distrust the empty spaces as much as Letje, Fasolt and Arcene did. Her father, strapped over her shoulder in his duffel, was also unusually silent. It appeared everybody was feeling the pull into The Void that seemed to permeate everything that once was home to the creator of the fastest growing religion humanity had ever seen.

All that was left was dust.

And silence.

Varik's home was certainly impressive, but nothing on the scale of The Commorancy, and Fasolt, having spent centuries holed up underground within its walls, knew its secrets. Not that he needed to implement much of what he knew as most of the building was open — only select Rooms were securely locked, and he opened them easily, having watched through The Noise as much of his son's home was built or re-purposed for his own dark needs.

They wandered from room to room, greeted only by the gentle swirling of dust or the obvious result of ransacking from those brave enough to venture inside what they once thought of as a holy space. Most of The Sacellum was untouched by looters though, Varik's legacy ensuring that even though he had finally lost his god-like status The Eventuals were still too superstitious to commit such blasphemy.

There was a lot to explore. The morning had seem them only just touching the three hundred and sixty five rooms that comprised The Sacellum. Fasolt kept quiet about his own personal cave where he had been incarcerated for more years than he cared to remember.

Letje turned full-circle as fast footsteps clattered away into the darkness — it was obviously Arcene. When she tried to be all sneaky she made more noise than George would have wearing wooden shoes.

"Arcene! Where do you think you're going? You come back here. Arcene!"

"Just going to have a look at The Inside Out Room, it sounds cool." Her voice trailed off as she rounded a corner and made full speed for the Room Fasolt had described. She wanted to see the tree and she wanted to see The Sacellum from the rooftops, plus where Bird used to live. Bird seemed to pick up on this and took flight after her, his huge wings almost touching the walls of the expansive corridor.

Letje and Fasolt looked at each other and shrugged, like they had a choice other than to follow.

~~~

"You should know better than to run off by now, it could be dangerous here," scolded Letje. "Oh, wow." Letje stared up into the branches of the huge silver tree, its slender trunk reaching impossibly high, the curved walls of Varik's exercise room making it seem even taller than it was — no mean feat for such a huge, obviously Noise-manipulated specimen.

"Where is she Fasolt? Can you see her?" Letje stared into the branches, searched in the dark alcoves running up the steep space, but it was hard to see anything in the gloomy interior. Bird flapped noisily up high, a loud *screeee* giving Arcene away.

"Up here, you should see it, it's really cool. C'mon." Arcene peeked out from behind a thick branch, seemingly oblivious to the height.

Letje stared at her half hidden face, suddenly understanding something. "You've been in The Dangerous Room, haven't you? I thought you said you'd wait until you were older." It was no place for a child.

"You use it," came the defensive reply. "Don't see why I can't. I've got The Flow too now, and anyway, I only used it a little bit."

That girl, she's going to get us all killed one of these days.

Fasolt shrugged. He was used to Arcene's antics and wasn't surprised in the least.

"You coming?" Letje asked Fasolt.

"I think I'll wait here. I know you want to go up anyway." He smiled as Letje eagerly began to climb the ancient tree.

"Oh wow, nice view."

Letje settled onto the branch with Bird and Arcene, a tiny image implanted in her mind from Bird showing her where he had once lived, where there were still bad memories of when he lost his chick. Bird had been busy since, Letje didn't even want to think of the state of the roofs dotted around The Commorancy with the ever-expanding number of eagles that were all related to Bird.

"It's no Commorancy but The Sacellum is pretty impressive, right?"

"It is," agreed Letje, staring out at the convoluted rooftops.

While Arcene continued to chatter away aimlessly Letje felt a connection to the tree itself growing. It wasn't doing so well. Varik had spent a lot of time with it, exercising and playing in its branches on a regular basis, giving it an impossible amount of energy via The Noise, allowing it to grow into something it otherwise could never have achieved. Now it was floundering, already its once silver bark, almost the color of Arcene's hair, was getting dark patches and its leaves were mottled with the beginnings of disease. It couldn't maintain its forced growth-rate without help, and it would surely die in a few years.

Letje reached out, watched almost as if a passenger to her own abilities, as life-enhancing energy passed through her from The Noise into the tree. She was sure she could hear it sighing gratefully as it sparkled with life once more. Letje focused in on control of her power and sent it though the whole tree, from the tiniest of roots to the highest of branches, imbibing it with a slow release that would allow the ancient tree to flourish for years to come without more intervention.

It opened to her, showing her its gratitude, the knowledge it had, the way it had grown as Varik spent more and more time within its branches. It was an unusual thing — to watch the development of Varik along with the flourishing of the tree, but the sense of finally coming this close to what it felt like to live a long life and watch events unfold around you was certainly more than worth it.

With a slowing, then a cessation of power flowing into the tree, she said her goodbyes and came back to her reality.

"Oi. You aren't listening to me, are you?"

"Sorry. What did you say?"

"I said let's go into the church, that's where anyone will be if they're still alive, right?"

"There's nobody here, I can feel it. But yes, let's go take a look."

Arcene began her descent, a crazed half-controlled fall comprised of swinging carelessly from branches and seemingly without any concept of the fact that some people were afraid of heights. "Be careful," shouted Letje, aghast at the way Arcene made her way down.

Arcene landed on the ground and smiled up into the branches. "What? C'mon lazybones, you're so slow."

~~~

"Does it feel strange Fasolt?" asked Letje. "Being here, now Varik's gone?"

Fasolt took his time answering, searching within himself for the right words to convey how he really felt. "This is something I have struggled with Letje. Not being here, but how to feel about the fact that my son is dead. There was a time when I don't think I would have given it a second thought — I was a bad man. But now?" Fasolt scratched his head through his thick hair, wondering if it was something Letje was really interested in.

"I am Fasolt, I want to know, and you haven't really talked about it much."

"I don't suppose I have, no. Well, there's the connection you see? Now I am what I feel is a real human being I think about these things, and the truth is that he was my son, and I guess that I really did love him. I just didn't know it for such a long time. Do you stop loving someone because they do bad things? Especially if what they did is partly because of the way you treated them? It makes it hard. After all, bad people shouldn't just be allowed to carry on without them being stopped, but should you stop loving them? Can you? It's not as easy as that, although I have certainly tried.

"Some of it is guilt, but the family bond is not to be ignored. Parents love their children, often no matter what they do, or have done. I don't know where you draw the line as to forgiveness, and I'm not even sure I forgive Varik, just as I don't know that I am truly forgiven by you for what I have done. But there is acceptance, and maybe that is something, at least. Life is so complicated, and it's easy to see why some people just want it over with, but I can't forgive him truly for how he acted, what he did, what he wanted to do. It's best that he is dead, but I wish things could have been different. I guess that's the best I can do really." Fasolt looked into Letje's eyes, for the first time truly trying to understand how she felt about him; something he guessed he just hadn't really wanted to know all these years, afraid of what he would see. After all, her and Arcene were his whole life now — his family.

"I forgive you Fasolt, I really do. You're family, and as you say, family can still love, and yes, forgive, even if bad things have been done. You aren't who you were. We're a team."

"I love you too Fasolt," came Arcene's voice from behind a pillar as she peeked her head out.

"Hey! I thought you were off exploring? It's rude to eavesdrop you know?"

"I didn't want to interrupt," said Arcene, pouting at the unjust accusation.

Fasolt smiled, amazed at the undeserved affection and the chance to have a new life that the two young ones offered up so freely. "Thank you, I don't deserve it, but thank you. Come, let's finish our search and leave this place, leave it to its ghosts and its terrible memories."

~~~

They wandered the vaulted spaces of The Sacellum, the architecture overpowering them with its carefully designed spaces. Everything was constructed to make you feel insignificant, that who you were was nothing but a pointless stain on the planet. It was hard not to be sucked down into surrender and a fog of imposition — that you had no right to be alive when there were things so much more important.

The whole space was made to make acceptance of Varik's religion easier. Indoctrination went smoothly under such a pressure of belittling.

A weight hung over them as they wandered the main church, peeked behind doors and walked the corridors. It was as if their thoughts grew heavy and confused, unable to think clearly under the vaulted spaces. How easy it would be to allow it all to overwhelm you, to accept that if a building was more important than your own life then what right did you have to do anything but further the end that should have come with The Lethargy?

"Let's get out of here, I feel like I'm drowning in misery here." Fasolt hated it, hated it more than he had hated anything in his life. What had his son done? Such a terrible place, sucking the life out of people that could have been anything, done anything, if given hope rather than been taught all there was left was a depressing end to a race that did nothing but despoil their surroundings.

Arcene and Letje walked beside him in silence, and it wasn't until they were outside breathing the fresh air again that anybody had the inclination to speak.

"Let's never come back here again," said Arcene. "What a horrid place this is."

"Agreed," said Fasolt, a tear falling for his son and the things he had done to the minds of others.

"I'll come back, maybe in five years, to help the tree. But I'm never, ever, going in that abomination of a church again. Ugh." Letje thought about the poor creatures that had been indoctrinated in The Sacellum, wondering what chance they had when even without people it made you want to just give up, lie down and offer yourself to The Void.

The Way of The Blade

"Hold on, hold on. HOLD ON!"

Wuppa wuppa wuppa wuppa wu—

"Letje, you are not supposed to turn off the helicopter until we have actually landed," offered up Fasolt helpfully.

"Oh, really? Thank you ever so much for those words of wisdom Fasolt. Maybe next time you'd like to fly the stupid thing?" Fasolt wilted under Letje's glare, zipping his mouth shut, trying not to laugh as Arcene smirked from her cramped position behind him.

Letje was sweating slightly, her internal control shot to pieces under the stress of flying the helicopter. She had forgone her ability to stop such an obvious stress reaction to focus on flying what she was now convinced was the design of the devil. "And I thought the hot air balloon was bad," she muttered under her breath, flicking switches, still rather amazed she had managed to land the contraption upright, even if it had been a rather bumpy landing.

~~~

"Well, that was a waste of time," said Arcene, piling food onto her plate.

"I wouldn't say that but it sure is good to be home, eh Fasolt?"

"Yes, this is home isn't it? Now more than ever I am grateful for that, and for you two young ladies too."

"Hey Fasolt, we're a family, you're like my mum and dad. Sort of," said Arcene hurriedly, as she got dirty looks from Letje and Fasolt. "C'mon, you know what I mean. You're the grown-ups, and I'm, well, getting there. Yum, any more of this?"

"No, that's the last of it Arcene, and we wouldn't have minded eating some too," scolded Letje.

"See, just like real parents," smirked Arcene, stuffing the last of the beef into her mouth before it was too late.

"Um, hello?" came a voice from the kitchen door.

Fasolt had to stop himself from attempting to shut the person down instantly, but he was across the black flagstone floor in a flash, knife pulled from his satchel and at the man's throat faster than was possible for those merely Whole.

"Whoa, whoa, take it easy. Nobody came, I waited, so I walked and ended up here. And, um, can you take that away from my throat? You're liable to do yourself an injury." Gammadims spoke with confidence, like he knew he could turn the tables on Fasolt if he had to.

"Letje?" asked Fasolt.

"It's Gammadims, Fasolt. My first Orientation. Let him go please. Sorry Gamm, you surprised us is all."

"Hey Gamm, how you doin'?" said Arcene, jumping up and running over to the big man.

"Um, oh. It's Arcene? Gosh, you've grown. Er, I'm fine, just a little confused. Nobody was there to meet me. How long's it been?"

"Yes Arcene, how long has it been? Didn't a certain somebody who was in charge of monitoring guests and telling me when they were due out say that Gamm may well be in his Room for fifty years?"

"Fifty years? I need a sit down, it didn't feel that long." Gamm ignored Fasolt and took a seat at the table. "I'm starving." He eyed the remains of the meal greedily.

"Help yourself," said Arcene. "Man after my own heart."

"Arcene? Stop avoiding the question?"

"Oh, um, er, yeah right. I um, maybe got it a little wrong." Arcene squirmed uncomfortably, looking around for a way to escape. "Hey, so, how about that helicopter ride? Letje was rubbish wasn't she."

Silence.

Gamm cleared his throat to break the uncomfortable situation.

The silence continued.

"Alright, alright, I'm sorry okay. I may have got my numbers a little wrong, it was a long time ago you know? I wasn't as good at reading all the data back then. It won't happen again, promise."

Letje gave Arcene the evil eye then turned to Gamm. "I'm so sorry about this, it's been a little over four years Gamm, which is quite a short stay for a lot of people. But if you got to the end of your Room then it was time for you to come out. Heck, the fact that you got out means it must have been time. Otherwise you'd be a dead heap on the floor and still inside. Sorry about this, I would have come to greet you personally." Arcene got an extra hard stare for making Letje feel like a bad host.

"Honestly, that's okay. I can't thank you enough, for the Room, for allowing me to stay. For Awakening. How did you know? How to do the Room I mean, what I wanted, well, what I needed anyway? It was incredible."

"Haha, all part of the service. There's a lot to it actually, but they're Commorancy secrets I'm afraid. Oh, help yourself to something to eat, if Arcene left anything that is. Arcene, where are your manners? Get Gamm something to eat please."

"Don't see why I have to be the one to do it, I'm not a slave you kn—" Arcene was cut short by yet another look from Letje. "Fine, no need to get all starey."

"You must have gained some pretty impressive skills Gamm, to have made it from your Room to here. Most people would be very dead by now if they'd tried." Arcene put a plate in front of him: fresh bread, homemade cheese and pickles that Arcene was proud of making, and every one else ate under sufferance so as not to hurt her feelings.

"Yes, I saw some very dangerous things as I made my way here, it was... Ugh, excuse me." Gamm descended into a prolonged coughing fit as he tried to deal with the vinegar heavy pickle he had just swallowed. Letje pushed a glass of water his way which he finally managed to drink. "That's a... a very interesting pickle."

"It's good isn't it? I made it myself. I'm going to make some more soon." Arcene brimmed with pride at her obviously excellent culinary skills.

"Oh, goodie," said Letje.

"Can't wait," said a grumpy Fasolt, who came and sat at the table now it was obvious Gamm was not an intruder or threat to his happy home.

"You went in a helicopter?" asked Gamm, once he stopped exhaling vinegar vapors. "Didn't know such things still existed."

"Oh yes, well, we have one anyway. It was awful though, Letje can't land to save her life. And it was all pointless anyway, everyone's gone, really gone."

"Arcene!" Letje couldn't believe her, but it was too late now.

"What do you mean, gone?" asked Gamm, his euphoria after the stay in his Room replaced by a terrible sense that the good times were over.

"Oops, sorry."

"I think I better get you something stronger to drink, it's vino o'clock anyway, let's go to The Evening Drinking Room."

"Letje, it's not five o'clock yet."

"Well, it is somewhere. New Rule."

~~~

Letje felt the warmth of her second drink and it was needed. The day had been long, depressing, and also a little bit deflating as her first guest had not been given the full Commorancy treatment. There were standards to maintain, strict ones, and now they just looked like a bunch of amateurs.

After explaining the situation to Gamm, the four of them and Constantine had settled into a pensive silence, each lost in their own thoughts of how best to approach the situation.

"I don't know what I can do to help, but first I need to go home. To check on things, see if anything has happened, maybe report back to you? If that's alright?"

"Of course, of course it is, just be careful. What of, I'm not sure, but something has obviously gone very wrong somehow. We just don't know what."

"You're all Awoken though, aren't you? And you didn't find anything to follow up on?"

"I'm not, not yet," said Arcene, who had been pestering Letje for years now to show her how to. Letje had told her she should wait, enjoy her youth before she concerned herself with such things and that she was lucky anyway as hardly anyone was even Whole.

Fasolt explained. "I am very old Gamm, I see into the minds of men, can control them as easily as I brush my teeth. I see pasts, presents and countless futures, just like Letje now can, and there is nothing. Not a tiny hint in The Noise, not a wisp of the people that are now gone, there is only emptiness. No people, none that I can find anyway. There are the guests of The Commorancy, that is all."

"That's impossible. People don't just die and disappear like that, over what, a few years at most?"

"Less, there were people not long ago at all. But we hadn't been keeping track of all the Whole, so it could have been going on for a number of years. Applications certainly slowed down for Rooms that's for sure."

"So it's a mystery? We need a detective."

"I know what that is, Sherlock Holmes right?"

"Yes Arcene, Sherlock Holmes," said Fasolt, impressed as he knew Letje or Gamm had no idea who it was.

"Sherlock who?" asked Letje.

"A character in a book Letje, he was a great detective, and he did drugs too, did you know that?" Arcene smirked at her oneupmanship.

"No, I didn't. But don't you go getting any funny ideas."

Gamm left the next day, promising to get in touch once he got home and saw for himself what was happening. Letje had the distinct impression he was relieved to escape the madness. She couldn't really blame him.

Where'd it Go?

"Hey, have you been moving my stuff again Arcene?" Letje was sure she had put down her scarf right on the desk, but she couldn't find it anywhere.

"What? I don't move your stuff. Why would I do that?"

"Because you are a terrible child and very naughty, that's why," said Letje, only half joking.

Arcene pouted and swore that she hadn't moved Letje's things on her desk. She had enough to be doing without playing childish games. Arcene poked her tongue out at Letje and said, "I was just coming to see if you fancied a game of table tennis, I'm getting quite good at it now. Be nice to have a break from work," she hinted.

"Yeah, sorry. That does sound good." Letje got up from her chair, back making creaking noises it ought not to for one still so young. A break from work was just what she needed. She followed Arcene out of the Room saying, "It's weird, stuff keeps moving, or I keep losing things, not sure. You definitely aren't up to anything are you? You can tell me, I won't be cross."

Arcene stopped and turned, arms folded across her chest. "Letje, in case you haven't noticed I am a lot more grown up now, I don't do such silly things any more."

"Okay, sorry. Come on, let's play. I'm gonna beat you though."

"Wanna bet?"

As they left the Room there was a shifting of shadows and a glint of a knowing eye as a thief moved as silently as it could across the floor then crept out after them. Watching them make their way around the corner it headed off in the direction of its home, deep in the depths of a part of The Commorancy its current owners didn't even know existed.

It took with it the scarf from the desk; it would come in useful.

Dreams Turn to Ash

Letje lay on a mountain of bones and ash, naked, covered in the dust of human beings dead and cremated. Some had gone to The Void hundreds of years ago, others were much more recent additions to The Room For Ashes — those that still dared to try to enter The Commorancy with hatred in the heart and death their goal.

Letje slept, exhausted, uncaring that she was lying on the most uncomfortable bed, sleeping the sleep of the dead. Penetrating her dreams, warping her clarity in The Noise, the ghosts of those she lay upon reached out impossibly from The Void, many already reborn into the past, the future, countless variations on the timeline currently running for Letje as she slept.

She was the gray woman.

She was death.

She was the most powerful person alive, and was but twenty two years old with centuries if not millennia ahead of her — if she didn't go mad in the process of being the gatekeeper between life or extinction for the now minuscule number of creatures left alive that could call themselves people.

Letje's mind, already completely re-wired since her Awakening five years ago, ran fast now. Millions of new neural pathways had been created, linking in ways only those like her could ever know. Nobody had told of the occasional crash from living such a life, although Marcus, and Fasolt, not to mention his son, should have been warning enough of what happens to those that Awaken — none of them were what you could call normal people. Far from it.

It meant that Letje needed downtime, and there was nothing to do to stop it. It explained why Marcus would suddenly just go from being full of energy to excusing himself and falling asleep, snoring loudly a few seconds later. She was getting hints of what was to come if she lived an extended life. The more she used Awoken abilities then the more her body reacted, taking defensive measures she was mostly unable to stop; reconfiguring to accommodate new skills, new knowledge, the overload of information that permeated everything and gave up its secrets to her often whether she wanted them or not. This was the curse and the reward for being at the vanguard of human evolution — it came with its own price that had to be paid, often in tears, sometimes in blood.

So Letje slept, dreaming the dreams of The Awoken.

They were endlessly disturbing. Reality was fleeing, she was already finding parts of her life lost in a maze of pasts, presents, countless futures, glimpses into what could be, making it hard to live in The Now, sometimes knowing what came next before it happened. Who wanted to live like that? It was boring; life should be a surprise. She was finding out that control was needed as her Awoken state didn't mean everything came easily, there were struggles to cope with what it was she saw, what she knew, and the energy burned meant that she needed to rest sometimes very suddenly.

She was the dreaming woman.

She was lost.

Letje dreamed of people, countless people, happy people. But not really happy, not deep down in their core where emotions welled up and reflected external stimuli. Letje dreamed of happy people that were made to be happy. There was a presence, not malignant, not necessarily evil, just wrong.

Wrong, wrong, wrong.

There was madness permeating the air, infecting everything, destroying realities and warping futures until they could be anything at all, not necessarily what they ought to be. Consequences of actions no longer linear, one thing no longer led to another, flowed as it should.

Letje awoke with a start, her side hurting until she shifted and moved the femur, the head of which was jabbing into her side as if looking for comfort from the only warm body in the Room.

Sliding down the clattering pile Letje felt refreshed, her Awoken body recalibrated to take into account ever changing functions both mental and physical. She wondered how long such a metamorphosis could last, and if she could stand to live like this for much longer. Could it take hundreds of years of such changes before she reached her ultimate potential? If so, she knew she would be mad long before then. How did Marcus cope?

She needed to spend some time with The Book, this was no way to live, not being in control. What was the point of being Awoken if it affected you in such ways?

And the people, the dream?

There was more to it than her subconscious filtering data and allowing her to continue her warped life — somebody was out there, skewing reality, making the future impossible to know. Infinite timelines were being let loose and there was no saying what would happen.

Everything was possible, even the end of all things.

~~~

"Madness," read Letje, scowling at the thick tome in front of her, weightier than many others but dedicated not to running The Commorancy or detailing The States Of Awakening, but focusing solely on

Marcus' inner battle with demons that would drag him kicking and screaming into otherworldly insanity and never let him surface again.

Letje stayed isolated for a week while she read it from cover to cover, refusing to be interrupted, taking food and drink gratefully when it was brought to her, but staying put, reading until her eyes grew heavy and slumber gave her a welcome respite from her ever more depressing — yet illuminating — studies of how Marcus coped with the true effects of becoming more powerful than any other person had ever been, until now.

"Well, how was it?" asked Fasolt, as Letje walked into the kitchen looking like she needed to sleep for a hundred years.

"Not sure. Fasolt, how do you deal with it? The changes?"

"From being Awoken?"

"Yes. What do you do to stop just sort of switching off to let your body get used to it? How do you deal with the things you can do and see? How did you stop the madness?"

Fasolt sighed, he knew Letje wasn't going to like the answer. "Letje, I was a bad man, bad before I Awoke, very bad once I did. I spent I don't know how many years never washing, never leaving a cave deep beneath The Sacellum, constant depravity going on above me. I spent most of my time in The Noise, exploring it, manipulating the minds of others: animal and human. I played in the chaos and let it consume me. I killed and hurt and humiliated and teased just for fun. Then I died, and came back reborn. And now here I am. Do I look like the right person to ask about madness? Actually look at me. Properly."

Letje looked at the man sat in front of her. A big boned but very thin man with huge hands and a face lined with effects of age. A naked man apart from a small loincloth and an ever-present battered leather satchel. A man with thick coils of dreadlocks that wandered away on the floor under the table and dangled over the back of his chair. Pure madness.

"I never thought of you as mad."

"Well, who's to say? I don't feel mad. I feel like I *was* mad, back when I was the old me, but then, at the time it all felt perfectly normal. I feel normal now, but when I take a step back? Think about what normal used to mean? Back before The Lethargy? It certainly wasn't a man walking around naked in the presence of two young women. It wasn't living in this crazy place and it wasn't entering the minds of people and controlling them, seeing the screams of the grass and the cheers of the grasshopper, the sensation of a caterpillar ripping itself to pieces to live as a butterfly for a day and dream of being as free as the wind.

"So, the answer? Either let the true Awakening do as it will with your body and mind, or take the offer while you still have it and become just a young woman, Whole, nothing more nothing less, and live a normal life. Grow old like everyone else and take your place in The Void when your time comes, rather than be the outlier that defies time and warps it for your own end. I believe those are the only choices really."

"Well, that makes me feel a whole lot better!" Letje poured a cup of coffee and sat down heavily. "Wish I'd spoken to you first. You summed up what took me a week to read in a few minutes." Letje rubbed at her red eyes, the dark skin underneath feeling thin and as if it would melt from her face.

"Haha, I know you too well Letje Sandoe, you would have still read Marcus' book anyway."

"True, I guess you're right. Well, suppose I'll just go with it then, see what happens, try to hold onto who I am, what I am."

"A wise move if you don't mind me saying so. Who knows what the future will hold? The main thing is to be aware and act accordingly. This part won't last, you are probably close to being all that you will be. Then you settle into your own new self and it will get easier. But don't forget the joy, the gift you have and the fact you should be grateful for being allowed to see the world we live in with such clarity. It is a blessing indeed."

Fasolt turned when there was no reply.

Letje was fast asleep in her chair, the coffee not even touching her tiredness. Fasolt grabbed a blanket from by the fire and draped it gently over her, then put another log on to keep the kitchen warm and went to think about the things that were coming to him in his dreams — things that hinted at a future he was no longer getting the slightest glimpse of. Something was messing with reality and he knew that life was about to get interesting. He was pleased Letje was so interested in the effects of her new life, it might just be enough to stop a descent into madness. He hoped so at least, and if she did halt it then she would be the first. How do you keep a personality when you live so long, know so much, and forget so much of your life, your actions and your feelings, even the people you knew, when the human brain can only hold onto so much?

Well, we all make our choices. Just have to get on with life, that's the most important thing.

Fasolt closed the door quietly behind him, leaving Letje to her, for once, dreamless slumber.

Damn Gamm

Gammadims was a solitary man, not by choice, but because of the total lack of other people still alive. He was a large man, almost a giant compared to the average person. His six feet five inch frame in no way looked disproportionate though; if anything he could have done with being a bit taller for the weight he currently held. Gamm had spent his adult life involved in strenuous physical activity to simply relieve the boredom of a very mundane existence.

There was just nothing to do.

He got bored of reading book after book, got fed up with having to deal with ever less efficient solar panels, so cut right back on using the TV to watch movies or shows about a long dead way of life. No matter how futuristic the concepts of the things he watched, they all seemed so dated and pointless — they really didn't have a clue back then what the future could be like for humanity.

Gamm had gone right back to basics a long time ago as he simply got annoyed with trying to cling to a past that wasn't even a part of his memory. Once he turned to more practical matters, using his strength and his mental abilities, he actually found that he lived a more technologically based life than he had before.

In his early twenties he relocated to an old collection of buildings on the side of a fast flowing river. An old water mill that gave him a project that took him five years to finish. He completely rebuilt the wheel, learned how to use it to generate more electricity than he could ever find a use for, and after getting so annoyed with constantly whacking his head on the low beams in the warren of rooms in the dark interior he stripped bare the main house and attached storage barns, opening up the spaces right up to the rafters, knocking down walls, connecting the buildings to each other, and installing new heavy joists and running tension cables from wall to wall to keep the structure intact now its layout was so drastically changed. The end result was a light and spacious building full of quirky features and different levels that was sparse, clean, and gave him the freedom of movement he needed for his large size.

Then he got bored again.

He didn't really like being inside all the time anyway, and although he occupied himself using the woodworking tools that could now be run easily thanks to his endless supply of energy, he soon gave up the hobby as it was nothing but a distraction from a mundane life he knew he had to do something with.

Every day he dedicated an hour to hard training with whatever big and bulky objects he could get his hands on, and over the years he grew in strength and size, and so did his appetite.

Gamm became an expert hunter and expanded his vegetable plots until all around his renovated home were fields of various crops so at least his meals were plentiful and varied. He took up husbandry, wondering why he had spent years honing hunting skills when all he had to do was capture a few animals and let nature take its course. Soon he had more pigs than he needed, chickens were always underfoot, and the adjacent fields not given over to crops were full of livestock that he cared for daily and thanked for the protein they provided so easily.

It was a good existence, plentiful, energizing now he had settled into a way of life that suited his personality. He was so goddamn lonely he thought he would shatter he felt so brittle and empty inside.

Out of necessity Gamm put himself in danger on a regular basis as he really felt that he had no choice in the matter. He was a solitary man by fate's whim, not out of choice, and he craved human contact so much sometimes that it became soul-crushing to stay alone for another day. It meant that every time it got too much to bear he would travel away from his safe little pocket of tranquility and venture not just into small villages and towns but to large cities — once thriving metropolises that held the most reminders of a civilization now mostly forgotten by all but the most ardent reader of what was now ancient history.

Days, sometimes weeks, were spent rummaging through libraries, scouring the bookshelves of once middle-class homes for items of interest, and generally wandering aimlessly, entering buildings just to see if he could be surprised by what he found. Much of it became mundane, but now and then he would make discoveries that made the hairs on the back of his neck stand on end. The detritus of a once so called civilized society was terrifying in its wickedness. The things he saw locked behind doors in what were once thought of as average suburban homes were startling. People used to get involved in all kinds of acts of depravity whilst obviously living seemingly outwardly normal lives.

Not that things were any better now though. Gamm had lived through the latter days of The Eventuals, then the total cessation of the Inked devils in the short time he was still at large in the world before he finally got his Room. It was like they disappeared off the face of the planet once Letje had taken over from Marcus — news he got quickly as he left his computer connected to the fractured Web just in case anything new did ever turn up. Run from within The Commorancy, it was a tiny fragment of what had been an amazing source of information, now limited in scope but at least he got the news that Varik was dead,

Marcus too, but that The Commorancy was accepting guests once more. He had jumped at the chance.

Loneliness and the inability to find people, company, a woman to share his life with, meant that he would do whatever he could to Awaken so he could use such abilities to seek out voices in The Noise and hopefully find a lifelong companion.

It was just a shame that the first news he got after he left his Room was that everyone was gone. Not exactly what he wanted to hear — quite the opposite.

Gamm thought about it all when he returned to his home after leaving The Commorancy, his time in his Room, his life before that and the few encounters he had with people after he found himself alone when his mother died as he was just entering puberty.

Exhausted from his trip back home, yet keen to check on the small family unit he had known for years now, Gamm sat and drank a warm cup of tea and his thoughts drifted back to the time he met the strange people just a few miles away from his home — it may as well have been another world entirely.

~~~

Gamm came from a lineage where most family members had been like him: large and strong. The three hundred years since The Lethargy had resulted in quite a few extreme body-types as the gene pool shrank. Descendants of the same family lines often had children carrying many of the same genetic markers as their parents and their parents' parents. As populations shrank, so inevitably those that remained become closer and closer related by blood, it was unavoidable.

Deformities were fairly common as it got extreme, but most children died in childbirth from The Lethargy whether they were from close family lines or as diverse as possible. Even so there were extremes, and one of the strangest, yet in no way disturbing once you got used to it, was when he met an extended family that lived just a few miles from him yet he had been totally unaware of for most of his time at his now comfortable home.

Halfway through his extensive renovations he had taken some time away from the work to clear his head and do a bit of exploring. He often roamed the countryside just for the sheer joy of it, stopping in at small villages or random isolated houses just out of curiosity.

This excursion was somewhat different.

He came across a convent, a large Gothic piece of architecture all stern stone and imposing scale. As he walked up to the entrance — the construction date of 1890 carved into the lintel above the door — he wasn't expecting to find much of anything inside; after all, what would a bunch of nuns have anyway? After all this time it was sure to have been taken whatever it was.

He was wrong.

He should have known before he stepped foot inside, but so pre-occupied was he with the building itself that he failed to note the well kept condition of the immediate surroundings. There were no plants gone rogue, no trees growing where they shouldn't, no mounds of rotting leaves from centuries of drifts against the house; just gravel and a neat exterior. He just didn't think about it as he had no thought of finding it inhabited.

As he stepped up to the door to check if it was locked he was shocked to see it open, the loud creaking hinges of the ancient metal groaning under the weight. A child's head poked around the door from out of the gloom, obviously as surprised as he was. He noted a small gardener's basket in the tiny hands of the child before the door was slammed shut suddenly when she caught sight of him. Strange that such a child would be wearing a nun's habit though, he had always thought it was for adults only from what he had read of the ancient religion. But centuries of faiths being warped, and even the sudden change in beliefs right after The Lethargy, meant that it wasn't really a surprise. You only had to look at The Eventuals to know that anything was possible when it came to religious practices.

Then something registered in Gamm's brain — it wasn't a child, it was an old woman. Since when do kids have wrinkles on their hands and faces? Yep, definitely an old woman, just a very small one.

Gamm walked down the steps, wondering what to do next. He didn't want to intrude where he wasn't welcome, so maybe he should just leave and come back another day? Or maybe he should go and knock politely and say that he was just passing and didn't know anyone was living there?

Or maybe he should just go and —

The next thing he knew he was flat on the ground with about a million tiny hands running all over his body and the only thing he could think of was that this is what it must feel like to be attacked by the monkeys he had watched in some old program about the animals that used to be so abundant all over the world.

Except these monkeys were chattering away to each other and had trussed him up like a pig ready for the spit before he had the foresight to maybe kick and punch his way clear. Could you do that to nuns, even if they were tying you up and none of them seemed to be over four foot if he was being generous with his estimate? *Probably, you idiot,* came the reply from his own mind. *They may be little, they may be nuns, whatever that means any more, but it doesn't mean they are little friendly nuns, now does it?*

Too late. Even as he was thinking about the idiocy of his own actions he was being rolled over onto a kind of large mat and dragged over the gravel by some grim looking wizened old ladies, all with gray habits on and hands smaller than a child's.

It would have been funny if it wasn't so uncomfortable — he didn't like to use the word terrifying as that would mean he was scared, which, of course, he was.

The last thing he remembered was bumping down steps, then he blacked out as his head slammed into the bottom step that led to a path around the side of the convent where there were even more tiny people: men and women.

They had pointed teeth and wrinkled faces and all he could think of as he blacked out was that they looked like tiny demons his mother had warned him about when he was a little child, to stop him from straying too far from home.

Guess you were right mum.

Nuns are Always Nice

They were lovely people.

Small, scary looking, certainly inbred to a dangerous degree, but once you got to know them The Sisters of The Lethargy were actually good company, unless you were one of their men, then it was a different story entirely.

There was a very strict matriarchal pecking order that was ruled with a hand of iron by the smallest person he had ever seen, even by The Sisters' diminutive stature. She was all of three feet tall when wearing her shoes, yet had the bearing of the most beautiful and statuesque woman there had ever been. The ancient woman stood as straight as an arrow and twice as deadly. A wild frizz of gray-white hair peeked out from beneath her habit, almost as washed out as her hair but perfectly starched and without a crease.

Gamm was something of a freak for The Sisters, they hadn't seen the likes of him — ever. This was a closed community and had been for a long time; he came to learn there had been no outsiders for generations. The Sisters went nowhere, had no interest in the rest of the world, just performed their daily duties, worshiped what turned out to be Mother Lethargy, and prayed that their small island of Wholeness would stay that way. So far it had worked out well and they were certainly uninterested in what was going on beyond their convent.

Gamm spent a number of days with them, being released once he had convinced them he wasn't there to do them any harm. In the end it wasn't his words that gained him his freedom, it was a nod of the head from Mother Superior after she had watched his mind through The Noise and was certain he was a kind and honest man. Mother Superior was the only one who was Awoken, but each and every Sister was Whole, and as far as he could tell it had always been that way, right back to the beginning when those that remained untouched by The Lethargy took it upon themselves to keep their order alive by inviting the caretaker of the property into their sanctuary — a man who had what he was told was called progeria, a rare genetic condition that was passed on to the first of what would become the new order.

The condition mutated across the generations as some children died from it or from The Lethargy until all the remaining occupants carried at least a remnant of the condition. But it wasn't the progeria as such that caused The Sisters to look so strange, it was the mutated cells combined with the severely limited gene pool that caused all of them to be diminutive in stature, have large bulbous heads which made them look like babies, and wrinkles that made them look a lot older than Gamm found out many were.

Gamm didn't ask, and didn't want to know, just how limited the gene pool was, but he suspected that the way children were treated, never having a mother as such, more a communal upbringing, that the Sisters themselves didn't know, or care about who bred with who. If they were old enough and interested enough to try to reproduce then it seemed that this sat absolutely fine with their version of a religion that had morphed from a form of Christianity into something completely different entirely.

Gamm kept quiet about the way the convent was run as it was obvious that there was nothing he could say to make them approach their way of life differently, and although the tiny men were obviously seen very much as second class citizens there was no doubt that they were happy with their lot — knowing no different after who knew how many generations being locked away from the outside world.

Apart from the occasional stealthy cleaning of the immediate area outside the convent the inhabitants stayed strictly behind closed doors, be that inside the building or in a huge compound to the side and rear that nobody would know was there unless they were very dedicated to gaining access. Gamm didn't want to think about what may have happened to anybody The Sisters didn't like if they had ever managed to scale the huge walls — original walls that surrounded the rear of the property combining a great courtyard with cloisters, walkways and gardens where they grew everything they needed and kept livestock to feed their small hidden community.

It was a strange few days for sure, and much as he craved human contact he couldn't bring himself to think of these strange folk as people in the traditional sense. They had strayed too far from the path of what was acceptable, locking themselves away, hiding from the world and keeping their lives secret. Whatever it was that kept the majority of them Whole, living long but normal standard lives apart from Mother Superior, he had no idea, he just knew they were like an alien race to him in the end. When he left he knew that he wouldn't be returning any time soon.

Yet that was the reason why he sat in his living room drinking tea wasn't it? He could have stayed closer to The Commorancy, have remained and helped, or done any manner of things now he was Awoken. Specifically, try to find a companion with his new powers of entering The Noise, but here he was. He needed to know if what they had told him at The Commorancy was true.

Gamm drifted off to sleep; he would check in the morning, first thing. It had been a long day, come to think of it it had been a long few years, four or more, and an evening sat in his favorite chair, with a nice cup of tea, dozing by the fire felt like heaven on earth to him right now.

~~~

He awoke with a start, the last embers of the fire dying away slowly as dawn came creeping across the water and lit up the window to his living room. The tea was as cold as the room. He must have got up in the night and grabbed a blanket as he was still warm, but his breath told him that some wood on the fire would be a good thing.

Once the fire was roaring again, and some more fresh hot tea was drunk, Gamm set about getting ready for his trip.

Then he suddenly realized — couldn't he just find The Sisters through The Noise? He had that skill now, it was why he had got a Room in the first place, wasn't it?

Nothing. Emptiness, silence, not a hint of human presence. Weird, he had found the kitchen in The Commorancy because of his new skills, seeing people via The Noise just like he was staring through walls and watching them.

He tried again, maybe it was his lack of practice? Maybe he was just tired. Had he showered since he got home? A sniff told him the answer to that question so he decided that some much needed morning ablutions would probably get him ready for the day and maybe let him find The Sisters in The Noise. If not then he would at least be clean to go and see if he could find them.

As he stripped off in his, for him, luxurious bathroom, Gamm caught his reflection in the mirror. It never ceased to shock him when he saw his naked skin — wondering yet again why he had allowed The Sisters to mark his body in the way they had. It was just the acceptance he guessed, even if he did have his reservations about the strange people when they had shown him how they themselves were marked, a sign of their devotion to the energies that controlled everyone's lives. He took them up on their offer and two painful days later it was over. He would never be the same again.

Running his fingers over the strange tattoos Gamm asked himself not for the first time if he truly liked his markings or not. He guessed that deep down he did, they were certainly beautiful.

All over Gamm's densely muscled upper body, across his chest, abdomen, shoulders and crawling down his back were beautiful lines, sweeping in majestic circles around his muscles, spirals, wavy lines, some bold and thick, others impossibly delicate like wisps of smoke. All were the same impossibly bright blue — a homage to the sky and to the oceans. Sometimes it felt like the wind itself was blowing over his skin, caressing gently the graded wisps that swept over his body. It was multi-layered and impossibly complex, a fractal tattoo that was never ending in its detail yet bold and simple on first inspection. It always amazed Gamm that the surface of his skin wasn't raised where the ink had been forced underneath, it looked so three dimensional that it was impossible not to think of it as a physical thing.

The Sisters were adamant that it be done, although of course he could have denied them if he wished, but they insisted it was important. It tied him to them, and to their beliefs. They told him he would be more of a person for accepting the markings — closer to the natural ways of the world, linked to the cycles of life and death, and although they didn't go as far as to talk about magic there was definitely an underlying current of a belief that the marks held a power of sorts. Gamm just liked the look of them, and although he had his doubts once his body was permanently stained blue, he accepted them as a part of him now, marveling at the vivid color and the impossible patterns.

Dressed, and feeling better for the shower, Gamm sipped yet another cup of tea and tried once more to connect to the presence of The Sisters — they really were gone.

Time to do a little investigating.

No Habits Here

The front door was locked and Gamm knew nobody was at home even before he walked up the lichen covered steps. There were drifts of leaves, the plants hugging the walls were in need of pruning, and the climbing decorative ivy was beginning to creep over the windows. The Sisters, or more to the point Mother Superior, would never have allowed the mess. The subservient men would have been ordered to cut back the growth as soon as it began to get out of control.

Nevertheless, he walked around the side of the building, then peeked through into the rear after a rather energetic climb over a wall. The grass was long, the weeds were rampant, and the vegetables had long ago bolted then rotted. They were gone, and a good while ago by the seems of it.

But where? And how? People didn't just disappear, especially without leaving any kind of a trace behind them. There were no bodies, no signs of a struggle, no broken windows or smashed down doors. No sign of marauders stealing or some kind of mass suicide — not that The Sisters would ever do such a thing. Gamm couldn't consolidate the people he had known with them suddenly taking off voluntarily either. There were people who upped and left their homes as life got too hard in one place, but The Sisters had stayed put for hundreds of years in their strange little pocket of isolation. They wouldn't leave.

They knew next to nothing of the outside world and showed no interest in much away from their tiny community, so there was only one conclusion he could come to: they had been taken.

Gamm prided himself on being quite a proficient tracker so spent the remainder of the morning, and then well into the afternoon after stopping for lunch, searching for clues as to what on earth could have happened.

It felt like a lost cause. What trace would remain of whatever had happened after months let alone maybe years? Still, he persisted, believing that something, some hint of what had happened, would reveal itself. Gamm found nothing before lunch and decided that he would widen the search for the afternoon. He tried to think logically about how the Sisters could have been taken and decided that the only way out would have been by the overgrown roads that led to the convent.

Tucked away in the countryside, access was by small lanes that were impossible to use, or had been. As Gamm followed the only real way out of the convent unless you went cross country as he did, something finally began to reveal itself to him. One of the lanes was open, cut back to allow vehicles to pass, something he hadn't ever seen before. It would take quite some time to clear the overgrown hedgerows and fallen trees from the road, meaning somebody would have been driving tractors or much heavier equipment to get the job done. It was more than a clue, it was a sure sign that they had been taken as the nuns would never have done such a thing — it would be like advertising their presence.

It was a literal dead-end though. The intervening period since the work had been carried out had seen the hacked back greenery sprout with renewed vigor. Soon enough the way was blocked once more for vehicles, but he managed to scrape past and there were hints of the path somebody had taken. Then the road met a main junction where chewed up asphalt made the perfect home for mosses and the meetings of trees large and small; the trail went cold. The kidnappers, for that is now what Gamm felt had happened, could have gone in a number of directions and whichever way he turned there was no sign of anything large, or small having gone any further.

He picked a direction and walked. Maybe he would get lucky and he would spot something further down the road.

~~~

Days had passed and Gamm was exhausted. He had tried every direction he could think of and nothing he tried gave up any more clues. The trail had gone cold and had been for a long time. The vigor of the plants ensured that everything looked the same as it had for decades. There was no way to know where The Sisters had gone or even if they really had gone by land. Could they have been taken by air once they had traveled a short distance? It was a possibility he supposed but what kind of vehicle? He hadn't heard of people traveling in the skies apart from in books, and had never experienced anything apart from the small helicopter Letje had told him about at The Commorancy.

Were there large versions, ones that could take away whole small communities? Surely not, and where would they land such a thing anyway?

Then it clicked, that's why the lane was cut back, to allow movement on foot of the people but then maybe they had taken to the skies, using the road as a place to take-off and land? If so then he had been looking for clues in the wrong way — he'd been looking for signs of vehicles or people on foot, not something that could fly. He just had to have a think about what to actually look for, as obviously he couldn't track where something went if it left the ground.

Another day passed and this time he gave it up as a lost cause. There were no signs of vehicles, ground or otherwise; he was all out of ideas. If they had been taken along the roads then he couldn't find any sign of them. Gamm decided to get off the open space of the road and go into the safety of the woods. If there were people out to kidnap the unsuspecting then hiding should have been his first priority all along but he hadn't really given it a second thought, not believing he could be considered worth the taking. But then why were The Sisters? Why was anybody or everybody if what he had been told at The Commorancy was true?

Gamm picked up speed and marched up the steep bank that flanked the road and immediately felt at peace as the silence of the forest enveloped him and the light turned to a gentle dusk, the cooler air a welcome change from the warm day and the constant buzzing of insects. It was amazing just how much heat the ancient crumbling tarmac still gave off, even after so many years.

A mossy rock looked very inviting so Gamm sat and took a drink of water. A glint of white poking out from beneath the loam caught his eye and he kicked it absentmindedly. The bone didn't budge so was larger than he had assumed. He stood and scuffed away the rotting leaves, loose moss and soil, realizing that there was a large patch of mushrooms shyly poking out from beneath the surface, tiny white-capped things that were easy to miss.

This was a clue, he was sure of it. He got onto his hands and knees, scooping the soft ground away from the skeleton. It was a horse. A horse!

That explained a lot. There was no hi-tech kidnapping, The Sisters had been taken by horse and traveled across country for the sake of secrecy just as he now was. No wonder he couldn't find any sign of their passing, such a trail would have gone cold after the first winter.

At least it was a clue though, a sign that maybe, just maybe they really had been taken. The only questions remaining were was it against their will, and where were they now?

Virtual Conversations

"I just spoke to Gamm, he thinks he's onto something. It was a bit garbled to be honest, I think his keyboard must be on the blink as letters were missing. Either that or his hands are too big to use it properly."

"He never had any problems with his questionnaires," offered up Arcene, being smug for some reason.

"Um, okay, sure. Anyway, he thinks he has found something; a clue. The people he went to check on? The Sisters, he called them, well they're gone too. He couldn't find any sign of them but some of the roads were cleared for a bit and then he thinks they headed across country, and he found the remains of a horse."

"That could mean anything or nothing," said Fasolt, twisting and turning a cube of various colors in his hands, frowning at it, eyes dark as coal, before twisting it again.

"It could mean nothing, but at least it's a start. Maybe people are being taken by horse... somewhere. And what if—"

"Damn!"

Thwack.

Fasolt got up from his chair and stared down at the colored cube. He pointed at it accusingly. "That is the stupidest thing that has ever been invented. Ugh, it's taken me weeks and now I find there is obviously a defect with it."

Arcene came running over. "What is it? A game?"

Fasolt stared at the offending object again and said, "It's a Rubik's cube. I found it and apparently all you have to do is turn the sides until you get all of them to have just one color only. But it's broken. I am a powerful man, Awoken for centuries, able to communicate in The Noise like no other, and I have been wasting my time on this child's toy only to discover it is broken and—"

"Like this?" asked Arcene, holding up the cube, each side full of a single color.

"What? How? That's impossible," spluttered Fasolt, color actually rising on his cheeks. "I've been trying to do that for countless hours. Days."

"Um, excuse me, if you two have quite finished?" Letje stared at them, hands on hips, her best evil stare seemingly having lost its potency.

"Oh, sorry Letje," replied a joyous Arcene, holding the cube high, her prize gleaming with perfectly aligned little brightly colored squares.

"Sorry," said Fasolt, staring first at the cube then at Arcene. "A clue you say? Horses? It could be how everyone has disappeared, could be. But why? Where? And how anyway? Surely there aren't people just going around the country grabbing everyone? Plus I haven't felt a thing in The Noise, have you?"

"No, nothing," admitted Letje. "But it doesn't mean it isn't happening does it? I mean, something's going on, all these people can't just vanish into thin air. And let's not forget that we have felt something, that things aren't quite right are they? Not as they are supposed to be, the timeline's out of sync somehow."

"You're right, it's like the future has hit a bump and is moving in a slightly wrong direction, but it happens more than you would think. It's why you can never truly tell what the future will hold; the tiniest thing can alter the course of things dramatically."

"That's just silly," said Arcene. "Are you telling me that even a tiny ant changing direction could alter the whole history of everything. Daft."

"Well that's where you are wrong Arcene, so very wrong. Let me tell you a story."

"I'm not a child any more," pouted Arcene.

"But this is a good one, promise."

"Okay, but it better be." Arcene sat cross-legged on the ground, waiting for Fasolt to begin.

"Letje?"

"Fine," sighed Letje. "But we do have things to do you know? We need to make a plan, I need to reply to Gamm too."

The story of the ant went something like this...

The Story of The Ant

"You know I was a bad man once? No need to answer, I was, and you know it. Well, once, hundreds of years ago, I changed the course of the future. Or if you look at it another way then the ant did."

Fasolt sat and thought for a moment, his eyes sparkling with the beginning of tears he wiped away and refused to let flow. He told his story.

It was only three or four decades after Varik had built his church and before Fasolt had lost himself totally to the world, becoming a foul hermit entirely. He was sat outside of The Sacellum, eating a chicken leg, the grease dripping down his face, wiping away the mess on his sleeve every now and then. As usual he was only half present, the other half of him dancing in The Noise.

He chewed absentmindedly on the chicken, pieces falling to the floor. It just so happened that of the infinite spots a particular morsel of chicken could have landed, it landed directly in the path of a single tiny ant

— a female belonging to the worker caste that was out hunting for food for its colony. Investigating the unexpected bounty the ant took hold of it and began to carry it back to the nest, leaving a pheromone trail behind so others could follow its path.

Soon enough hundreds of other worker ants had made their way to the spot where there were now many more tiny gobbets of chicken flesh, each ant picking up a piece and heading off back to the nest. Some of them followed the trail right up to Fasolt's mouth, so lost was he in his games in The Noise that he was sat as still as a rock with the chicken leg clenched between his teeth. As his beard began to tickle, and the chicken fell to the floor, he brushed frantically at the tiny menaces, which bit him in return, trying to defend themselves.

Fasolt grew angry. The angrier he got the more he was attacked. He pinched an ant between his fingers; unbeknown to him it was the original ant, the cause of the whole battle of man vs insect. As his pressure increased so the ant bit him, the final bite that sent Fasolt into a rage. He dropped the tiny insect and before they drove him mad he jumped into the stream that he had been sitting close to. The ants on his body drowned. Fasolt was soaked. And angry.

"That's not much of a story," said Arcene. "And anyway, how did you know it was the same ant?"

"I knew," said Fasolt cryptically. "Now, listen to the rest of the story please."

As Fasolt emerged from the water he saw a dog grab his chicken leg and run off with it. He didn't want it now anyway, so just resumed his position on the rock, even though he was cold from the water. The dog ran off and its adventure was almost as exciting as the story about the ant, assured Fasolt, but it would have to wait for another day.

Letje and Arcene looked at each other dubiously, but remained silent.

Fasolt told that while all of this was happening more ants had shown up and were dodging water droplets as they took what tiny pieces of chicken they could and returned to their nest. Angry and feeling meaner than usual, Fasolt followed the line in the dirt and easily found the nest. He could see all the tiny tunnels entering the ground, hear the hollowness beneath his feet where the soil had been excavated. He was about to stomp on it all when a tiny pinprick of fractal glory caught his interest in The Noise and he was lost once more to his otherworldly pursuits, wandering off, all thought of ants or his wet clothes forgotten.

Two weeks later, a young acolyte was walking where Fasolt had been and caught his foot in a collapsed section of the nest that the ants had abandoned as they couldn't maintain it with fewer workers since Fasolt drowned them. He broke his ankle as he twisted it in the hole and as a result had to be laid up for months. While he recuperated he grew fat, eating to console himself, to ease the pain. But he also caught the eye of Varik who spoke with him one day in the infirmary, Varik realizing that this was an intelligent and highly motivated man.

As the years went by the man grew both in rank and girth, until he was granted the honor of being referred to as Bishop, as all others of such rank were known.

This particular Bishop happened to be out in the woods years later at Varik's request, chasing down a foe. He came up with a cunning plan to distract his enemy while at the same time putting into motion orders that would see him rise even higher in position when he succeeded. He didn't succeed, and Fasolt killed a number of his men, Bishop's enemy killing others. But a terrible price was paid with the blood of the innocent that day, and it was all because of the chance dropping of a tiny piece of food that happened to fall directly in the path of a single female worker ant.

"What was the future meant to have been then?" asked Arcene. "You know, if the ant hadn't found the food and the hole hadn't collapsed, and the man hadn't got fat then killed people?"

"It would have been different, little one. How different nobody knows, but without the ant, or me, one of us at least, then things would not have been the same. Everything traces back to some such seemingly inconsequential event, so never believe that you are not to blame for your actions, or that the tiniest thing you do cannot have the most far reaching of consequences.

"Infinite futures are played out in this way. Every event happening in ways just slightly removed from the reality we now find ourselves in. And at the moment Letje is right, our timeline is not quite our own, it's off somehow. Maybe only by the actions of a single ant or by the marching of every ant in existence, it doesn't matter, the smallest thing can lead to the biggest of changes in the future."

"That was an apology, wasn't it?" said Letje, tears running down her face, hugging Constantine tight to her chest.

Fasolt nodded silently, staring deep into Letje's eyes, never looking away. "I never did say sorry, not properly."

"It's okay, it wasn't your fault. Things happen, we can't be held responsible for everything we do. Or maybe that's not right, we may be responsible, but we're not always to blame."

"What's going on?" Arcene looked from one to the other, neither saying a word. She thought about the story, then she understood. "Sy, right? That was all about how Sy died, because you got angry with an ant?"

"Yes, yes it was Arcene. All because I got angry with an ant."

I miss him Daddy.

I know you do my dear, I know you do.

Jobs You Hate

Letje hated this part of being the most powerful woman in the United Kingdom. What self respecting oligarch had to butcher her own meat? It made a mockery of such power and influence, which was exactly why she insisted on doing it on a regular basis. She even cleaned out the impossibly luxurious Rooms the animals had the great fortune to spend their lives in. It was all part of being a well-rounded despot, she insisted, when Fasolt tried to offer to take over the roles. Even Arcene offered to be in charge of the butchery but Letje shivered at a vision of Arcene wielding sharp knives and hacking away like a demented murderess at the unfortunate carcass she would surely desecrate.

So quite often Letje butchered the meat herself.

It was in The Book — Marcus was quite insistent on it, and after a few months of grumpily learning the skills she understood the importance of such seemingly grim but necessary work. In her previous life she had gutted animals, but it was always reluctantly and without any kind of skill or consideration. Large animals she had never really butchered, unless she was fortunate enough to get a deer or boar on occasion, which was very seldom, and until her father passed he had been the one to do such work.

Marcus had dedicated a whole chapter to the art of dissection of each animal she was likely to come across. Rather disturbingly the only exception, the only thing missing from this chapter, was human anatomy — which was given an entire two chapters of its own, along with a lot of warnings about the risk to your sanity of cutting up human flesh, also the rewards if you approached it as a spiritual exercise. Letje had decided she could do without such a path to enlightenment.

Back to work.

Letje honed the edge of her blade on the sharpening steel and became as one with the knife. Her pastel green leather apron, of course with matching gloves, leggings and galoshes — she had really begun to understand the importance of a fine wardrobe, part of Marcus' legacy — was at odds with the spattered blood, but it set the right atmosphere she felt. She made her incision, no energy wasted, the cut perfect, slicing through the joint in just the right place so there was little resistance. She put the slab to one side and resumed her work, each movement perfect, each cut impeccable.

It was all about respect, and honesty.

To eat meat was to understand the process, to pay your dues and to be thankful. What right did those that would turn away from such parts of the process have to eat the final product? Marcus had been insistent on this, even writing that for a period of twenty or so years he had become a vegetarian as he felt unable to perform the butchery. Letje understood the importance of the work, it was a ritual, all about understanding the cycles of life and death and she now performed such a task with the care and attention the carcass before her deserved.

She sharpened the knife again, performing a few final cuts before putting the blade aside and grabbing a huge cleaver, the wooden handle worn as smooth as glass after centuries of use. Letje adjusted the carcass slightly, centering it on the huge block, then flexed a bicep and chopped through the thick cartilage in exactly the right place. A few more well placed moves and her work was done.

Shaking her head to move her hair from her eyes, her gloved hands too gore-stained to use, Letje took a step back to check on her work — perfect. She busied herself packaging the various cuts, going as far as labeling them before they were taken to one of the many freezers or The Freezer Room, depending on when she thought the food would be eaten. Bones, head, parts she wasn't keen on eating and knew Fasolt and Arcene weren't either, were bagged up ready for some of the animals that she knew would appreciate them. That was another task that needed attention, or tasks really: the breeding programs and guard animals that Marcus had invested centuries in perfecting. Maybe there could be another George at some point? Then again maybe not.

With armfuls of well wrapped meat Letje stacked packs in the huge freezers then carried a large rack of ribs into the freezing cold Room. Marcus' taste in meat had been something of a revelation, and it was surprising what they had found as they explored the Rooms that stored all manner of foodstuffs, perishables and long term stocks of anything from grains to a Room dedicated to tiny little birds that she had to admit were absolutely delicious brazed slowly, then served with carrots and fennel.

What a place, she thought once again, never ceasing to marvel, even after five years, at the incredible complexity of the systems that kept so many people well fed and everything running like clockwork. It was still mind-blowing and she guessed it always would be.

Work complete, Letje stripped off her stylish utility clothes and decided that after a shower she really needed to wear some thinking clothes. A plan was needed and she had to spend some time really thinking about how best to approach the disappearance of everybody else. There was no way she was going to allow the UK to just carry on without people — it was why she did what she did after all.

What's happened to them all? People don't just disappear, they fade away because of The Lethargy, not vanish entirely.

~~~

Letje stopped, messing with her hair as she suddenly realized she had been walking aimlessly. For how long she had no idea. She had been lost deep in thought about the problems facing them all and hadn't taken any notice of where she was going. She did it quite a lot, if nothing else it was a great way to get to know The Commorancy; there was still plenty to explore even now.

She looked around the Room. It was mostly empty, rather coarse in comparison to a lot of other Rooms. It consisted of rock and an open pool, shallow as it crept over part of the floor, incredible depths hinted at as the water darkened in the middle. A spring she supposed, where part of the many underwater streams made it to the surface.

Strange thing to have a Room for, but then, there were things more surprising then a Room with a spring in it in her home, much more surprising. She peered curiously into the shallow water. Crayfish, British crayfish, but there was something more going on here. Marcus had said something about crayfish hadn't he? Something about being nice to them if you met them? She remembered feeling worried at the time, as she had once gorged herself on their sweet flesh as she roamed the country before being accepted as a guest by Marcus.

Letje squatted down, peering into the clear shallow water. She entered The Noise, let it consume her, went in deep and recoiled at what she found. She fell back, her hands splaying behind her. She crouched again, peering into the tiny black orbs of the crayfish staring intently at her, eyes that were part of a vast intelligence too alien to truly understand.

Reaching out from the small creature before her a complex sentience expanded, a huge hivemind spreading out beyond the walls of The Commorancy, through streams and rivers and small pools until it was all over the UK and beyond.

It was what was once a man, now impossible to communicate with, so different was he to anything that had come before.

Letje felt the deep, ponderous intelligence, felt its tiny unimportant single entity components spread far and wide, each one dispensable, but together making up a whole so much more than its individual parts. The intellect was vast and deep, yet impossibly alien.

It was knowable. For her.

Doing the impossible, Letje focused as deeply as she ever had, deeper than she had known possible, her truly Awoken self revealing just how different she was from the girl she had once been. It surprised even her, hinting at impossible energies that could be released, the potential to know things no other person had ever known, let alone understood. Letje spoke to the creature, no longer could it be called a crayfish, or a family, this was a new life-form albeit one housed in tens of thousands of crayfish, once an endangered species throughout the British Isles.

It spoke to her through The Noise, too alien to truly commune with, but there was a sense of palpable relief. The creature, once a man, a guest, had thought it would never be able to tell of its life, the things it had seen, the knowledge it now had. It spoke to her in words that were not words, pictures that were not pictures, as much feelings without emotion as it was anything else. It gave knowledge — took some in return. It wasn't truly a conversation at all, it was company for the ex-man, it was an expansion of awareness for Letje, a hint of what was possible for those that truly wished to explore the boundaries of what the human mind could accomplish if it was daring and brave enough.

Letje crouched for hours until even her bodily control told her it was time to move and she risked overloading her brain with too much exotic knowledge. There were limits after all.

Farewells were said, thanks given from both parties, then the single human brain and the complex system that made up the alien being went back to what they now knew as their own realities, both the better for a richer grasp of understanding the incredibly diverse ecosystem they found themselves playing a tiny part in.

Letje closed the door behind her, wondering about what was safe to eat and what may just contain a mind that was more intelligent yet too far removed from what it had once been to ever be considered human again.

Better take lobster off the menu, just in case. Letje took a moment outside of the door to remember what she had been doing before the strange encounter. Darkness had fallen and the evening lights lit the way down a corridor unfamiliar to her. She really should make a concerted effort to memorize the maps she had finally uncovered in The Book, but it would take some of the fun and surprise out of her new home.

Maybe another time.

Hunger

Orientated, finally, Letje decided that a quick change of clothes and a shower would have to do — she was so hungry she felt like her legs were going to give out under her soon. Going so deeply into The Noise meant her brain consumed calories at an alarming rate; she needed to refuel soon, and a lot. She began to salivate at thoughts of all the food she craved like a mother-to-be with an unlimited larder.

Clean and with clothes not at all suitable for thinking — as had been her intention earlier in the day — Letje made it to the kitchen on wobbly legs and began grabbing food and eating before she even managed to lay it out on the table.

It was late so she was alone. Arcene was probably asleep long ago, and Fasolt, well, he was a mystery — she wondered if he truly slept more than an hour or two a day now. Constantine was tucked away in his corner of the kitchen by the fire, a nest he had been spending more and more time in of late. Her father had been quiet for some time and she wondered if it was because the tortoise part of him wanted nothing more than to hibernate. It wasn't the right time of year but her father had forcibly stayed awake through the last few winters to help out with such a monumental task, more for guidance and company for his daughter, but Letje knew there was only so long he could continue for before he had to face the reality of the body he found himself in. It seemed like that time was now.

Hiccup.

Hiccup, hiccup.

Letje drank a glass of water and sat down, then expanded her diaphragm to stop the interruption to her eating. She took it slower, enjoying the food rather than gulping it down.

She carried on eating until she felt her body restored, then cleared away the remains of her meal.

Goodnight Daddy, sleep well.

Yabis was lost in dreams of a very tortoise based nature. He dreamed he had succumbed to The Lethargy once more and was slowly fading away from himself, replaced by the mind of a patient tortoise that still had plenty of living to do, just not as a man that should have been dead long ago.

Letje closed the kitchen door behind her, turning out the light as she did so.

Who You Talking to?

Arcene was chattering away into the big chrome microphone on the desk.

Letje stopped as she passed the open door to the... what was the name of this Room? She had no idea. Come to think of it she hadn't seen it before, how come it was here now? She shook her head — she was getting used to things, but it was still a lot to get to grips with. Arcene seemed to accept it a lot easier than she did, and was getting used to the layout a lot quicker as well. Not that it was a strict layout, which was the problem — this Room definitely wasn't here before behind this door, it had been something else she was sure.

Letje peeked her head around the door and studied the Room.

It made her head hurt just looking. The Room was cramped, the walls lined with metal shelving, piles of junk in the corners, cables and strange pieces of equipment in various states of assembly, or disassembly, scattered all over a heavy wooden workbench, a thick magnifying glass attached to a thick base distorting the dissected innards of a piece of equipment clamped to the bench. Arcene was on the other side of the Room where the mess was minimal, seemingly where finished or repaired equipment was given some kind of deserved attention once it was complete. Above the desk was a single shelf with a handful of neatly arranged and very shiny pieces of equipment, some familiar, most totally unrecognizable to Letje.

She recognized what Arcene was talking into though, it was a microphone of sorts, all bulbous chrome and a thick black cable winding away from it under the desk.

"And then there was this crazy ride, Fasolt calls it a roller coaster, and it took me outside and high into the air and around in loops and I thought I was going to fall off at any second. Over."

There was a pause while Arcene listened, then she replied. "What? Oh, no, it was great fun, I wasn't scared at all. Well, maybe a little, not much. Then I went into this Room. The roller coaster just stopped right up high, the tracks ran out and I was in a Room with all kinds of things that Marcus had put there about his past and I found out that he—"

"Arcene! What are you doing? Who are you talking to?"

Arcene lifted a hand to her mouth and jumped out of her chair, looking guilty like she had never looked before.

"Letje, what are you doing here? How did you get here? I didn't know you knew where this Room was."

"I didn't, it's moved. It isn't usually here."

"Damn, I knew the quantum track needed looking at. I wonder if I can fix it. Hey, fancy something to eat, I'm starving?" Arcene stretched and yawned, rubbing her belly and walking away from her seat.

"Oh no you don't. I'm not that easy to distract. What is going on here? Who were you talking to Arcene? What have you been up to?"

"Leave me alone, just leave me alone." Arcene ran out of the Room, brushing past Letje, swatting her hand away as she tried to grab her.

"Arcene!" It was no use, she was gone.

Spiders crawled up her spine, tickling nerves and whispering of the horrors that were to come.

Just you wait, they whispered. *We'll get you, we'll get you all. Each and every one of you.*

The Silent Treatment

"Hello, is anybody there?"

"Who's this?" The voice at the other end sounded curious but not really that interested.

He already knows who it is, thought Letje. *He knows my name.*

"You know who it is. But I don't know who you are."

"Ah, well, I guess I do know. Letje isn't it? Arcene's such a nice girl, so friendly. So talkative."

"What's she been telling you? Who are you?"

"Sorry, have to go."

Click.

Lèse-majesté

"You're a traitor. It's treason, sedition against your home, your family, your ruler."

"You're not my ruler, you're not The Queen, and you're not my mum." Arcene broke down sobbing again, her face red from tears, her hair wild, the pigtails half unfurled, snot running down her nose, her cuff soaked where she wiped at her face ineffectively.

"Lèse-majesté," muttered Fasolt, thinking the French more apt, reflecting Arcene's lineage.

"What?" snapped Letje.

"Nothing." Fasolt may have been the most powerful man alive but he knew better than to cross an angry twenty two year old woman, let alone one with Letje's abilities. He shuddered slightly, shifting in his chair. He was beginning to feel sorry for Arcene; Letje really did have the scariest of stares.

They were in The Room For Traitors and it wasn't going well. Arcene had trailed along reluctantly, not liking the sound of the Room one little bit. She tried to act defensive when confronted with her clandestine activities but had given nothing up in terms of who she was talking to or how long it had been going on.

Letje wanted the truth, and she would get it.

"Do you know where you are Arcene?" said Letje in a clipped tone.

"The Commorancy," sniffed Arcene.

"That's right. Who runs it?"

"We do, you, me, and Fasolt. Constantine helps too I guess, though not lately."

"Who really runs it?"

"What? I just said didn't I? Jeez."

"I said, WHO REALLY RUNS IT?"

"You do," admitted Arcene. "I know you do, alright? And I know you give me jobs to make me feel better, to be nice."

"I do, but not just to be nice or to help teach you, but because I love you and I want you to grow up to be intelligent and to make your own choices in life. To have options."

"I know, I love you too."

"So, so... WHY THE HELL HAVE YOU BEEN GOING—" Letje felt an arm on her shoulder. She turned to Fasolt. "What?" she snapped.

"She's a child Letje, so are you to some degree. Control yourself, be kind. Patient. Arcene is fifteen, she knows she has done wrong and will tell us what we need to know. Isn't that right Arcene?"

"S'pose."

"YOU 'S'POSE'?"

"Letje!"

"Okay, fine, sorry. I need a break, I'll be back in a minute."

Letje got up and left by the door behind her, hidden in the shadow of a carved devil that hung heavy over the lintel and suitably intimidated anybody that had the nerve to look up from the floor when in The Room For Traitors.

Clunk.

The echo from the door closing died as fast as some people had in the Room.

Silence.

Heavy, depressing, bone aching silence.

It lasted for lifetimes, gnawing away at the air, chewing it into lumps that filtered into your heart and weighed your body down until it begged to sink to the floor and dissipate through the ancient flagstones.

"I'm sorry, alright?" managed Arcene, feeling so alone she thought she would die from it.

"I know," said Fasolt, letting the thick absence of noise return. "It's not always enough though."

Arcene sobbed.

Her knees hurt from kneeling, her hands hung limp by her sides. She was exhausted, scared, ashamed.

~~~

It was an hour later when Letje returned, all part of the plan she had decided on with Fasolt. Letje hadn't felt so awful in her life. She knew Arcene was only a child, even if she was fifteen. But this was important, and they had to be in no doubt that Arcene would tell them everything they asked — their lives may be at stake, everyone else's certainly were.

They had discussed it after Letje told Fasolt what she had found, both coming to the only obvious conclusion: this man was responsible for whatever was going on. The Fluctuation.

Letje had known it the second she heard the man's voice. Here was the cause of all the problems. And Arcene had been talking to him, probably given away secrets that had helped him do what had been done. Who knew what information he had? So Fasolt and her had agreed to play good Awoken, bad Awoken, just to ensure that Arcene gave up all she knew. It was a terrible thing to do but there was a part of Letje that also felt Arcene deserved severe punishment, she really had been immensely stupid to have done such a thing and hidden it from her.

Really, really stupid.

The Room For Traitors was a rather intimidating Room, Letje had to admit it. There was something about it that made everything feel heavy, like the air, the walls, the floor, were all trying to suck you down into confession, like a big box that could help absolve you if only you gave up your secrets and told of the bad things you had done.

Absolution.

Power through architecture once more, as depressing as a church was humbling.

Of course, Letje had already absolved Arcene — mostly. Arcene just didn't know it yet, and wouldn't for some time.

Letje sat down in the thick wooden chair, high up on a judges' dais, Fasolt at her side.

Arcene was down on the floor, ignoring the chairs behind the desks and kneeling. There was a small wooden fence between her and her Judges: a courtroom, Commorancy style.

"Let's start at the beginning. Arcene Robideaux, please be seated."

Arcene looked up in confusion, the formality strange to her. Nevertheless she took her seat and placed her clenched hands on the desk, knuckles red like she was trying to wring more tears from her palms.

"How long have you been talking to that man?"

"Dunno, it's been a while."

"Arcene, you need to answer me, you know how serious this is, right?"

"I don't see why I have to sit here like a criminal. It's not fair and—"

"ARCENE!"

"Fine, I've been talking to him for years alright? Since maybe after the first year we got here. So four years maybe, about that."

"What! All this time, you never thought to tell anyone? Why not?"

"Because it was my thing, for me. Something private. And I just, well, I felt clever for working it out, for finding someone to talk to."

"How did you find him? How did you know what to do?"

"Well... um, I didn't find him exactly, I found the Room. And I was playing about with stuff, you know, just looking really," said Arcene hurriedly, "and all of a sudden there was this voice coming from some equipment, so I went over and pressed a button and we got chatting."

"You got 'chatting'," said Letje, rolling her eyes at Fasolt. "They got 'chatting'."

"I heard."

"I was eleven okay. I found some cool stuff and just wanted to have some fun. We talked to each other; he sounded nice."

"What's his name?"

"He said it was Devan."

"Did you believe him?"

"Why wouldn't I?" Arcene was getting defensive again, which Letje thought understandable, but it wasn't the time or the place.

"Just answer the question Arcene, we need to understand what is going on, and now."

It was as if a neural pathway suddenly connected the dots in her brain and Arcene put her hand to her mouth, pale eyes as scared as a rabbit caught in the lights at night. "He's the one, isn't he? The one taking all the people, making everything funny."

"What do you think? Who else could it be? You've been telling him things, private things; Commorancy business. It's secret, you know that."

"I didn't mean to, I'm sorry. I just thought I had another friend, a private one, something for me, someone to talk to when you were being mean or Fasolt was off doing... dunno, whatever he does. What do you do?"

They ignored her question, trying to understand quite how deep Arcene's unknown treachery went.

Slowly, the whole story unfolded; it was no wonder Arcene had kept her friendship secret.

It was nothing less than the grooming of a child for despicable purposes as far as Letje could tell. Arcene had been used, her naivete the key to unlocking secrets of The Commorancy and who knew what else? Well, it was obvious to Letje now, this man, this infiltrator, this 'Devan', had gained access to things he should never have been able to, and once inside he had used the knowledge to find and somehow take nearly everyone who lived away from The Commorancy.

He had stolen souls and blemished a young child's — who was just too damn friendly for her own good.

Letje should have seen the signs, should have known something was happening, but how? As Arcene told her story Letje softened more and more. She remembered when she first met Arcene, how impetuous a child she had been, unable to really grasp the danger of strangers, that talking and trusting those you didn't know could have dire consequences. She had assumed her experiences in the world — especially when kidnapped — had taught her the value of caution, but a year under the protection of Letje and Fasolt had allowed Arcene to let her guard down and revert to the trusting and innocent, maybe rather unthinking and instant-to-act child she used to be.

At what cost though?

"Now, what exactly did you talk about? You need to tell us everything, and I do mean everything Arcene. How did this friendship develop? What did you get out of it?"

Arcene told her story. Letje got mad, Fasolt got angry, Arcene got absolution.

~~~

There was no doubt about it, the man had taken advantage of Arcene's innocence and abused it. She may have been capable of surviving from a young age out in the world all alone, but the one thing she lacked was much in the way of skills when it came to people. She had simply never met enough to be capable of reading the signs they gave off. Sometimes she seemed like nothing more than an excited puppy — oblivious to the signals of danger. She trusted too easily, let her insatiable appetite overrule her instincts, and got into trouble as she was nosy, impetuous, curious and mostly fearless. Yet she lacked knowledge or real understanding of tone of voice, facial signals or body language. Not that Letje herself was much better in that regard, but she had done her best to rectify the situation over the years.

Arcene was, and would always be, a person that wanted to see the good in people, and her trusting nature had been abused by what was becoming clear was a very intelligent and very manipulative man.

It had all been going on for years, warping small parts of her mind, always reassuring her that although they had a secret there was nothing wrong with it. Did Arcene really think Letje told her everything? Of course not, everybody had secrets. Everybody.

As the story came out it was clear that Arcene had taken delight in her secret, thinking she just had a remote friend. He told her that he lived alone but was a bit of a technical wizard, just like she surely must be to work the contraption. He said he would help her in any way he could, he was great with numbers and with anything to do with computers or machines of all types. He told her he was bored and lonely and really enjoyed talking to her and that he didn't mind that she was still young. After all, he was Whole and so was she, so very soon she would be a grown woman and then he wouldn't be talking to a young girl any longer, would he?

The more Arcene told the more unnerved Letje became.

So much made sense now, things that seemed incongruous to Arcene's nature. It was obvious why Arcene grew so good at numbers and data collection and collation — she had outside help. When asked, there was a long nervous silence before Arcene admitted that she had shown him things to get some help and that she hadn't thought anything more of it. It never crossed her mind until now that the things she had shown the man could have been used against them. How could it? Just a few bits and pieces put onto The Web with password protection so only he could look at it and help her figure some stuff out — she never gave him top secret information, never let him look in their own computers or get access to cameras or anything like that.

Letje tried to explain that he could have hacked in. After being shown bits he may have found a way to get access to everything digital in The Commorancy. Or maybe after talking for long enough he had been able to just figure out Arcene's passwords, get access that way.

"You did use a secure password didn't you? Like I told you to?"

There was silence, than a spreading redness that rode from Arcene's cheeks down her neck and disappeared beneath her clothes.

"Well? Answer me."

"I never changed it from when I was young and you first gave me proper access. It was silverprincess."

"And I bet you told him about your name being French and what it meant? Not that he couldn't figure out it meant silvery anyway. He could have found out your password just by trial and error. What were you thinking?"

"I'm sorry. I never thought of stuff like that happening."

"Don't be too hard on her Letje, it's an easy oversight," said Fasolt, shifting in his chair.

Letje stared at him. Realization dawned. "Why, what's your password Fasolt?"

"Password."

"No, what is it? What password did you use?"

"Password."

"Just tell me what... oh, you didn't? You are not telling me that your password is password?"

Fasolt just nodded, as ashamed as Arcene.

"What is wrong with you two? Seriously?"

"I just never got around to changing it, I don't really use the computers. I prefer The Noise."

"Fine, okay. Look, I think we have enough of an idea now to know that it must be this man that is taking everyone, warping everything. I don't know how, or why, but it's him, it has to be. Arcene, I don't blame you, I'm sorry for being mean, but we had to find out what had happened, and you needed to be honest with us. But it's over now, you weren't to blame, he took advantage of a child; you weren't to know. He groomed you."

"He didn't, I've never even met him and if I did I certainly wouldn't let him brush my hair like I'm a horse."

Letje couldn't help but smile. "No, grooming in this context means—"

"I know what it means, I'm just playing. And I am sorry, truly sorry. I would never have done it if I thought it would get us into trouble, mean things got worse. What are we going to do?"

"Well, that's obvious isn't it? We're going to go and find him and get everyone back."

Fasolt turned to Letje. "How are we supposed to do that? I can't find them in The Noise, they're shut off. I'm not powerful enough to get deep enough to break whatever is protecting them, I can't find even a hint of them."

"That's easy," said Letje, "we just need to go find Marcus. He'll help."

Dreams of Butterflies

Letje lay on a bed of butterflies, her naked skin glistening in a thousand hues of orange, green, blue — all the colors of the rainbow in countless variations. The gossamer-thin wings were so delicate as to be almost transparent, creating a kaleidoscope of color as she peered around the Room through the wings of her dream companions.

Letje was in The Room Of Dreams.

There was nothing in the Room. No bed, no light, no dark, no butterflies, no her, nothing.

Emptiness.

And dreams.

It was one of the most dangerous Rooms in the whole Commorancy — The Book warned of it. Marcus himself had never used it for more than a minute, the result being that he was sure it was what tipped him over the edge into a downward spiral of insanity. When Letje read the entry concerning the Room, Marcus recorded that he often wondered if it wasn't this Room that eventually made him question everything about his life, often no longer sure if he was him and mad or there were two Marcus', but still probably both mad. At least he had company either way, but one thing he made absolutely clear was that this was not a Room to take lightly.

Once, just once, Marcus had put a man inside and left him for all of three hours; a man that had tried in a very nasty way to end his life. Marcus never forgave himself for the gibbering wreck he created — the thing that came out certainly couldn't be called a man in any normal sense any longer.

Letje had thought long and hard about entering such a space, finally deciding that she was strong enough to not let it overpower her. She needed answers and if she was unable to locate Marcus by any other means then she would have to do so through dreams.

Two days she had prepared for the Room, meditating, going over her exercises repeatedly, checking and double checking the control she had over her own body, her mind, and most importantly of all: The Noise. This was not a task to be undertaken by the novice — even Fasolt had balked at the idea of Letje entering, and had in no uncertain terms declared that there was no way he would venture into such a Room.

Letje wasn't scared as she entered The Room Of Dreams, if she had been then she had no right entering. This was what Marcus referred to as a specialist Room, just like The Dangerous Room, The Discombobulated

Room, and a few others. If you didn't have complete control then you would fail. Injury, madness, or death would be the result — a foregone conclusion for those not up to the experience. With her heart-rate under control, her mind as empty as The Void, sweat glands slowed, adrenaline set at regular levels and as many precautions taken as she could think of she had entered silently and closed the door behind her while Fasolt and Arcene waited nervously out of sight, peeking around the corner believing Letje didn't know they were there. It was still amusing how even Fasolt seemed to forget what she was capable of now — the wall may as well not have been there, so clear were they through The Noise. Still, it was nice to know they were thinking of her.

Inside, Letje stripped off her clothes to be greeted by a gentle warm cycle of air that made her skin feel adorable. The delicate breeze hinted at perfumed summer days laying on the grass, staring at the sky lost in daydreams of nothing — little fluffy clouds.

Air blew through her hair, lifting it from her eyes, tickling her ears with loose strands, caressing her neck like the gentle touch of a lover she had never known. It touched her thighs, tickled her behind, and she heard the gentle sound of insects buzzing away in the background — out of sight but the perfect accompaniment to a perfect day.

Letje noted the butterflies through a dream-haze that had already descended — impossible to fight just as the Room itself was an impossibility.

They wrapped themselves tight around her — a second skin.

She sank.

Through the cloud floor and out into nothingness, the butterflies splitting into tiny reflective shards, trailers shimmering endlessly as they dissipated in the nothingness that was all there ever was and all there ever would be.

What was Letje became something else.

Her life so far was wrapped up tight — a long piece of string compressed into a hard ball. Experiences, emotions, her life, all criss-crossing randomly. A new order was created that ignored linear time or cause and effect — as if her brain itself had been unwound then connected back up without concern about ever making sense.

She bumped down on the soft ocean floor, sand and the dust of creatures turned to nothing, undisturbed for eons floating up and away as she upset their unknowing peace.

Dark.

Heavy yet buoyant.

A place to relax and feel the power of the planet root you in place while you slept on the history of evolution of species dead for millions of years.

A voice.

Slow.

Ponderous.

Lost in its own dream-life of longevity and unthinking weight.

A huge creature — at one with the deep and the never ending adventure of freedom as it traversed the waters in search of nothing more than the next Now; all there ever was.

Letje opened her eyes as the tiny fish nibbled at her toes, eating away at her, bits floating off into the darkness, tiny motes of her self lighting their own way as they settled onto the ocean bed. Her feet were gone, then her ankles, her calves. Nibbled and sucked until they returned to dust, pointless and unnecessary for one such as her: a dreamer who had awoken to the end of everything.

Her knees were gone and then her thighs. She was a half woman, a thing out of place, not meant to be so deep. An intrusion.

Letje was calm. The dream was all there was yet it was only a dream. She was in there somewhere, dreaming of a dream in a Room of impossibilities — there was a quest, a point to her dreams of oceanic hunger that was taking her away piece by tiny piece and when she was all gobbled up and spat out there would be nothing left of the woman named Letje, only an emptiness that could never resurface.

Not that there would be anything left that would want to.

~~~

The huge eye was almost touching her head, it consumed her vision and told of impossible dreams of lives untouched by concern for what she felt was so important.

This was no ordinary creature, it was not even one, but it spoke to her and she listened.

It told of a Room, hidden deep and accessed only once, sealed away behind fake walls and eradicated from the memory of the only man ever to set foot in it.

Then it was gone.

A blink of an eye and nothing was left but emptiness and the nibbling away of her body. Most of it was gone now and Letje watched it without a care as tiny pieces floated away happily on the gentle currents. She was a head with arms, the fingers already mostly gone, and when she was all eaten up there would be nothing left to do but enter The Void and have everlasting peace.

The Room. The Room. The Room.

The voice beat like a sonorous drum at the base of her skull.

Boom, boom, boom. The Room, Room, Room.

On it went, pounding and throbbing and reminding her... of what? Of her purpose for dreaming?

She was dreaming wasn't she? She wasn't just a head and... just a head now, the fish hanging off trailing flesh that dangled like she was an octopus. They nibbled upward, they were at her chin now.

Boom, boom, boom. The Room, Room, Room.

Butterflies swam through the thick water, turning it to air as they danced their dance and left trailers of gold sparkling in their wake. They gathered up all the bits of Letje and put them back together piece by tiny piece. Letje's arms grew, rebuilt one tiny mote at a time. They lengthened and were covered by butterflies all the colors of the rainbow.

She lifted, floating in the nothingness and her body resumed its shape.

Then she woke up.

Naked.

Letje.

The girl that dreamed and came back to herself.

So very nearly lost.

Never to be what she had once been.

Friends?

Artek Ligertwood, born a hundred and fifty years after The Lethargy encompassed the globe, had waited all of his twenty seven years for this moment — at least that's what it felt like. He was destined for greatness, he knew it from the minute he was old enough to understand such things. He was born for this, born to Awaken and become an exceptional human being, more exceptional than he already was. Which was difficult because if Artek knew one thing then he knew that he was one really rather exceptional fellow.

As the door closed behind him and he took stock of his — he had to be honest, amazing — Room he knew that very soon he was going to be even more incredible in almost every way than he already was.

If he had any doubts about his future then he didn't show it. Artek had made it his first vow as a man to not regret any decisions, never to look back and think about the might-have-beens, but to keep on looking forward, on the bright side. His, some would say unfounded, confidence in himself and the way he lived his life meant that he would face whatever the world threw at him with his full attention, hope, and a clarity of vision most Whole could only dream of.

Soon he would be Awoken.

He couldn't wait.

~~~

Marcus walked back to Orientation after seeing Artek into his Room, and sat in his checkered chair, matching his shirt and socks, complemented by a rather subdued thigh length coat and tan boots that had seen better days.

He had doubts about his most recent guest — he never let them have a Room if he had any doubts about them. It was why his research was so intense and why it was so hard to even find out how to apply to The Commorancy — it needed people who were determined and showed skill. Then there was Orientation itself, the final hurdle that usually meant you got accepted, but not always.

There was just something... that was the problem, he couldn't put his finger on it, couldn't actually think of a single reason why Artek shouldn't have a Room — he was the perfect candidate and that itself was the issue he guessed. Nobody was a perfect guest. Nobody.

Confidence was a good thing, Marcus knew he was himself a rather over-confident person in some regards, although in others he was certainly rather shy. This man seemed quite incapable of not believing he could excel at everything he set his mind to, and although commendable it wasn't really a very realistic way to approach life as far as he was concerned. But then, it had got Artek this far and he seemed like a rather nice man.

During his Orientation he had been gracious and answered all the questions in the right way, although that was never the main goal of such meetings, it was more to see what was behind the answers, what the person was really like.

Marcus couldn't fault him, and he supposed that was exactly what gave him cause for concern: he should have had his faults.

It was as though nothing really shocked the man. He took everything in his stride assuming everything happened for a reason and that everything would work out 'just dandy' in the end as he rather elegantly put it. He hadn't batted an eyelid at George, just rubbed his ears and stroked his horns, admiring his fine coat and bushy tail. George had taken a liking to him immediately and spent most of Orientation nudging his hand to continue if he stopped playing with his ears. And George was as assured of himself as Artek, so never acted subservient for long with people he didn't know well or really, really like.

Even a game of croquet out in the small quadrangle hadn't phased the man, and he almost won too, which did irk him, Marcus could tell. But he took his defeat graciously, stating that now he had played the game he was sure he would win if they ever had a re-match. Marcus had been baiting him really, taking him outside, playing games dead for centuries. A lost game that hinted at a gentility and warm summer days with blankets spread on perfect grass and picnics. Lifestyles that were now dead and buried.

Marcus never took people outside, but he had wanted to... what, intimidate the man with the overpowering wonder of what he had built? Or was it that he wanted to show off? To make the man think highly of him? He did have that kind of effect on you — you wanted him to like you, to approve of you, to be impressed.

Marcus sat back and laughed at that. Here he was, sat in his chair surrounded by the single greatest achievement of any man and he reverted to a child wanting to impress the popular boy in school so he would like him and be his friend.

You had to see the funny side of it.

Marcus thought back to when he first met the man, when he went to pick him up. It had ended up being quite the adventure, rather a revelation too, for Artek was no idle man, he had been busy in his life and had made sure that he lived well while he made his way through the ravages of the country he was born into one and a half centuries too late, as he told Marcus. He felt he should have been born to enjoy all that modern society could have offered an enterprising young man such as himself, but he did the best he could and tried to make the most if it.

He had certainly done that, Marcus was impressed. He had never seen anything like it, apart from at The Commorancy, of course.

Wheee!

While Marcus dealt with pressing matters back at The Commorancy, Marcus had decided it would be a good idea if he went to collect the guest in person. It was a break for them and something to talk about, and they did like to try out the various equipment kept in hangars dotted around The Commorancy.

The solar glider had only been up a few times in the years since Marcus had found it and brought it back, and he was excited to get up in the sky and feel as close to being a bird as you could get without risking your life in a paraglider or occupying the mind of an actual bird.

He wheeled out the glider from the hangar, checked that the batteries were still fully charged from the day before where it had been left outside to soak up the clear blue sky's energizing rays. He manhandled the ultra-light fiberglass wings into their slots and ten minutes later he was putting his tools away and climbing in after pushing the glider out to the short runway. The hatch closed, Marcus checked the simple controls and started the motor.

There were no fumes or nasty odors, this was clean technology and he wondered why it hadn't, haha, taken off as a means of transport for more than a lucky few.

A few minutes later he was high above The Commorancy and marveling at his own ingenious creation before he shut off the engine and glided in silence. He could feel a strong thermal tugging at the wings so took advantage and with a few small adjustments climbed higher and higher. If need be he could start the engine again to climb and search for the thermal currents, but for now he traveled over the water to the mainland without any sound other than the air forced out of the way of the sleek glider.

Artek lived somewhat out of the way, which had been quite a surprise as he seemed like the kind of man that would always want to be where the, albeit rather limited, action was. That would mean being near to a large city where there were more opportunities for surrounding yourself with the remains of man's achievements, but Marcus knew him to be an intelligent man, and intelligent men didn't live in places were there was a much higher risk to their life from those that would kill you, rob you, or worse. The cities always seemed to attract people that were less than friendly, probably as food was so much scarcer than out in the country where land for growing crops was certainly in plentiful supply.

Artek had set up home in a strategic location but well away from the worst of the crumbling city centers. As Marcus circled the man's extensive home he had to admit that he was impressed. From what he could tell the house itself was well maintained and so were the grounds. As he swooped lower, picking a suitable spot to land, it was obvious that Artek had already put in place systems to ensure his home kept running while he was away. There were row after row of solar panels that adjusted slightly to track the sun, large feed hoppers that led to various well-fenced pens, enclosures and pasture land that would ensure the continuation of his collection of animals that were clearly thriving.

Orderly fields were filled with crops and around the house were military-neat lines of vegetables sparkling with late morning rain after a warm shower that had just now cleared.

The house was a fine example of Georgian architecture for what had once been known as the landed gentry and as he exited the glider Marcus was greeted in a suitably gentlemanly manner.

"Cup of tea?"

Marcus smiled. Now that was how you greeted a guest. "Mmm, yes please."

"Milk? Sugar?"

"If you have them then yes, please."

"Of course, of course."

"Hi, I'm Marcus."

"I'm Artek, pleased to meet you. Come, let me show you the way."

The two men shook hands then walked up towards the house.

~~~

"Haha, well, yes, it is a bit bigger than your home, you'll see soon enough. But I must say you have been busy here, especially um... it's just you?"

"Just me yes. Not that I haven't tried finding company, I've searched and searched. It sadly isn't that easy, people are so spread out, and there aren't many anyway. And as you know not all people are, shall we say, of a friendly disposition anymore."

They chatted away amiably over their tea, the confident young man gracious and keen to show off the work he had done. As they wandered around the grounds Marcus offered little bits of advice on how to keep things running, although he did explain that it may all be for naught if Artek's stay ended up being prolonged.

"Oh, don't worry about that, I'm sure I will do well and only be a guest for a few years at the most."

Marcus didn't insist, there was no point pressing the matter. Some people stayed for a week, others for more than a century — it was what it was and he didn't want to dent the man's indomitable spirit.

Soon enough it was time to go, and with just one small bag, which was the allowance for all guests without exception, they took to the sky.

The trip back was uneventful even when Marcus allowed his companion to take a turn flying the glider. He was, as Marcus suspected he would be, a natural. Artek was blindfolded for the rest of the flight just as others had been and would be in the future, so had no idea where he was or what awaited him below. Marcus was tempted to allow him a peek at the expansive Commorancy but stopped himself, knowing it was showing off and him being bizarrely eager to impress the well presented young man.

Which was another thing that drew Marcus to him: he dressed well.

There had been a discussion about clothes, longer than about anything else, and Marcus had reassured Artek that whatever he had wanted he could have. Marcus felt the connection and knew that Artek held clothes in as high regard as he did. *What would he make of The Room For Clothes?* wondered Marcus, again realizing he was keen to show off.

The difference between the two was that Artek wore one style only and always the same colors, even if the cut of the cloth varied. As they walked along the corridors towards his Orientation Marcus glanced sideways at the man. He seemed perfectly relaxed in what was, even to Marcus after all this time, an impossible to ignore idiosyncratic series of spaces.

Yet Artek held his excellent posture, looked around politely, and made suitably complementary comments on what Marcus had achieved — the perfect gentleman.

His hair was neat and cut into a tight bob that came to the nape of his neck. He wore an emerald green shirt that complemented his fire-red hair, and had a neatly trimmed mustache and wisp of a beard. Trousers were tight fitting and of dark denim, with functional handmade boots of dark leather obviously very well maintained. Over it all he had a three quarter length overcoat of dark black and a silver belt buckle gleamed at his waist. Artek was slender and only lightly muscled, almost boyish in his build, yet he held himself with the bearing of a military man, and his flawless appearance further reflected this.

Marcus had, of course, delved deeply into the man's life, his history, the lineage of his family and what had happened to them, and everything about it was reflected in the man that strode confidently beside him. His family had a long history of holding military office, often graduating straight into well placed roles that reflected money and connections. The Lethargy changed everything and the family was severely reduced in size as the good old days vanished in an instant. But the main line mostly remained Whole with only a few exceptions, although finding suitable partners appeared to be a stumbling block. There was a stubborn streak and a sense of having a right to things that no longer tied in with the society, or lack of one, they had to make their way in.

Upper class sensibilities didn't work in the men's favor and their reluctance to sever ties to ancestral ways of behaving meant that they still looked down their noses at those they deemed of the lower classes. The line mostly ended — it was his mother that kept things going. She was a woman of indomitable will, one of the few that Awoke, and had lived a seemingly long life, long enough to bring up her son until he was capable enough of finding his way in the world alone.

Through the years the new family home expanded and everything was organized with military precision, one of the spill-overs from what now seemed like a different time altogether.

With Artek, the remains of the past were present, yet he was very much his own man, keeping the traditions he felt were right, discarding anything that felt out of place or like relics of a past he never knew and frankly didn't really care about.

His overriding goal in life was to continue his family line, something that was a must as far as he was concerned, and allowing others to do likewise. He felt strongly that people had a better chance of survival if they could only find the right person to spend their life with.

Marcus had no doubt he would succeed, he wasn't the kind of man to change his mind about something.

Not Much of a Holiday

"Well you didn't last long did you? I must say I'm a bit disappointed." Marcus' green eyes had changed, they were almost blue now, but when Letje looked again they were back to green, then as dark as the ocean, then as green as a frog, as gray as a winter's sky. Was that orange? She felt like a child again — stared at by a man that knew what it was to be many things and no things. It was really unnerving.

"Were you really a whale?" asked Arcene, peering at Marcus as if he was about to blow water out the top of his head. She stood on tiptoe to get a better look.

"Not just any whale, a blue whale. It was only for a few weeks though, a mini-vacation really." Marcus stared accusingly at Letje. "It was supposed to be permanent, not a short trip into the depths. I assume Marcus is dead?"

"Yes, he died," interrupted Arcene. "We were there, all of us. Varik chopped his head off. Your head off. Well, not you, the other one. Hey, there really were two of you then? Cool. We have your head. In a box. Do you want to go see it?"

"Arcene!" Letje nudged her in the ribs.

"Ow! What?"

"Stop babbling, of course he doesn't want to see his head."

"Well, I wouldn't mind actually. Do I look alright? Is it a nice box?"

"Oh, well, erm, yes, I suppose. Look Marcus, sorry to bring you back, I know you wanted to go away, be... a whale? Sorry, that sounds weird. Things have happened though. Strange things. Bad things."

"People, right? I can feel it, they've all gone. Can't you find them? Or Fasolt? You are both powerful enough now."

"That's the problem though, we can't find them, they've gone. Somebody got access to information from The Commorancy, sensitive information, and we think maybe they used it to find people, at least some of them, the last of them, and well, they took them."

"How could they get in? I've got, I had, excellent firewalls, no end of failsafes and false backdoors, safety feature after safety feature."

"I know, and all that's well and good but it doesn't help when your password is password."

"When your password is password? You don't mean that your password was password?"

"Not mine. His." Letje pointed at Fasolt.

"I said I was sorry." Fasolt felt he would never be able to do anything but hang his head in shame ever again.

"Okay, maybe we ought to start at the beginning. First things first, I hope you haven't been reorganizing The Room For Clothes or anything as obscene as that?"

Letje suddenly realized that her fingernails needed staring at.

"You wouldn't? You haven't? Oh my god, things are worse than I feared."

"We only changed a few things, you probably won't even notice the difference."

Marcus stared through Letje's eyes, into her head, then out the other side, leaving a gaping hole in his evil stare's wake.

"We'll see. Come on, you're all coming with me. And how can all of this happen in just a few weeks anyway? I've only just left."

"Marcus, you've been gone five years. I can't believe you haven't noticed how much I've grown. Look, I'm nearly as tall as you now." Arcene pouted her bottom lip so far out it looked like her tongue.

"Ah, yes, well, things have been a little... unusual, I may not quite be myself yet." Marcus began to walk off, in search of clothes. He stopped and turned. "Oh, yes, another thing, just how exactly am I here anyway? I never did know how there were two of me. I wiped such memories and I wasn't even sure if there was such a thing as more of me. Are there? Were there? Can I see?"

Silence.

Shifting of feet.

Cough.

"It's, er, a bit of an odd story actually," said Letje, looking warily at the others.

"What? I was supposed to expect something else? Something normal? Haha."

"Well, you see, it started like this..." Letje explained how Marcus happened to be Marcus after having his head chopped off and the other him becoming a whale and his body eaten by crabs as it rotted away on a shoreline somewhere along the southern coast of England.

~~~

"You went into The Room Of Dreams? Well, that was brave of you."

"Don't you remember? I met you, the whale. You told me of the Room, where the, you know, the yous are."

Marcus scratched his head, his eye color changing rapidly, flickering through the spectrum as if searching for one he liked. "Nope, don't recall that."

"Um, Marcus, can you speak a little faster? This is taking ages."

"Huh? What do you mean?"

"I mean that we are all getting starving, you've been stood there for four hours now and we've only had a short conversation. Speak faster." Letje stared at him intently; he really didn't realize.

"Is this true?" Marcus asked Arcene and Fasolt.

"Yeah, you're really, really boring when you talk so slow Marcus. It's driving me mad, and I need to go pee too."

Fasolt just nodded, understanding the effect a life in the depths could have on a man.

"HowisthisanybetterIthinkifItalkwithoutthinkinga boutittoomuchthenitshouldcomeoutaboutright."

"Whoa, no, I didn't get hardly a word of that, that's too fast now."

It took another few hours before Marcus finally managed to get his mind working properly and could speak at a normal speed that everyone could understand.

Then he said something that sent Letje cold, fear gripping her before she fell to the ground unconscious.

"You can wake up now Letje, I think you are finished with your dream."

~~~

Letje woke up in The Room Of Dreams, naked and shaking.

Somebody was knocking at the door and all she could hear apart from the insistent banging was *Boom, boom, boom. The Room, Room, Room.*

Ow!

"That hurt, what did you do that for?"

"So you'd know you're not dreaming now. See, you're awake." Arcene pinched Letje again.

"Ow! Stop. You didn't have to do it again," moaned Letje, rubbing her arm.

Fasolt was deep in thought, staring at Letje as if she would be eaten by fish at any moment. After hearing her story of the dream and that she had thought she was awake and they had brought Marcus back to life he was showing deep concern.

"What? What is it?" Letje couldn't get her mind to work properly. She had told them what she could remember of her dream, but was worried that she had thought she had been awake and that it felt like days had passed and that Marcus really was back. She still kept expecting him to sit down and ask for the sugar.

Fasolt stirred uncomfortably. "You should never have gone into that Room. Forced dreams like that are dangerous. You said it yourself that in The Book Marcus warned it had sent people mad, or worse."

"I know and I was almost gone I'm sure. If those fish had eaten much more of me I don't think I would have been able to come back."

Fasolt twirled a dreadlock idly. "Hmm, that's the problem though isn't it? How do you know you're awake now? How do you know that this is real and that it isn't all a dream?"

"Well, because I know I'm awake I guess," said Letje, doubt creeping into her voice.

"See, you don't know do you? Your whole life, me, Arcene, The Commorancy, Marcus, even your dream, it could all just be a part of a dream now. You could still be in there, or maybe you never were but are dreaming in The Void about a life you haven't yet lived. That's what you're thinking, isn't it?"

Letje admitted it reluctantly. "Yes. How do I know?"

Letje's arm shot out and grabbed Arcene's before she pinched her again.

"Just trying to help," smiled Arcene.

"You don't," said Fasolt, "and that's why I told you not to go in there. Some things are best left alone, and messing with dreams is high on the list. You will never be the same, you will always have that doubt. A little piece of you will always be wondering if everything isn't just a made up story that you are dreaming while you wait to live whatever life it is that you actually have. Or that you are right now at home, laying on the grass, dozing in the sun while butterflies search for nectar with your tortoise next to you and your mother and father making supper. Sorry, that was cruel. But you should not have done what you did."

"So there is no whale? No Room that we need to find? No way to get Marcus back? It was all for nothing?"

"What? No, of course there is. I don't doubt for a second that what you dreamed will actually happen; that's the whole point of the Room. You spoke to Marcus and he told you how to find out how to bring him back. Let's go find it."

"Huh? But you just said it was a dream. Now you are saying it was real?"

"No. I'm saying you had a dream and parts of what happened in it could be real, could happen, if we do what you did in your dream. So, what do we do first? Where is the Room that has the... What did it have? Was it full of Marcus' waiting to be animated? Some kind of clone bank or something?" Fasolt sat forward eagerly. Arcene was staring so hard it was as if she was trying to drag the information from Letje's head before she spoke.

"Well, that's the problem, I didn't see what was in the Room. The dream jumped, it told me where it was, then the next bit was us all stood around Marcus and him taking hours to speak a line. I don't know what was actually in the Room at all. But I do know where it is."

"So let's go. What are we waiting for?" Arcene moved to stand but Fasolt put a hand to her shoulder and nodded in Letje's direction. "Oh."

"Let her sleep, she needs her rest."

Arcene looked at Letje, fast asleep and starting to snore. "But, but she's just been sleeping for so long already, she can't need more."

"That was different," explained Fasolt. "That wasn't sleep for the need of sleep, it was sleep for dreaming and it doesn't count."

"Oh."

Letje dreamed she was dozing in the garden, or she dreamed she was asleep in a chair in The Commorancy, she wasn't really sure which, or if it even mattered any longer.

It's About Time

Letje woke a few hours later trying to get rid of the terrible sense of her whole life being a lie. Maybe the Room had been a mistake? She felt out of things, disassociated from time and reality, as if she was only half a person, the other half still being eaten by the fish then put back together by butterflies, an endless loop of dissipating and resurrecting only for it to happen over and over.

Coffee, that was what was needed.

A few cups later, and with Fasolt and Arcene getting more and more impatient, she finally felt up to going to discover if her dream really had told her what she had wanted to know.

They went to find The Room For Marcus, not The Marcus Room, which was a different Room entirely.

Three hours later, wrong turn after wrong turn, after walking down endless corridors only to find them leading nowhere, after entering countless Rooms and exiting them into even stranger ones, they finally came to the end of their quest.

It was a bit of an anti-climax.

~~~

"Is this it?" said a disappointed Arcene. "It's just a dusty drape, look." Arcene tugged on the material, a dull white that spat out dust as it was disturbed.

"Careful, it might be booby-trapped," warned Letje.

Arcene kept pulling and the drape slid along the rail to reveal a plain pine door that had never even been painted. The yellow wood was so uninspiring that nobody would try very hard to discover what was behind the door. "See, it's fine, just a stupid door."

"With somebody inside. Snap." Letje and Fasolt stared at each other then laughed nervously, both of them saying the same thing at the same time.

"It's not fair, I want to be able to do that too. When do I get to be Awoken?"

"Soon. As soon as you stop being naughty," said Letje.

"So, never," said Fasolt, smiling.

"Look, I said I was sorry."

"Oh, no, I didn't mean that. You know, that you gave away secrets and stuff," said Letje, trying not to sound mean. "I meant going off and pushing buttons and pulling levers and generally trying to blow everything up."

"Oh," was all Arcene could think of to say. "Okay."

"Ready?" Letje felt her stomach flip over as she looked for reassurance from her friends, her family, her responsibilities.

Two heads nodded in the affirmative.

Letje looked at the door, seeing the complex circuitry hidden within. She placed her left hand on a panel, her thumb tight into the profile, her other hand flat, middle finger not touching the wood, angled so that she made the shape of a butterfly. Her stomach somersaulted again, next there would be fish coming from the floor and eating her feet. She stared down at her feet, tapping away like they were trying to dance away from being eaten. "No fish."

"Letje? You okay?" Fasolt gestured at the door.

"Oh, right. Sorry." Letje let her middle finger touch the door and complete the circuit and then removed her hands.

Psst.

The door slid into the wall to the right, only to reveal another door, this time dull gray and looking like it would take some serious explosives to budge it. There was no embedded circuitry that she could see, no handle, keyhole, or even a crack where it met the frame, a seamless solid piece of steel that meant business.

"Well, that's a bit annoying. Thought it was too easy. How are we supp—"

Whoosh.

"Arcene!" yelled Letje, as Arcene pushed at the door and it *whooshed* up into the ceiling revealing the interior.

"Oh."

"Hello, you took your time didn't you?" said Marcus, sitting behind a simple wooden desk, immaculately dressed and matching his surroundings as always.

"Marcus, it's really you? I'm not dreaming?"

"Hello Letje. No you're not dreaming, although that was a dangerous thing you did going into The Room Of Dreams."

"Your eyes," exclaimed Arcene, "they're just like Letje said they were."

It was true, Marcus' once green eyes flicked through the spectrum constantly, flashing every color and no color. There was something else too, Letje just couldn't quite think what it was.

"You're younger? Older? What is it, I can't tell?"

"Just different Fasolt. Different."

"How so?"

"Because I'm the real Marcus, the original."

~~~

"You mean you haven't been out of your Room since you built the place?" asked Letje, still not believing it really, truly was Marcus, not just a dream.

"That's right. Marcus, Marcus plural that is, locked me in and I haven't been able to get out since."

"For what, like three hundred years?" Arcene couldn't imagine being in one Room for that long, but knew others had stayed in The Commorancy for similar amounts of time.

"Give or take a few years, yes. It was part of the deal, the plan, although I must say I wish I'd never agreed. I expected one of them to come back and get me at some point, but I guess the memory wipes worked like they were supposed to."

"Care to explain?" said Letje.

"Only if you tell me what's happened. I've been watching you since you arrived but there are still a few missing gaps, like exactly how I died, where the other me really is, that kind of thing. I've listened to most of it when you've talked but there are some things I still don't quite understand."

"Haha, things that you don't understand. What about us? We've known you to die, assumed, no, knew, the other you was dead, now here you are again. I mean, c'mon, your head is in a box in The Orientation Room."

"Ah, yes, about the head..."

Not Just Any Room

Marcus' Room was unconventional to say the least. As he invited them in and busied himself gathering chairs — he had never had guests — and returning some time later with pots of tea and coffee, it was obvious that he hadn't just been cooped up in a single space. Doors and entryways open to corridors hinted at extensive living quarters.

Marcus explained what he had been doing and how he happened to be locked behind a door for so long. Locked in by himself, two of them.

He did his best to explain but it was no easy task. As soon as he began there was utter confusion, so he tried again.

"Now, let me try to get this right, sorry about getting it jumbled, I sort of missed the end of everything so don't know exactly what I, they, did."

"So you couldn't... feel, see, download what they were doing?" Letje always wondered how Marcus managed to know what the other one was doing, or had done.

"No, they were connected. Each lived a life but updated almost instantly to the other so they both always knew what they were doing. But over time it got a little frayed around the edges so to speak, and the longer I, um, they, lived, the more confusing it got. The more of an impossibility it seemed until I, they, didn't really know if it was real any longer. Nevertheless, they had a connection, and it wasn't until one left with you Letje for the mainland that the link almost broke, then it did. Poof, no more connection.

"From then on they didn't know what each other did, and I didn't know what either of them did. I was cut off; blind. Alone. You know it really did get lonely then. I was surprised just how attached to those guys I got."

"Well duh, it was you Marcus."

"Thank you Arcene, most helpful my dear."

"You're welcome," beamed Arcene.

"So, I never saw what happened to them once the connection broke, once The Final Decision was made. Although, obviously, I guessed what it would be, as it was what I would have done if I had the luxury of two choices, which I suppose is exactly what I did. One went off to have an adventure on his own, right? And the other sacrificed himself so the right future would happen. So you would be the new owner of The

Commorancy and run things." Marcus was looking at Letje, his dancing eyes mesmerizing.

"Right. He, you, um... He let Varik chop his head off and Bird killed Varik and we came here."

"Smart man wasn't I?"

"What do you mean?" Letje didn't get it, neither did Arcene.

Fasolt interjected. "He did it so you would come here and get the original him. You. Right Marcus?"

"Well, yes, that's right. At least it's what I would have done."

"What do you mean? What are you talking about?"

"Look, the other Marcus', they wiped their memories of how there were two of them, right? Well, actually I wiped them, just to be sure. And they wiped memories of who was the original, believing it was one of them, and they got rid of even the memory of agreeing to do it, of how there were two of them, of how any of it worked, and this is the most important bit, they were wiped clean of any hint that there was another one of them or any kind of a chance of one of them coming back."

"So..." Letje didn't get it.

"So... I let myself be killed so that you would run The Commorancy and come and find me."

"Hang on, that doesn't make sense. You just said Marcus didn't know there was another him, you, so why would he sacrifice himself so I, we, would come looking for you? He didn't know."

"Aha, he didn't know that there was another me, but he knew that there were two of him. Yes?"

"Right."

"So he knew that there was a way it had been done. So he knew that even though he didn't remember doing it, or how it happened, or how to do it again or where to look, he knew that here somewhere there was the answer. So he allowed himself to die so that you would find out the answer and bring him back."

"That's crazy. What if we didn't want to, or didn't find out how to? You could have been in here forever. It's pure luck we found you."

"Is it? Is it really?"

"Well, yeah, isn't it?" Letje turned to Fasolt and Arcene. "Isn't it?"

"Don't ask me," said Arcene, "I got lost at the bit about wiping his memory."

Fasolt spoke up. "I think Marcus knew that at some point something would happen and we would try to find him. Since we knew for sure there were two of him, or mostly anyway, then given that there was an option then we would try to see if we could bring Marcus back. Right Marcus?"

"Exactly. You knew that there was a chance, so at some point you would try to find me. It stands to reason doesn't it? If you think there is help then you will go looking for it. And here I am. I'm here to help. I must say it is going to be such fun, I'm so looking forward to it. When do we start?"

"This is making my head hurt," moaned Letje. "You're saying that you had your head chopped off so that we would maybe come and find another you?"

"No, not at all. I'm saying that after three hundred years of running The Commorancy and dealing with an extended life and two of me that I went mad and was happy to end it all and pass on the responsibility to somebody I felt was up to the task. Especially as they had help from friends and would probably at some point find me."

"Oh, so you were mad then?"

"Well, I was a little eccentric at least," smiled Marcus. "Now, about the other Marcus, what happened to him?"

"Judging by Letje's dream, and by what I felt when you faced Varik, and a strange conversation I believe was real when I was staring out to sea, which I will have to tell you about properly," said Fasolt, trying to come to terms with meeting the man his son had killed, "I believe you went into the deep. The ocean," offered Fasolt helpfully.

"That makes sense, I assumed as much. Before their connection broke then that was what I had wondered about — an adventure, something totally different. I wonder how I'm doing, what it's like?"

"It's slow, and dreamy," said Letje. "In my dream of finding you I saw your whale eye, it spoke to me, told me where you were. You are big!"

"Well, that settles it then. It was what I had being wondering about."

"Marcus?"

"Yes Arcene?"

"How did you know what the other Marcus' were doing though? Have you got all their memories as well as your own? Are you bonkers too?"

"I am the one that created them, gave them me, made them me, so the connection was strongest from them to me. I felt things exactly as they did, experienced what they did. They just didn't know. Even though the thread was there, they were told to ignore it, to not see it. They never did as far as I can tell."

"Okay, so you were them but they weren't you?"

"That's right. What I did, this me?" Marcus tapped his chest. "They never experienced that, only each other."

"And Marcus?"

"No, I don't think so, not quite mad yet, but I am a little bored. Let's go and have a cup of tea, somewhere away from here."

Letje got to her feet, curiosity overtaking her. "Can we maybe have a look at where you've been living all this time first, if that's okay?"

"Well, I suppose another day or two won't make much difference, although we will have to do a bit of a rush tour if we are to get going on our quest."

"A couple of days!" shouted Arcene. "I thought it was just a big Room?"

"What, knowing I was going to spend who knew how long in here, maybe longer than I have? Oh no, it's quite expansive. Not Commorancy big, but I did my best before they locked me in. Come on, but let's have another cuppa first, I'm parched after all this talking. It has been three hundred years since I had the chance to chat with anyone."

~~~

"Psst. Psst... Oi."

"What? What is it?"

"I think he's more mad than the Marcus we knew. Have you seen his eyes?"

"Yes, I have. And yes, I think you're right."

Marcus wheeled past them on his scooter, trundling off into the gloom, shouting for them to follow if they wanted the guided tour.

"I think you're absolutely right Arcene, he is kind of fun though, don't you think?"

"Oh yeah, it's going to be great."

Settling In

Marcus felt strange, he hadn't had company for so long.

Yet at the same time he had always had company, had lived three lives spanning centuries each — meaning he had in fact lived through almost a thousand years accumulatively — and seen more, done more, than any other human being alive or dead. He saw so much, understood so much, could do many things he still thought somewhat magical himself even though he knew otherwise. Yet, when it came down to it, it was still the first company he'd had for over three hundred years.

It was the conundrum of being who he was, or rather, what he had been. He had lived the lives of the Marcus', did and felt everything they did as though he were doing it himself, which to all intents and purposes he was. Their lives were his life, yet his was not theirs. When they finally cut the cord that linked the triumvirate it was doubly hard for him as he was saying goodbye to two best friends not just the one. It was like having two of triplets suddenly leave your life, making it empty and hollow, and oh so slow.

Living a life such as his meant that even when he personally wasn't busy or doing much of anything there were always things being done by the other him or hims, making life fast-paced, never boring, even a little exciting at times. There were days, months, occasionally even years where one or the other dropped out from his experiences, secrets they never even admitted they had to each other, yet Marcus knew they were being kept, didn't begrudge them their personal alone time and personal memories never to be shared.

For the most part though he went about his life in triplicate, yet always once removed from the closeness as the other Marcus' never knew of the connection. Still, he was them so it didn't really change anything.

The difference was that the others had been interchangeable, never knew whose memories or experiences were whose, but for Marcus he always knew, as the life he lived behind closed doors was his and his alone. Even that got warped over time.

It was a complicated business indeed and there were many times that he sat down to think through how it worked only to come to no other conclusion than that he had a very bad headache. Some things were simply impossible to truly understand — but it didn't stop him trying. Marcus was the other Marcus', he lived their lives, did what they did, he was them. Up until they were no longer connected to each other or to him. He had slowly faded away once on the mainland, not a sudden death so much as a dissipating into The Void, slowly going back to nothingness. At the same time he had been losing his mind while alone at The Commorancy after killing countless Lethargic and pining for the other him. He had experienced the meeting of himself, the agreement to live his own lives, knowing that each had chosen a death of sorts, one more final than the other. Also knowing that he wasn't actually going to die, that at most a few weeks or months out of an impossibly long life would be missing from his memory.

That wasn't so bad was it? Even normal people had months and years where they couldn't remember what they did — it wasn't possible to remember everything. He had made a decision to also have the adventure of a lifetime, albeit in different form, and that was something he really wished he could do, but of course he had, was, is doing exactly that, just not the him that was right now showing his guests around his home within a home.

There was a difference however, a difference between all of that direct experience removed from physical self and real, genuine, hands on visceral experience of the actual life, solid and real, that he personally was living. It was, when all was said and done, an impossible life on so many levels that he thought he had done quite well to have not completely broken down into insanity right at the moment he became a tri-split personality.

Or maybe he had.

How would he know?

What he did know was that it was uplifting to finally have real, solid, living breathing company that was actually here, really here. However real his other lives had been it somehow just wasn't the same, even though it should have been.

Time to forget about the past, time to live in the moment, begin again.

After all, he did have his freedom at least, didn't he?

He was free wasn't he?

Or was he now merely a prisoner in a larger cage? An animal in the zoo moved to a bigger enclosure, still just as captive as ever, just with an illusion of liberty, still locked down tight if the truth be told?

Well, whatever. At least he could experience his work firsthand for the first time in centuries.

Although he already had hadn't he...?

Here I go again, thought Marcus. *Around in circles never getting anywhere but more confused. Just enjoy the beginnings of a new life Marcus, you are reborn into a world you have been away from for far too long.*

And it really is beautiful Marcus, although we are going to have to figure out exactly what has been going on with all the people.

Aha, I was forgetting just how strong a woman you now are Letje, but no peeking at my thoughts, it's rude you know.

Sorry, you just kind of spilled over, it's because I haven't been around you before, I picked it up. I'll block you out, promise. I know how wrong it is to listen to people's innermost thoughts. Sorry.

That's okay Letje, I guess we both have a lot to get used to, right?

I don't think it ever ends does it?

No, I don't suppose it does Letje. I don't suppose it does.

~~~

"It's almost as big as The Room For Clothes," whispered Letje, the sacred space forcing respect and allowing for nothing but hushed voices.

"Well, not quite, but near enough. I knew I was going to be in here for a while, although I didn't know it was going to be quite so long," said Marcus, eyes flashing through colors as he looked from outfit to outfit, absorbing colors as he stood in one of the infinite seeming aisles where each row was organized by color first then categorized in numerous sub-sections — impossible to be understood by anyone apart from Marcus. "Most of the things here in The Slightly Smaller Room For Clothes were picked up when the larger Room was mostly completed, but of course I haven't been able to add to it since then. Still, there has been plenty to allow me to change when needed."

"I bet," said Arcene. "Wonder how long it would take to wear every outfit you own Marcus?"

"Haha, I don't even want to think about it. I don't know that anyone could live that long."

"You might though. We all might," said Arcene hopefully. She tugged at a pigtail for a moment, eyes staring inward before she asked what was obviously on her mind. "Marcus?"

"Yes Arcene?"

"How long can people live for? I mean, people like you and Letje, Fasolt? Truly Awoken?"

"That's something I have pondered myself over the years my dear, and the answer is that I have no idea. I also don't know when you would stop being you. For Awoken I can't really see how long they could live. There are plenty of people as old as me and Fasolt with no sign of slowing down. And for us? We are different, you too Arcene, you will be like us when the time comes. Our lives obviously cannot be infinite in human form, but it could be millennia, longer, until maybe we join with the animals or the birds, or even the planet itself and become something different."

"Could I be a tree? That would be cool I think."

"Oh it is Arcene, being a tree is a beautiful thing."

"You've been a tree? Cool!" Arcene couldn't imagine such a thing.

"Not been one, but I speak to them. If I recall correctly then you once asked me what it was like to be me?"

Arcene stared at Marcus in confusion, then understood. "Oh, at Letje's house? The you that wasn't the you here? Yeah, and what you said was sad, and scary."

"Well, it was me, is me, sort of, but let's forget about that for a minute. What I told you wasn't the whole truth Arcene, at least not for me personally." Marcus tapped his chest. "This me."

"Um, okay."

"There is more, much more. Things have happened to me that didn't happen to the others. Couldn't happen unless they lived how I lived. But the other me, they spoke to the trees, just as I do. I have a Room For Trees you know? Here in my little part of The Commorancy. We are very good friends now, although I think they will not miss me as much as I will miss them."

"Where you going?"

"Oh, you know, away," said Marcus, gesturing at nothing in particular. "We all are aren't we? Off on an adventure, out into the big bad world to find out where everybody has gone. Although I must say it does feel like I've just been out, but it was what, five years ago?"

Letje found herself twirling a wide-brimmed hat in her hands idly as she spoke. "Five years, yes. It seems like a lifetime ago to me though. So much has happened here since then; we've learned so much."

"And there is certainly a lot more to learn Letje, but before any of that we must find out where the people are. There's no point being humanity's salvation if there isn't a humanity to save anymore, right?"

"Right," said Letje.

"Let's go get 'em," Arcene shouted enthusiastically, then clasped a hand to her mouth. "Oops, sorry."

"No need to say sorry, this isn't a church, just a place for clothes and stuff."

"Well, I don't believe that for one second," said Arcene, smiling as Marcus delicately took the hat off Letje and placed it back on it's perfectly lit pedestal.

"I think you know me all too well Arcene. Haha."

Arcene smiled outwardly, but the pain in her eyes was obvious. It was clear that she really didn't want Marcus to see the main Room For Clothes if he was so fussy about a single hat. Arcene tried, but she had to admit she really wasn't the most organized of people in some regards.

Marcus turned to Fasolt. "You're quiet my friend, are you alright?"

"Yes and no Marcus. I feel like I must apologize all over again for the things I have done, the pain and trouble I have caused you. So much is my fault, my doing, my terrible legacy."

Marcus put a hand on the slender bare shoulder of Fasolt. "Do not worry Fasolt, this life is full of surprises. We do good and we do bad, the main thing is that we understand ourselves and accept our nature. Yours is a good one now, you have made your apologies and I accepted them then as I do now. There is no need for you to dwell on such things."

"Thank you Marcus. For everything."

"Come, let me give you the rest of the tour, then we have some planning to do. I have something in mind that should help with our quest."

~~~

Three days later they emerged through a door the size of small skyscraper into a world that made their experience of The Commorancy so far seem like nothing but a stay in a cheap hotel then moved to the penthouse suite at no extra cost.

But there was always a price to pay.

Always.

Some Project

"Um, well, wow," was all Fasolt could manage.

"Crikey," said Arcene, staring at Marcus as if she truly did believe he was a god.

"Well, you've been busy Marcus, this is quite some project you have been involved in." Letje thought she had become advanced with her powers in The Noise, had seen and understood more than most ever did in their lifetime, but it faded into insignificance when she thought about what Marcus had achieved. Not thought, witnessed, experienced, become immersed in.

"Thought you might like it, had to have something to pass away the time." Marcus' eyes danced crazily, a flickering candle reflecting color as if a disco ball was spinning at top speed.

Letje settled herself; her heartbeat slowed to a normal rhythm, adrenaline lessened, her brain became sharp and open, then she shut down the heightened senses — it was too much, she wasn't ready for such an experience yet and she was wise enough to understand it. Before she had a chance to say anything Marcus did it for her.

"Well, that's it, time to go."

"Wha... what! Um, aren't we going to stay for a bit?" Arcene looked expectantly to Marcus then Letje and Fasolt, all three shaking their heads.

"No Arcene, I just wanted to show you all, but Letje isn't ready, Fasolt maybe, but you definitely aren't. I just wanted you to understand what you are, what you will be, what is possible."

"But I want to stay!"

"Well, I don't, come on." Letje grabbed Arcene by the arm and dragged her back out the door. Marcus and Fasolt followed, the deeply carved door, a living thing, part of the Room, part of its interior, part of everything, shut behind them with a quiet thump.

Letje heard the Room whisper its goodbyes to her as she left.

Goodbye, I will return.

We know, we know, whispered the Room to her as it settled back into its impossible life.

"The Living Room," said Marcus.

"But that's—"

"Yes Arcene, I am well aware of the double meaning. What good is life if you can't have a little fun?" Marcus smiled conspiratorially and winked at Arcene, his open eye as pale as the hair on her head. "Come on, I believe we have a plan to make. Ooh, this is going to be fun, it's about time I had a bit of action myself. First time really, the last major thing I did was build The Commorancy, now I get to really save people, matter of life and death stuff, it's gonna be great."

Letje watched as Marcus skipped off down the corridor, Arcene nudging her and twirling a finger by the side of her head.

"He's been a bit isolated is all, I'm sure it will all work out fine." Letje hoped so, once again things were moving faster than she could keep up with.

Well, it beat sitting in a chair waiting for The Lethargy to take what little you had left, and Marcus was the one that had given it all to her, to so many others. Now they were going to find those people and all the others that somehow seemed to have disappeared from the face of the planet.

Pick a Ruler

Marcus and Letje had left the others in the kitchen and were settled in The Space Room, somewhere they both felt suited their discussion. The Space Room was made up of emptiness: empty chairs, empty sofas, empty tables and empty walls and floors — no distractions.

It had the exact opposite effect. The lack of things, the echoing Room, the non-furniture without much in the way of comfort, meant that it was impossible to settle and focus on any kind of meaningful conversation.

"Shall we move?"

"Oh yes, please. Marcus, I have to say it but I don't think this Room was a success. Sorry," said Letje.

"Well, nobody's perfect. You can't win them all," smiled Marcus.

~~~

"Ah, that's better. Right?"

"Oh yes, it's nice to be in more familiar surroundings. Um, one minute." Letje got up from the couch they were both sat on and picked up a black silk cloth and draped it over the head of Marcus in its clear box. She returned to the couch and plonked down, feeling better.

"No need to do that on my behalf Letje, after all it was me that asked for my son to, you know, do it."

"It doesn't bother you? Staring at your own cut off head?" Letje knew for a fact that it would bother her immensely.

"Can't say it does, not really. There are worse things, and besides, I'm still here aren't I?"

"Ugh, I don't even want to think about that. This you isn't that you is it?" said Letje, pointing at the draped box.

"Well, no, not exactly, but I am him. Just more so."

Letje sat, thinking about it and eventually just dismissing it. She had never gotten used to believing that there had been two and they were the same person, now there was another one she couldn't even bear trying to think about who he was, which one, if any. "I can't really come to any kind of resolution when it comes to this, it's too weird."

"I understand. Imagine how I feel. I bet you're wondering how many more of me there are, aren't you? Maybe another one will peek out from behind the drapes over there and I will be the one in the dark, never knowing there was another me that experienced all I do and the other Marcus' too."

Letje couldn't help but stare at the heavy red drapes, half expecting Marcus to materialize and be caught in a never-ending loop of new Marcus after new Marcus, one behind the other fading into infinity in never ending madness of oneupmanship. "Don't even joke about it."

"Haha, spooked you right?" Marcus stared at the drapes. "Actually I spooked myself too. How do I know that isn't true? After all, the others didn't know about me did they?"

"No, they didn't. And I still don't get how you knew someone would find you eventually. You could have been stuck in there for eternity."

"I knew myself only too well, and I knew that I would find a way. It would have been the absence of knowing that would have made Marcus sacrifice himself. He knew that as he didn't know how there were two of him that there must be a place in The Commorancy where it happened, so it stood to reason there was a high chance he could be brought back, somehow."

"And if not?"

"Then I guess I wouldn't have known myself as well as I did." Marcus leaned back and put his hands behind his head and smiled, confident in himself, but more than anything obviously happy to be back in The Orientation Room where he had been so many times before, yet never really been for too many years to even think about having lived.

"So," said Letje.

"So," said Marcus.

There was silence, each wondering how best to put what was obviously a very important issue.

"So, who's in charge now? Who runs The Commorancy?"

"You beat me to it. It's a bit of a problem, no?" Marcus smiled. Letje was sure it was deviously.

She smacked him playfully on the arm. "Are you trying to mess with me Marcus Wolfe? Poking fun at the youngster?"

"You're not such a youngster any longer though are you? A fully grown woman no less. That's pretty grown up."

"But still young to be running such an important place. The only place that can truly help people. Well, could, if we knew where they were."

"You have been doing an excellent job Letje, I couldn't have asked for more. I have been watching you know?"

"I know, and that still feels weird. All of it does. You being here, my dream, you being dead, in the ocean, all too strange. But back to my question."

"Well, you were given the responsibility by me, right? I would not have taken such a momentous decision lightly I can assure you, and I never intended for me to run The Commorancy. This me." Marcus poked his chest, just so Letje was sure who he meant.

"What? But it's what you built it for, to run it."

"Yes. And no. As I was constructing it and came across the means to never be alone — the other Marcus' — things changed, everything changed. Yes, in one way I ran it, but in another, for me locked away, then I had no part in what happened, couldn't influence anything, take actions."

"Surely you could have, you know, got out really? If you wanted to." Letje couldn't believe the man sat across from her didn't have a way out of his self-imposed exile if the need arose.

"Oh no, absolutely not. I made sure of it. It's why The Rules are so important, the ones about the doors and opening them," hinted Marcus. "The same Rules applied to me. Everything was set up so I couldn't leave, I had to be let out. You rescued me Letje, my Saviour." Marcus leaned forward and kissed Letje gently on the forehead through her hair.

Letje felt like she'd been shocked and jumped back, her hand automatically going to her forehead as if the kiss remained. "Hey, no funny business mister. You've played your pheromone tricks on me before, remember?"

"Ha, I remember, but I did nothing of the sort then, I promise." Marcus put his hand on his heart.

Letje stared at him suspiciously, the tingling still running through her body. "Okay, just you be careful," she warned.

"I will, promise," said Marcus, laughing.

He was unnerving her. He seemed almost too alive, too visceral — about ready to burst. She focused on the rather important matter of who now ran The Commorancy. "So, who runs it?"

"You do."

"Oh. Right."

Marcus stood. "Okay, now that we have that sorted out let's see about finding who is responsible for stealing all the people shall we? Gosh, it seems like no sooner is Varik dealt with than there's another crazy person out there doing things that are maybe worse. Come on George, let's go find out shall we?" Marcus walked toward the exit then turned and searched George's various hiding places.

"Um, I think maybe there's something we need to talk about first..."

~~~

"He what?"

"Sorry, I thought you knew." Letje shifted uncomfortably from foot to foot.

"Eh? Oh, yes, I suppose I did. Must be my age. I haven't seen him around for five years have I? Silly of me. Old habits I guess, sort of got used to him after all these years, even if... well you know, he wasn't actually with me."

Letje stared after Marcus as he left the Room, the now familiar *whoosh* no longer seeming quite so bizarre. She followed, wondering exactly how far gone Marcus actually was. There was no way that he could have lived the life he had and not had serious repercussions for such an existence. She wondered how it would manifest itself and how long before he too totally unraveled now he was at large in the world and could probably do anything he wanted to.

That was the question though. What exactly could he do? She had witnessed him bend time, pause it then move through the gaps like a mouse sliding under a door. And that Room, The Living Room, it told of depths she couldn't even begin to contemplate.

Letje was a little bit scared.

And excited too.

She touched her forehead.

It still tingled.

Letje suddenly felt her heart race, blood pounding in her ears like a giant's footsteps. What if she was still dreaming? Still in The Room Of Dreams? It would make more sense than this wouldn't it? Marcus locked behind a huge door for centuries and that impossible Room?

She hurried after him, wondering how she could confirm her reality.

Fasolt had been right, she never should have gone inside. Life had just got very complicated very quickly.

Well, that was The Commorancy for you.

She remembered she had better check on Constantine, he'd been very quiet.

A Burial

"Daddy. Daddy!" Letje knew there was something wrong as soon as she stepped foot in the kitchen. Yabis, father of Letje, long time inhabitant of Constantine Alexander III and reluctant tortoise, was absent from The Noise.

The body of the ancient tortoise was still in his little den, curled up as best a tortoise could, by the side of the huge fire where he had been half-hibernating for quite some time now.

He was dead.

Letje picked him up, hoping there would still be a spark of life there for her to maybe try to bring him back, but it was no use. The legs dangled listlessly, the head flopped to one side, eyes closed. The essence of what was once a man and a tortoise was already in The Void, already back to where they came from, where they would always be — apart from tiny blips in the continuum when they would inhabit the bodies of diverse beings throughout the Universe.

Letje sat down on the floor, the fire warming her tears as they dripped onto the shell of her best friend and her father. How could she have not known? Not seen that he was going to die? Constantine had been slowing for years now, sleeping more, hibernating through the winter months and taking longer to come back to her. But her father had assured her it was just part of being a tortoise and that he felt fine. Letje, constantly busy and never having as much time as she would have liked to spend with him, had simply taken him at his word and left him to his quiet and his sleep.

Now he was gone, forever.

Dead a second time with no chance of revival. Constantine too, her very best friend for so many years. How she would miss him, miss his slow blinking eyes, his funny little head that poked out all stretchy and crinkled and darted into his shell at the first sign of danger.

Gone, nothing but memories left.

"I should have seen it coming," said Letje, turning to Marcus who was stood beside her.

"You can't be everywhere, do everything Letje. Some things just take a natural course, happen. As they should."

"Natural? You call forcing your mind into a tortoise natural," spat Letje, venomous words she didn't mean. "I'm sorry, it's not your fault. I just don't want him to be gone."

"Well, I would imagine that he hung on as long as he could, stayed with you until he thought you were safe, happy, had friends around you. He did very well, living side by side with the mind of Constantine for so long. That's difficult to do you know? Stay yourself when you have the mind of the animal you are inhabiting always trying to revert to its natural state."

"I know, I just thought... that he'd be here forever."

"Nothing, absolutely nothing, lasts that long. Apart from The Void."

"Hey guys, you finished with your little chat? Oh." Arcene stared at Letje, stared at Marcus, and then focused on the listless body of Constantine held in Letje's lap delicately, limp and clearly no longer a part of their unusual family.

"I found it," said Fasolt, coming out of one of the storage cupboards with a small tin held aloft like a mighty prize. "Oh. Oh no. I'm so sorry Letje, so sorry."

"Thank you. I think I probably knew deep down, knew he wasn't the same as he had been so quiet. He usually liked to offer his opinion even when it wasn't asked for." Letje smiled at the thought of her father always trying his best to guide her, even when she didn't want him to.

She was alone now, the last of her family gone.

"We're your family Letje," said Fasolt, "you aren't alone."

Arcene crouched down and gave Letje a hug, then kissed Constantine on his shell and then just sat there by the fire with Letje, the family now one member smaller.

~~~

"You can get rid of it you know?" said Marcus.

"What?" said Letje, forehead creasing, her hair shifting.

"The pain, the sadness. Even the memory of it happening."

"You mean like Sy did? Forget he was ever here, that my father died?"

"If you want, yes," said Marcus kindly.

"No, I don't want that, I want to remember. It's what happens, what's supposed to happen, right?"

Marcus nodded slowly. "It is. Life, then death. The way of all things."

"Right, and if I forgot? Then I would remember him dying years ago. He would still be gone, only it wouldn't be true, would it?"

"It would be for you, but no, not really."

"Have you forgotten? Have you taken away memories of death and being sad and losing those you felt love for?"

"Well, that's impossible to answer isn't it? How would I know? But I don't think so, no. I remember so much death and sadness Letje, losing so much, those I loved more than anything else in the world."

"As the other Marcus' you mean?"

"Yes and no. I, this Marcus, I had more than my fair share of loss before The Commorancy ever came into being, and much more as it was constructed, more than you could imagine. I had sisters, a mother, a family, and I have lost those I loved in the most terrible of ways, and I remember it all. I don't want to forget."

"Neither do I. But thanks Marcus, and I'm sorry."

"What for?"

"For your sadness."

"Well, that's part of life isn't it? You can't be happy if you have never been sad. How would you know joy if sorrow never clutched at your heart?" Marcus stepped forward after Letje stooped and picked up a handful of dirt and dropped it onto the duffel bag that had been Constantine's portable home for so long. Arcene and Fasolt did the same. Fasolt turned to Letje and nodded inquiringly, Letje nodded in return and Fasolt shoveled the excavated dirt back into the hole that now contained the body of the tortoise and the memory of family and friendship.

"Love you Daddy. Love you Constantine. I'll miss you."

Arcene grabbed hold of Letje's hand and squeezed it tightly. Letje smiled at her and said, "Come on, lets go celebrate the life and times of Constantine Alexander III. He was a great tortoise, a great friend, and for a while he was a great Daddy too."

"You bet," said Arcene. "Do you remember the time he ate all that chocolate even though he knew it wasn't good for him in his tortoise body? Pooey, that was one stinky mess to clear up."

"I remember," said Letje smiling. "But who cleared it up?"

"Well, yeah, you did. But it was gross Letje," protested Arcene, "oh so gross."

"True, it was a bit whiffy wasn't it?"

They chatted away about their lost loved one as they made their way back to the kitchen. Letje felt the absence of her friend and father deeply, but knew there would be little time to mourn the loss. More than anything she was thankful for the extra time she had with a man that should have died years ago but clung to existence just so he could watch out for his precious daughter. How she had changed since that day, and how she would change in the future.

Letje stopped and turned as Fasolt shoveled the last of the pile of dirt. "Bye Daddy, love you. Always."

Screeee.

Bird sucked the air from the sky and landed on Letje's shoulder with an absence of sound that never ceased to be disconcerting. It was as if the ancient eagle sucked away the quiet, drawing a deep silence in his wake, quieter than quiet, more than an absence of sound. He broke it with another call to Letje and stared at her with pale eyes that had seen so much. He nibbled gently at her ear, offering his condolences. The understanding was there, the loss of family was something Bird knew about all too well.

"Hello my friend. You have been away a lot lately haven't you?" Letje tickled his foot just above a huge talon that was more than capable of slitting the throat of a human in a single slice if he so chose.

He was Letje's friend.

Bird stared at Marcus.

Marcus stared at Bird.

There was nothing more to be said.

Bird had seen too much to be surprised by any of the meaningless games of man.

Marcus looked to the sky and smiled at the silhouettes of the ever-growing family that had made The Commorancy their home. They would decorate the sky long after Marcus was no longer even a memory and the buildings crumbled to dust.

Bird and Family

Bird had moved his home from The Sacellum once Varik was gone and once his chick was fully fledged. He and his mate, and his expanding family, had set up occupancy in one of the largest of the many peculiar trees that were dotted around the grounds of The Commorancy.

It was like finally coming home.

Bird loved his new, and hopefully permanent abode. He spoke to the strange tree that wasn't forced into unnatural shapes like the one at The Sacellum, but rather had been given the option and was more than happy to oblige the man that had planted it and given it a tiny piece of The Noise to help it grow strong and big and allow occupants to spend time in its strange interior, if it wanted.

Bird was at one with his home, knowing that as he came and went from the nest atop the tree the games of man played out slowly in the vast empty spaces that made up its interior. People coming and going through the ages, the tree showing him of their play.

Bird cared little for that, but Bird cared greatly for his companion, another majestic eagle with a striking white stripe across her slender head. Now there was also a rather extensive family — his young growing large and proud as they filled up more and more of the sky above The Commorancy. Ever since the first year that Bird had brought his then small family to the peace and safety of The Commorancy their chicks had flourished. Food was plentiful, there were no extended — and forced — trips away from his new home, and each new brood survived and grew ever stronger.

So far none of his chicks had shown signs of being like him, but he didn't mind. Bird knew that as the years went by and the family grew ever larger, then at some point the newborns would become more than just graceful creatures of the sky. They would Awaken, like him.

For now he was content to merely have a family and know that they were Whole. Not a single one would succumb to The Lethargy — they would remain Whole and live out natural lives of grace and beauty.

He sometimes thought of how fleeting their lives would be, as already his oldest was showing signs of maturity as it finally became an adult after more than five years. It's life would be so short though, just like its mother's; forty years at most. But bird wasn't too sad about it, this was the way things were meant to be.

Lives lived then gone, back to The Nothingness where everything came from.

But now was an exiting time, for a new batch of chicks were about to hatch, and Bird knew, on an instinctive level, that inside one of the three large pale gray brown spotted eggs there was something special stirring, ready to break free first and gradually grow to be even larger than him. Awoken and immensely powerful.

His dynasty had begun and he saw a bright future for his species that now thrived even in the milder UK climate rather than its native Australia.

Bird was happy.

Bird was home.

Bird had a family.

Bird had a friend.

Existence was joyous.

He had a legacy.

When it Happened

"That's him, there. See? Bright red hair, very smart, nice posture. He was a bit of an odd one actually, but in a nice way. But there was something, well, I couldn't put my finger on it and he had a Room, but he was the first person I kind of changed my mind about at the last minute. By then it was too late. Artek."

Letje and Arcene peered over Marcus' shoulder. He and Arcene had been glued to the monitors for days now. Letje had been next to useless, unable to bring herself to contribute much, the final death of her father threatening to pull her down into a permanent depression. But life went on, there were important matters to attend to, and she finally got herself together after giving herself a good talking to, reminding herself she was lucky that she had the extra years with her father even after she had already thought him dead once before. The truth was that it hadn't hit her as hard as it had the first time she had thought him dead —

losing the same parent twice meant that the second time was never going to be as heart wrenching as the first.

Still, it hurt. But she had responsibilities and there were more important things than her own sadness to deal with, so she had returned to The Room For Seeing What Was Happening to discover how Marcus and Arcene had been getting on.

For days they had trawled through footage from within The Commorancy, trying to see if events on the outside had been reflected internally. There was a lot of footage to go through even when fast-forwarded, but Marcus had been convinced that such a momentous thing as everyone somehow being taken was bound to be tied up to his home somehow.

Working with Arcene, he had tried to pin down just when it was that applications for Rooms had begun to wane, and then they worked back a number of years from that point, watching Orientation after Orientation, speeding through the years or decades of people locked in their Rooms, watching them Awaken, emerge, leave.

The more they viewed, the more obvious it became that many more than Marcus had realized had simply dropped off the face of the planet some time after returning to the mainland. He had thought nothing of it, assuming they had simply moved location, gone off to live their lives with their new Awoken states driving them toward goals he knew little of any longer. But the scale of it meant that there was definitely something underhand happening somehow. One minute they were there, the next they were gone.

There was no sign of people being taken from the various live feeds dotted all over the country — people simply vanished. The cameras were sporadic at best in their functionality, and not really of that much use as the recordings could not possibly be kept indefinitely, so most of what had gone on out there was ancient history and there was no way of retrieving the deleted data.

But everything ever recorded within The Commorancy was kept. Records and digital archives spanning centuries were locked down and retrievable at a push of a button. So they focused their attentions on the Room that was designed to monitor activity inside The Commorancy.

They searched. And they searched, and eventually something jogged Marcus' memory.

Artek.

"This is the man we need to find," said Marcus, tapping the screen. Letje and Arcene peered closely at the rather formal looking man. Handsome, immaculately dressed, and with a rather bizarre hairstyle, bright red hair cut into a very straight bob, not a hair out of place.

"How do you know it's him though?" asked Letje. "And why would he do whatever it is that he's doing anyway?"

"I don't know why, or how, but I do have a feeling it has something to do with him, so we must find him."

"Yes, but why do you think he has anything to do with it? What's the connection?"

Marcus and Arcene explained what they had been up to, that they traced back the beginning of when things appeared to have got a bit strange — Letje couldn't help stifling a laugh over their choice of words — and looked back over the guests that had been there before the disappearances had begun, or when they thought they had at least. When Marcus saw Artek he simply said that he knew the man was involved, but had no idea why.

"We can at least go to his home and see if he's there. I picked him up, I know where he lives, or lived. If nothing else then it's worth a look, it could be a lead, it could be the answer."

Letje felt that there was something she wasn't being told, that there was more to this than Marcus was telling. Why this man? Why would he have anything to do with it? Why would it have anything to do with people that stayed at The Commorancy?

"Okay Marcus, I think you owe me, us, an explanation. Something isn't fitting right here, you're holding out on us and I know it. Don't try to deny it. Why on earth would this man be the one responsible for taking people and doing who knows what to them?"

"Okay, I guess I should be a little clearer, but it's him, I'm sure of it."

~~~

When Fasolt arrived back in the kitchen after Letje let him know about the meeting through The Noise and he was up to date on events thus far, Marcus tried to explain just what had led to his conclusions.

"I know this is going to sound odd, but he's the middle." Marcus got nothing but blank faces so continued. "I met Artek when he was twenty seven years old, and he stayed here for only two years. He left about a hundred and twenty or thirty years ago, and was born right about a century and a half after The Lethargy first became known. It's not exact, I may be out by a bit, I'd have to check his records properly, unless Arcene remembers from the time-stamps on the recordings?"

"Sorry, we saw so many, I'd have to check too," said Arcene.

"Okay, never mind for now. But look, he's like the crux, the mid-point for us all. Well, for The Commorancy anyway. He was born almost half way between its inception and now."

"Give or take, what? Ten twenty, or more years," said Fasolt dubiously.

"Well, yes. But Fasolt, you more than anyone should know when something simply feels right. That you just know." Marcus took off his felt hat and scratched the corner of his eye, ripples of red blowing across the pupil like dust in the desert.

Fasolt merely nodded.

"It's more than that. We've checked, me and Arcene, and guests began to dwindle not long after Artek left."

"How long after?" asked Letje.

"About ten or twenty years, it's not easy to pinpoint exactly, it was never linear by the looks of it," said Arcene. "Some decades were much busier than others, it seemed to go in waves."

"Right," said Marcus. "But there is definitely a downward trend not long after he left."

"What, you mean as Varik and The Eventuals really began to gain ground and more people joined his church?" Letje didn't understand how Marcus was jumping to conclusions in the way he was.

"Okay, maybe that's true, but it still doesn't explain one thing."

"Which is...?"

"I tried to impress him."

Letje just raised an eyebrow, not seeing the connection.

"Look, not to boast or anything, and no offense to Fasolt either, but you do know who I am, right? You live here, have seen what I created? I never, ever, ever try to impress people just because I want them to like me, but that's what I did with this man. Sure, I have tried to impress people countless times, it's part of the whole experience, part of the mythology, the whole thing, but this was different. I wanted him to like me even though I wasn't actually sure I liked him or even wanted him to have a Room."

It took a while but finally it seemed like the man, Artek, was really somebody a little unique. Impossibly self-assured, confident bordering on arrogant, but always polite and deferential. For some reason he couldn't explain Marcus had doubts about him after he was given his Room, but by then it was too late. Yet however much he tried to impress on them how somehow different the man was there was still a problem.

Letje spoke for them all. "Marcus, we understand, we do, but all of this, the man, it still doesn't give any explanation as to why you think he has something to do with people disappearing."

"Because he was too much like me, I suppose. I saw it in him, saw what was possible, but there was something missing. His one true desire was to Awaken and to continue his family line, ensure they remained Whole, maybe Awoke themselves, but there was more to it than that. I see that now. He wanted to be great, to be better than he was, better than everyone, better than me. Looking back at it I suppose the best way I could explain it would be to say that he believed he should be King, and had a right to it too. He wanted it all; to be the best at everything. He felt he deserved anything that he wanted."

"Okay, well, we haven't got anything else to go on yet, so let's go take a look at where he lived, at least then it will feel like we are doing something. Agreed?"

"Oh yes, I'm looking forward to it. You left me behind last time so I'm definitely coming this time." Arcene was jittery with excitement, she looked like she would happily run out the front door that very moment.

"You came to The Sacellum didn't you?" said Letje.

"Yeah, but not when you went in the hot air balloon and did more traveling."

"Hmm, okay. Anyway, as if we could do it without you. But calm down, we need to actually have some kind of plan in place first," said Letje, trying to slow down her very impetuous friend.

Don't Forget

Snick.

The door closed behind Artek and he was alone in his Room. Finally, he'd done it. He smiled to himself at his cunning and his intelligence, surprised at just how easy it was to have gotten access to such a sought after position.

But here he was, ensconced in the safety of The Commorancy, in a Room purpose built just for him, designed to allow him to become truly Awoken and go back out into a world that was sure to be even more ravaged than it was when he left.

Sitting down after unbuttoning his jacket, Artek swept a hand through his perfect hair and closed his eyes.

Let the games begin.

~~~

"Hello Marcus, how are you?"
"What are you doing?"

"Excuse me?"

"I said what are you doing? Why are you here, outside of your Room?" Marcus was somewhat flustered. He never got flustered. He'd run from the peace of The Peaceful Room after that damn Annoying Klaxon Sound had gone off and his tablet told him that a door that ought not to have been opened had actually been opened. By Artek.

As he made his way to the exit of Artek's Room he ran through in his head the timeline that should have been followed and how it could have changed. It was unheard of, never before in the almost two centuries of guests had a single one ever left their Room before it was their time. Marcus always knew when it was their time — he monitored his guests closely. The automated systems, countless sensors hidden in their Rooms, and other precise equipment, kept him up-to-date constantly on their progress with everything from heart rate, weight, fitness, their sleep patterns, their Awoken state and even complex brainwave patterns that allowed him to pinpoint almost exactly when it was right for them to leave their Rooms.

He had never been wrong. The door simply wouldn't open until he told it to. It was how things worked. He was in charge.

As he made his way to the exit door Marcus checked the systems on his tablet and there was no doubt about it, the door had opened. Artek had opened it.

"Have I done something wrong?" asked Artek, staring at Marcus with an innocence that made his guilt all the more apparent. "I felt it was time to leave so I tried the door."

"You tried the door? Even though the door didn't tell you it was time for you to open it? You just turned the handle and it opened, is that what you're trying to tell me?" Marcus could see the power that Artek now had, his aura glowing purple, flashing off from his body in all directions: phosphorescent yet definitely wrong somehow.

This man was powerful, more powerful than Marcus had expected him to be; than he should be. Everything Marcus had found out about the man pointed toward his Awakening being generous, but nowhere near to the level that it was now apparent he had ascended to. He would never be like Marcus, or many others that had been guests, but he definitely possessed something just a little different. Marcus didn't know what it was, yet it was his generosity and drawing out of the man's latent power in The Noise that had Awoken him and whatever it was that he now possessed.

"Well, not quite, no. I must confess I sort of made it open, I felt it was time." Artek smiled sweetly at Marcus.

Marcus wanted to punch him in the face. Actually just punch him and mess up his hair and make him wear a different colored shirt, and put some meat on his bones and stop standing like he was on parade and... Wow! When was the last time he felt like this about somebody? What was more annoying was that there was no rational explanation for feeling quite so angry about the man's personal appearance. For breaking The Rules, yes, but Marcus was old and wise enough to know that this was something different — personal. He really didn't like this guest of his one little bit any more.

He wanted him gone.

"Follow me," said Marcus, glaring at Artek over his shoulder as he walked away. He heard the precise footsteps of Artek behind him, confident strides that *clack, clack, clacked* on the flagstones.

What an annoying sound. It grated on his nerves and sent his heart rate up. He wanted to rip the legs off the man and stuff his feet in his mouth and tell him to stop having such an irritating walk.

Something was seriously amiss, you couldn't get that annoyed about how somebody moved their legs, surely?

~~~

"I forgot. Damn, that was what I couldn't see in him, the thing that made him different when he exited his Room early. He has the power to make people forget."

"What? But you said earlier that you remembered how you felt when you gave him his Room, what he was like and your doubts. How could you just forget he came out early?"

Marcus scratched his head. "I don't know. His gift once he Awoke, that was his focus I assume, what he really went in there for. Maybe. Who knows?"

"Well that's not a great deal of help Marcus, but I suppose it's a start. But why are you remembering now, after all this time?" A lot of things weren't making much sense to Letje at this point.

"Probably as I am thinking of him again properly, seeing him on those old recordings. It jogged my memory I guess."

There was a problem though, a glaring one to Letje. She wondered how long it would take for Marcus and Arcene to realize.

She waited.

"Hey," said Arcene, "but that wasn't on the recordings was it? Him leaving early?"

Marcus thought for a minute then replied. "No, which means I assume he somehow managed to get it deleted. Maybe I did it, you know, one of me?"

"Which means..." hinted Letje.

"That he can manipulate people into doing things, just like you can Marcus, you too Letje. Right?"

"I wouldn't put it exactly like that, but yes, I suppose you're right."

Letje was getting a seriously bad feeling about what a man like that could have been up to for over a hundred years with time to grow, hone his skills and powers. One thing was certain, if it was this man, or whoever it was, they had changed the timeline of the United Kingdom, and humanity, and it may just be irreversible. They simply had to find out where everybody was, however many that was anyway.

Letje felt like she was living on an empty planet, that she was amongst the last ever people to look up at the sky and thank The Void for the chance at a short but beautiful life.

"We need to go find him. Now."

"Well, you do," said Marcus, staring at Letje, then Arcene.

"What about you?"

"Oh, you won't need me, you have a new protector for your adventure. He'll be along any minute now."

"Ooh, surprises, I like surprises," said Arcene, staring at the door as if the mystery man would appear.

"I don't," said Letje.

New but Old

Marcus was in The Dangerous Room.

Exercise complete, he found himself in a very strange mood. He felt different to how he had expected. Emotions were mixed up and he didn't have his usual assured control over himself that was taken for granted

He had to accept that things were different now. All the time he had lived, the triple life, doing so many things, living so much, it all felt like a lie. It was impossible, yet he truly felt like this was the first time he himself had actually been in The Dangerous Room, which wasn't true. The other Marcus' had been in countless times, which meant he had. The memories were there, all of them, some more hidden than others, but he remembered. It was him.

Yet being here now? Actually having climbed and walked and landed and felt the lactic acid build? Well, it was different, yet that was impossible.

It was too subtle a thing to truly understand, yet the sensations were more real, vibrant and visceral. This was real.

The rest?

Some kind of a dream maybe? Where you lived the lives, thought of them as truly being you — that was how it should have been — yet when it came down to it those experiences paled in the face of the reality of actually truly, really, physically living the life yourself.

What actually constituted experience and memory? Nobody could ever pinpoint that. Marcus had lived through so much, seen so many things, always believing it was as much his experience as it was his doppelgangers', but true physical living through experience was, when all was said and done, just more real. Edgy. Meaningful.

Marcus looked back over the lives he had lived, wondering at the state of his mind. He had lived a life in this body for over three hundred years, all of that felt real, just like the other lives, but somehow this felt different, like the sharpness of reality had been turned up, the dial swiveled, making the world buzz and hum a little louder, the life-forces that made up everything vibrating a little faster, carrying more energy, bringing the world into stark clarity, a veil finally lifted to reveal just how glorious and how downright intimate it was to be a part of the whole that made up his small slice of the UK, the planet, the entire Universe.

He liked it.

He was the same person though. He'd left behind one part of The Commorancy now he had been released, but a life had been lived. He had never been bored, merely spending the time exploring The Noise, surpassing by a large margin the other Marcus' when it came to powers and knowledge. He had theirs too, they never had his. So how come he felt like he had just Awoken to find the contrast turned up and everything ramped up into high definition?

People. Company, chatter and emotions flying through the air carried on energy waves that effected, enhanced, changed everything, making the world come alive.

You had to be there, to truly be there, however much you thought you were. The conclusion he had to come to was that it simply was not the same as physically being present and experiencing the interaction with others on a firsthand basis.

Marcus had fooled himself.

The others? Well, they had never known any different. Maybe they felt as he feels now? After all, they were linked together totally, sharing everything. Maybe it diluted a little by the time such experiences made their way to him?

"Ugh, does it matter? The main thing is that you are home now Marcus, truly home, truly alive. And how it hurts." A tear fell like a star dying in The Void and Marcus pulled the knife from out of his leg. He watched with interest as the wound closed and the tissue healed. The pain had been exquisite, the sensation awakening him to the true depths of his new existence.

He really had come home. Resurrected from a life of loneliness he never even knew had existed, to be born once more into a world full of hurt, pain, emotional instability and a life full of infinite possibilities.

"Time to play," said Marcus, smiling happily, eyes flickering madly through the spectrum like a picture book full of pages of colors, turned at speed by the hands of a happy child.

"I'm a new me, free to run The Commorancy for a while, then who knows? I guess I will just have to wait and see. Once the timeline is back on track then there is no end of possibilities. But people, there must be people. Otherwise what's the point?"

Marcus was looking forward to a new life once more. He hadn't realized until now that he simply hadn't been living and experiencing fully all that the gift of life really offered if you just stopped and let it show itself, rather than moving through a precious life in a haze of pre-occupation and semi-awareness.

~~~

Marcus was young again. His thoughts drifted back, unraveling the centuries like peeling back the skin of that most rare of fruits now: a delicious banana.

He felt the years stripped away, the madness recede, the knowledge, power, brutality and dogged determination all faded to nothing more than a future possibility that was one of many outcomes for the boy — for that was what he was — that had Awoken to find himself one of only a few people left that wasn't going to slowly succumb to The Lethargy and be dead inside a year or two.

He was home. Back in a semi-detached house in a nondescript town as the world fell into sadness and apathy around him, closing in on itself. The autumn for humanity, winter just around the next blind corner.

As Marcus sat naked and joyous in The Vast Room For Growing Things, surrounded by the impossible, now taken all to easily for granted after the madness of centuries piled one on top of the other, he let himself slide between the gaps of his life and watch from an impossible viewpoint as the young boy that he had once been sought answers to his existence while the world fell into an impossible state of indifference.

Marcus had known something had happened to him when he woke from a restless sleep, the dirty mattress and sparse furnishings of his room greeting him depressingly as he shifted beneath the never sufficient covers and wished life could have been different.

He got up, his skinny frame shivering with the cold, his teeth chattering. He should have gone scavenging for wood again, but it seemed like there was always too much to do to keep up with all the chores. He made a mental note to make staying warm and getting blankets a priority, no matter what he had to do to get them. Not that it would matter, nearly all the neighbors were either dead and rotting in their homes or so far gone with The Lethargy that they wouldn't notice if he took the clothes off their backs. Not that he would. But it was time to start getting out and making some kind of life for himself. He knew that his time at home was coming to an end even as he tried not to admit it.

He dressed quickly, wrapping a blanket around his coat-hanger frame, and padded downstairs wearing his battered Adidas. He always wore them in the house now. There was a time when his mum would have had a fit about the thought of dirt getting on her precious carpet, but those days were long gone.

Sighing, Marcus walked over to the static figure sat on the couch staring blankly at the hiss of the TV — the power must have come back on at some point in the night.

Here she is again, sat there, doing nothing. Marcus hated himself for thinking bad of his mum, it was just getting to him was all. He wasn't coping too well since she had finally given up. The year that she had taken to slide had been hard, terrifying and just so draining that he dreaded each and every day that lay before him.

He just wanted it to be over, for the release that was coming sooner or later; just not yet.

"Morning Mum, you want anything?"

Of course she didn't; she didn't even know who she was any longer. The last few months had been the worst of his life — it seemed that as he grew and became something more so she joined everyone else and became less than a person. The Lethargy had taken just about everything from him, from everyone else too. Families fell apart slowly and it was sickening. By the time the world had actually realized what was happening and that it wasn't just some kind of normal reaction to the stresses of everyday life, it was already a different world to the one Marcus had been playing in just a few years ago.

Heck, less than a year ago he could still walk down to the park and play football with whatever kids were there, but the last few times he went all that greeted him were empty fields, wild dogs, and not a single person. Nobody walking their pets, no kids having a kick-about, no mothers pushing their kids on the swings on the way home from collecting them from school. Well, there wasn't even school any more — no teachers.

The loneliness was terrible. Marcus Awoke, a name coined by the media for what was happening to him. The newfound abilities, and a sudden realization that The Noise was real, meant he could be a part of it — manipulate the minds of others, especially those with The Lethargy. The TV still came on now and then, no schedule, but sometimes there would be a bit of news, reports mostly local as international news was pretty much impossible. It stopped in the end though. Nobody could be bothered to organize such a complex things as sending a news program out, there weren't enough people without The Lethargy for such systems to be set into action.

So Marcus just stayed home, looked after his mum, and sought answers through The Noise. He knew he was destined for something special, and understood that there would be huge responsibilities that came with being something more than what the reporters had called Whole, although there weren't even many of them as far as Marcus understood it.

The kitchen was a mess, his fault really, he should be keeping on top of the chores but he just didn't have the energy.

Marcus nearly had a severe panic attack, cold sweat pricked his skin as he staggered against the sink. Did he have The Lethargy? Was he going to turn into a vegetable like everyone else? He shook like a wet dog, checking over his body for signs. Would he know? How could you?

No, he was just tired, just run down and stressed out. Everything had fallen apart. He'd lost his sisters, there they were buried in the back garden, the mounds still too fresh for it not to hurt just standing there.

He didn't have The Lethargy, he'd just lost his family, couldn't bring himself to take care of the mundane, and needed to learn how to develop what was growing inside him like a cancer, eating away the child, turning him into something new, advanced, the next stage in human evolution. Not that he thought of it that way.

All Marcus knew was that he had to do something. It was too late for his sisters but he would save his mum, save those with The Lethargy, make somewhere safe and comfortable for himself, for everyone, do something worthwhile.

"Mum, mum, I've got an idea, guess what I'm..."

She was dead.

Marcus was alone.

He stepped out into the dirty and empty streets and began his new life.

~~~

Marcus smiled at the young boy back through the twists and turns of the centuries. It felt like watching the life of somebody else. It was a different world, in many ways a simpler one, at least for him. With age comes responsibility and its own kind of madness, but what he wouldn't give to go back and be a boy again, his sisters squabbling in their bedroom, his mum telling him off for bringing dirt into the house and making him do his homework before he went skipping off down the street to play in the park and promised to be home before it got dark.

"Love you mum, love you little sisters. If you could see your big brother now."

Marcus wondered what they would think, would they still call him beanpole and try to kiss him as they knew it made him embarrassed in front of his mates? Or would they look at him and not even recognize the man he had become?

Would he even recognize himself?

He was afraid of the answer.

Gamm Returns

Gamm was in two minds about even returning to The Commorancy. He knew that if he did he would be caught up in the madness. One part of him wanted nothing more than to stay at his home and continue his quiet life, the other was already feeling edgy at the silence and the boredom — itching for an adventure.

Who was he kidding? He wanted to do something epic, crazy, fun, maybe even frightening, and besides, whatever had happened to the nuns, along with everyone else, well, it had to be dealt with. If he was one of only a few people actually left out in the country fending for themselves then he owed it to the others, wherever they were, to try to help if he possibly could.

So he went back.

~~~

"Gamm!" shouted Arcene excitedly, hugging him tightly like they were best friends.

"Hey Arcene, how are you? Any news since I was last here?"

"Oh boy, you wouldn't believe what happened." Arcene stared up at Gamm encouragingly, frowning when he said nothing. "Well?"

"Well what?"

"Aren't you going to guess?"

"Um, well, okay. Did you find out where everyone is?"

"Ha, no, not quite. But I got really told off for talking to a man who I didn't know, probably the person stealing all the people, and I heard a story about an ant, and Letje was resurrected and dreamed of butterflies and whales and Letje's father died so we buried him and Marcus was resurrected too. He has been here all along, well, one of him, but you mustn't tell anyone, and now we are all going to go and find the people. You got some clues didn't you? Can you tell me, I think that—"

"Whoa! I think maybe we should start this again from the beginning, don't you? Let's go find everyone else and then maybe you can explain it all. But he's really alive? Marcus?"

"Oh yes, and you should see his eyes, they keep changing color like he's full of magic or something." Arcene beckoned Gamm to crouch down and whispered in his ear, "I think he is actually a bit mad. Don't tell him though."

"I won't, promise. How is he still alive though?" Gamm's head was reeling. If Arcene was to be believed then things were definitely about to get very interesting. Well, he wanted an adventure, right? Looked like he was going to get one.

"C'mon, let's go meet the others. Letje's still sad though after Constantine died. I liked him, he was a lovely tortoise. Even if I did want to eat him once." Arcene dragged Gamm after her, taking him to a meeting that promised to be one of the more interesting encounters he had ever had.

~~~

A few hours later and things made sense, at least a little bit anyway. Gamm wondered if this was just normal for The Commorancy or if the confusion of events was more of a one-off, all tied in to the other, revolving around the disappearance of what seemed to be everybody apart from those still residing in their Rooms within The Commorancy.

Gamm's world had just been turned well and truly upside down. He had to admit that he was actually enjoying himself.

What he didn't quite understand was why Marcus and Fasolt were to stay behind and entrust him with looking after Arcene and Letje, or maybe it was the other way around and Letje was to look after him and Arcene? She was certainly far beyond him in terms of knowledge and implementation of what The Noise offered to those who were Awoken.

"So what do you think?" asked Marcus. His eyes really were very disconcerting.

"I think that it's a lot of responsibility but if everyone agrees then I'm not about to say no," said Gamm, looking from face to face for signs of anyone not thinking he was up for such a task.

"I know it's a big ask, and I am sure you have your doubts Gammadims, but one thing I know is that Letje is more than capable of looking after herself and—"

"Me too. I'm not a kid any more," said Arcene.

"Yes, thank you Arcene. As I was saying. And I am sure that Arcene will do exceptionally well too. You are as experienced out there," Marcus swept a hand out into the world, "as anyone, more so than the rest of us actually, so I think that you will be perfect for helping get to some kind of understanding of exactly what is going on. This is very important. We can't just have people being taken, or whatever has happened to them. The world is so fragile as it is, if we don't get these people back then our country will be desolate in a few generations. There simply won't be enough people to sustain us and what Varik wanted will be a reality. Extinction."

"This is why it's a little overwhelming, such a responsibility." Gamm was having a hard time talking to Marcus, he was too different, too otherworldly, and way too odd. Since he'd met the man just a few hours ago he was already on his third outfit — "Catching up on the larger choices," was how Marcus had explained it, as well as a rather intense recap on what had happened to him, how he happened to be there at all. Gamm didn't even want to think about such a life, it was too crazy, impossible really. His world was being turned on its head and he was having a hard time staying centered and in control. The last thing he wanted was to just be swept up in something where he couldn't stay on top of things — think and act rationally.

"And you're not coming? You or Fasolt? Is that wise?"

"I think it's for the best, although it's crucial we find the people it's also crucial The Commorancy stays protected." Letje had been shocked at Marcus' suggestion that he stay, but it did make sense.

"Letje's right Gamm. The Commorancy has certainly been in fine hands while under new management, but the simple truth is that I know this place better than anybody, and I will be able to protect it better. I know its quirks. Much as I am not keen on dealing with any form of Contamination, and I don't think there will be one, the most sensible thing from an objective point of view is that myself and Fasolt stay to ensure that our guests, and who knows, they may be all that is left, are protected and there is always somebody here who can run The Commorancy if anything should happen to you."

It seemed odd to Gamm, but then it did make sense. At least he and Letje going to try to find the truth. Arcene was a different matter entirely.

"What?" Arcene squirmed in her chair, Gamm hadn't realized he had been frowning at her.

"Um, nothing. Well, okay, I should say it. No offense Arcene but you're still very young, and also... well, somewhat impetuous. Some would even say naughty. I can see it." Gamm hoped he wasn't causing too much offense.

"Well, let's look at it from Arcene's point of view shall we?" said Marcus. "First," he ticked off the reasons on his fingers, "I know for a fact she won't stay even if we tell her too." Arcene nodded in agreement. "Second, she is, at least partly, responsible for what has happened. She has been talking to Artek I assume, and so is at least involved in whatever it is that has happened. And third, she has grown up a lot and will be of assistance I assure you."

"And don't forget," said Arcene, trying to ignore the bit about blame, it seemed to Gamm, "that I am a great fighter now, and strong too." It was true, Arcene had spent more and more time in The Fighting Room (Simulated Meat) and had become a bit of a whirlwind when it came to hand to hand combat. When Letje had seen just how skilled she was with a sword she had been shocked.

"Well, alright then. If we are agreed?"

"Good," said Marcus. "Now, if you will excuse us for a while, I need to go over a few things, get up-to-date on a few changes," Marcus looked disapprovingly at Letje and Arcene, "that seem to have happened that don't follow strict protocol, and then we should start to formulate a proper plan for this expedition."

Marcus ushered Letje and Arcene out of the door and Gamm was left alone with Fasolt, who had been very quiet up until now. Gamm wondered what he had to say.

"I don't like this. Young girls shouldn't be doing this kind of thing."

"Well, from what I've heard they dealt with an awful lot before you all returned here five years ago," said Gamm.

"Yes, you're right," sighed Fasolt. "But at least they are safer if they stay here. They are very special young women and I like them kept close."

"Don't worry Fasolt, I shall protect them and they shall protect me, we will be fine. And one way or another we will discover just what has happened. Was Marcus telling the truth, that people will die out if The Commorancy is all that is left?"

"He was being over-optimistic I am afraid, the situation is a lot worse than he led you to believe."

Fasolt told Gamm the truth of the numbers of people currently residing in The Commorancy. Gamm realized just how empty the country would soon be unless they managed to find, and free, those that must have been taken. Why? Well, hopefully they would find out soon enough.

Polterwhat?

"Can I keep it, can I, can I?" Arcene was ten again, at least acting like it anyway.

"Are you mad? Look at it, it's bigger than you." Letje stared at the giant creature, wondering just how it was possible for it to be so huge. It looked like it could probably eat Arcene whole and still have time for the main course — which would probably be Letje by the looks of those gleaming teeth that were right now bared as it backed away, lithe muscles rippling beneath the surface.

"Come on, let's get out of here before it eats us for lunch." Letje grabbed Arcene and pulled her by the arm but she held her ground and refused to move.

"It's sweet, look at it's lovely head. I bet it wants a biscuit or something."

Letje couldn't believe what she was hearing. Was Arcene stood in front of the same beast as her? It looked anything but sweet and definitely looked like it wanted more than just a biccie. The giant creature moved, guarding its collection of stolen items, the poltergeist problem solved. "We should go Arcene, it's very dangerous."

"No. I like it, I always wanted one. Look, she just wants a cuddle, I'm sure."

"Are you serious? A cuddle? It's as big as you and a lot more scary. Come on." Letje tugged but Arcene still refused to move.

Woof.

The deep bark echoed around the small space, almost deafening them. Letje jumped in front of Arcene and was just about to enter the impossibly large creature's mind and try to take control when Marcus barged through the door.

"Oh. Ah... Hello there you. Gosh, I thought for a minute there was something wrong."

Letje thought she must be the only one that hadn't gone stark raving mad. She stared at Marcus in the gloom, guessing he had finally cracked. "Have you seen it? It's probably going to eat Arcene."

"Don't be silly, it's just Lilla. That's Danish for purple."

Yep, he'd definitely gone mad. "Um, I know it isn't very bright in here but that dog is blue, well, gray really, definitely not purple. And can we leave please?"

"Haha, it's a long story. But honestly, she's nothing to worry about."

"What is it? It's so big."

"It's a Great Dane, a blue one. Well, that's what they were called once. I managed to get it really rather blue/gray don't you think? They came from slim ones from Denmark crossed with the English Mastiff, and that's where I started."

"For pets?" asked Letje, incredulous.

"Oh no, for security. I thought I could breed some aggression into them, but it didn't work. I ended up stopping the breeding program and just letting them live at The Commorancy. There are proper fierce ones now to protect us, as you well know Letje."

"Yeah, thanks for that Marcus. It's been the one job I hate, trying to keep them under control." Letje dreaded having to deal with the very large, although not by this dog's standards, and very vicious wild dogs that roamed certain parts of The Commorancy, always ready to be unleashed on any uninvited guests — the same as the ones that now lived totally wild on the rest of the island.

"Arcene, be careful," shouted Letje, reaching out for her but it was too late. Arcene was crouched down, the dog dominating her, her hands around its neck, the dog licking her wildly and wagging its tail dementedly.

"See, she's a big old softy. Aren't you eh? You are so warm. Come and feel Letje, she's as soft as a bunny."

Marcus nodded at her and for the first time Letje looked at the dog with senses she should have used from the beginning. It was no threat, that was obvious now. In fact it didn't have a dangerous bone in its body.

The mind was nothing but fluffy and warm, gentle and caring, above all else it was lonely.

"They are a very loving breed," said Marcus. "She probably got out from where I have been living. I wondered where she'd got to. She's the last of her line, the last puppy born, aren't you Lilla my little beauty?"

The dog wagged excitedly and bounded over to Marcus almost knocking Arcene over in its excitement.

"Whoa there girl! I've told you before, you have to be careful; you don't know your own strength."

Lilla sat and hung her head until Marcus gave her a tickle under her chin and it seemed to set her off again into a frenzy of wagging, licking and general chaos. She ran over to Letje, gave her a fly-by lick then bounded onto her bed and started licking Letje's missing scarf.

"Ah, she just wants a fuss and some love, don't you girl?" Arcene rolled over onto her back and began wiggling her legs in the air. Lilla jumped on top of her and began licking her manically.

"Well, at least we know who's been stealing the things," said Letje, unable to stop herself from smiling, as much as anything just happy to see Arcene enjoying herself and admitting that it did lighten her until now still somewhat dark mood since her father passed.

Marcus flipped a switch and the tiny space, a cubby-hole more than anything else, was bathed in warm white light. Letje got a proper look at the dog for the first time.

It stood at least four feet tall at its back, had the dopiest grin on its face — not in the least bit threatening — and its short fur was a strange kind of gray that shone almost blue under the gentle lighting. Yet it wasn't a perfect coat, its left eye had a large white patch around it, giving it an endearing quality that simply made you want to smile. But it was incredibly large. And, as the antics continued, obviously very playful.

"How old is she?" asked Letje.

Marcus did a quick mental calculation. "A little over one now, fourteen months just about."

"Oh boy."

~~~

Letje could tell that she had absolutely no say in the matter, Lilla was staying. It was as if the dog and Arcene were meant to be together; already they were inseparable. It was a bizarre sight — Lilla walking by Arcene's side, constantly turning to check what she was doing, her head almost at the same height as the fifteen year old's shoulder, Arcene's hair repeatedly tickling the dog's snout.

Lilla's huge droopy jowls were constantly dripping saliva and her ears obviously had a mind of their own — they were the most expressive ears Letje had ever seen. The dog walked with a huge swinging gait, the massive pads almost as large as a mans feet. Arcene talked to the dog non-stop, whispering away at all the

353

fun things they were going to do and telling Letje how great Lilla would be at tracking down all the lost people.

When Letje told her not to be silly Marcus had interrupted her and said that actually Lilla was an exceptional tracker, and that was probably how she had managed to find her way to them, even if she had been naughty and hidden, probably as she knew she wasn't supposed to have left her home with Marcus. But she craved human company and couldn't help herself. The result? She had a new best friend with as much energy as her.

"But don't you want to keep her with you Marcus? She's your dog." Prompted Letje hopefully.

"Well, I think we can both safely agree that Lilla has found a new owner, and besides, Lilla obviously wants to protect Arcene. She knows that she is the youngest so probably just relates to her more. She understands I'm rather old and can take care of myself."

"Yippee. Did you hear that Little Er?"

"No, it's Lilla. Leel as in peel. Uh as in luck."

"Oh, right," said Arcene happily. "I think I'll just call her Leel. What do you think Leel?"

Leel wagged excitedly, seemingly willing to be called anything Arcene wanted.

"What?" spluttered Marcus, you can't just change her name and—"

"Leel. Leel, come on girl," shouted Arcene over her shoulder, running down the corridor, Lilla, now Leel, bounding after her excitedly.

Letje smiled. "Looks like you can change her name after all."

"Hmm. Guess so. Oh well, as long as they're happy, that's the main thing."

~~~

"Whoa, that is one very large dog," said Gamm, backing up into a corner of the kitchen as Leel approached him, sniffing the air then staring at his legs and sniffing up his entire body.

"She's called Leel," said Arcene happily, "and I get to keep her. Isn't she great?"

"Well, I guess so, she sure is big. Um, good girl, good girl." Gamm patted Leel on the head gently, the huge dog slobbering all over his trousers then rubbing her jowls into his hand. "Ugh, um, right, go see Arcene, there's a good doggie." Gamm cleaned his hand under a tap as Leel looked at Arcene and ran over when Arcene slapped her thighs with her hands.

"She's going to come with us, isn't she Letje?"

"Well, we haven't discussed it yet have we?"

Arcene did her best sad face and it wasn't long before it was obvious to Letje and Gamm that there was no way that they could leave without taking Arcene's new guardian angel with them.

"I think she really likes you Gamm," said Arcene, as once again Leel began sniffing him enthusiastically.

"Yeah, I think you may be right. She is a nice looking dog I suppose, just big. Very, very big. Hey!"

Leel bounded around the kitchen, front paws darting excitedly up in the air like she was a cantering pony, happily munching on the piece of chicken Gamm was just about to eat.

"Leel! You bad doggie, where's your manners? You say sorry to Gamm." The effect was instant. The dog dropped the chicken, put its tail between its legs and skulked over to Gamm. She put her huge head in his lap and stared up at him with eyes so sad she looked like she was about to burst out crying on the spot.

"Oh, um, it's okay Leel, don't feel bad." He patted her on the head and she rumbled happily. A second later, chastising forgotten, she was happily running around again stealing anything that looked like fun or edible and bounding about with it, throwing clothes, food, anything in the air and having a great time.

"I think she's going to be a very obedient dog... with a bit of training," said Marcus, smiling as wide as everyone else.

"Isn't she? I think she is just the best thing. Ever." Arcene danced around with her new friend, singing silly rhymes and lost in an innocence it was easy to forget she still possessed.

"Oh boy," said Letje. Again.

Dreams of Dreams of...

Letje found herself in The Room For Big Showers, she was glad to get the dirt and grime of the search for people off of her, and wondered what they were going to do now...

~~~

"Anything?" asked Letje, pulling up a chair and sitting next to Arcene.

"Nope, nothing. It's getting seriously creepy now, like everyone has just vanished. Whoosh."

Letje leaned forward and peered at numerous screens; there were too many to count so she didn't even bother, but these were their eyes to the outside world...

~~~

"Well, that was a waste of time," said Arcene, piling food onto her plate.

"I wouldn't say that but it sure is good to be home, eh Fasolt?"

"Yes, this is home isn't it? Now more than ever I am grateful for that, and for you two young ladies too..."

~~~

"So what do you think?" asked Marcus. His eyes really were very disconcerting.

"I think that it's a lot of responsibility but if everyone agrees then I'm not about to say n—"

"Wait, stop!" shouted Letje.

"What? What's wrong?" Arcene looked terrified, it was obvious to Letje that she felt the change.

"What's going on?" said Gamm, his huge frame rising from the chair, ready to confront the danger.

"You feel it too?" asked Marcus.

"Yes, and you?"

"Definitely."

"That broke it, I think," said Fasolt.

"Letje, I don't like this," said Arcene. "What happened? Why did you shout? This isn't what's supposed to be happening now, we should be... Oh!"

Letje stared at everyone in turn, only Gamm seemed to be totally in the dark, but then, he hadn't been back for long, had he?

"So you get it then?" asked Letje, turning to Arcene. "This conversation isn't the one we had, is it?"

Arcene was lost in thought, struggling with something. "Ugh, I don't like this. It feels like we should be saying something else, but something we've already said."

"It's there alright," said Marcus, standing, then sitting straight back down again.

"We're going around in a loop here. We already had the conversation we were about to have, it's like I just forgot. How long has this been going on for I wonder? It's not just me is it?" Letje had a horrible feeling in her head, like the future had already played out a million times and she was just repeating actions already lost to the past eons ago.

"It's not just you," said Fasolt. "As soon as you broke the conversation it came flooding in — the disruption."

Marcus' eyes had turned a creamy white, pupils contracted to the size of pinheads, irises devoid of the shifting colors.

"Can somebody please tell me exactly what is going on here?" said Gamm, already showing signs that he was coming to the same understanding as everyone else.

"Me too," said Arcene. "This is starting to feel really creepy you know?"

Then everything just stopped.

Frozen.

It was as if Letje had pressed pause on reality and could wander around a snapshot of existence, passing through The Void, nothing was linear, just crossing from the spiral of time, jumbled like a ball of wool, infinite points touching each other, connecting past, present and future until none of it made any sense.

"Well? What do you think?" asked Marcus.

"Huh? Didn't you feel that?"

"Feel what?"

"I missed your conversation, everything froze, like I could move, nothing else could." Letje noticed Marcus' eyes were back to their crazed flickering and Leel was no longer in front of the fire but was now stood beside Arcene, who was on the other side of the Room, not where she had been a split second before reality and the rules it followed were made a mockery of.

Arcene was opening the window by the sink, which, of course, was not a normal sink, or window. How could it be in such a place?

"Why are you opening the window?" asked Letje.

"What? Am I?" Arcene turned the brass handle and the hidden cogs in the frame *clumped* as the whole side of the kitchen opened outward before then sliding back into the void in the ceiling.

Bird flew in and sat on the counter, staring at Letje, then at the dog.

"Okay, this is getting too weird, even for The Commorancy. Why do I get the feeling that none of this is real?"

"What do you mean Letje, of course it isn't real. You're sleeping, you're dreaming in The Room Of

Dreams. You were warned about that weren't you?" said Bird, head cocked to one side, now perched on the head of Leel who looked like she didn't like it one little bit. Blood began to pour down the huge head, a red river staining the white patch dark.

Arcene smiled down prettily at her companion's new baptism in blood, and Letje slipped out of time between the cracks once more, to a place that would swallow her up and spit out nothing but an empty vessel — the body of what was once Letje, for a short period of time the most powerful of women, no match for the life she had accepted as her destiny.

~~~

"Wake up, you did it again." Arcene's face was so close Letje could smell the onions she had eaten with her snack.

"Huh? Oh. I had the strangest of dreams. Bird was on Leel's head, Marcus was alive and Gamm was here then time froze and..."

"Hello Letje," smiled Marcus.

Letje shook her head to clear the confusion, slowly coming back to her reality. "How long was I out for?"

"Oh, just a minute or so, don't get upset. It's the residue of The Room Of Dreams, just let it wash over you without it going too deep, it will pass soon," said Marcus, motes of stars playing across his pupils.

"I told you not to go to that Room," scalded Fasolt, his hair rising from his head, streaming toward the ceiling as if gravity no longer applied to the ancient dreadlocks.

"Uh-oh, here we go again." Letje felt waves of nothingness wash over her. It started in her feet before they disappeared, tiny pieces of her skin taking flight as they broke into a million black butterflies, floating away where gravity no longer existed, passing through the ceiling out into the empty spaces. She looked down to see the absence of her body creeping inexorably upward. Piece by piece she was being drawn back into her impossible dream of things that were not meant to be a part of what it was to be a human being.

She welcomed the nothingness as she crashed to the floor.

On the Road Again

A fifteen year old girl with a spring in her step and a large dog bounding by her side. A woman in her early twenties yet impossibly old with knowledge. A Bird and a heavy-set man covered from head to toe in tattoos inflicted on him by miniature nuns — all leaving behind the last piece of hope humanity now had; all off to discover who had been stealing people and had left the country in desolation.

What could possibly go wrong? thought Gammadims, as he hefted his pack onto his broad back and strode purposefully out onto the high platform where the wind was whipping strongly and the air had a pleasant salt tang.

Just about everything, he thought sourly, before suppressing such dark thoughts and trying to just let life fill him with wonder. *At least you have company now Gamm, and a purpose. That's what you wanted, isn't it?*

Isn't that what we all want Gamm, some meaning to it all?

He stared at Letje, not surprised in the least that she knew what he was thinking.

"I guess you're right Letje. Wise words."

"Thank you," said Letje, patting him on the back and jumping up into the harness. "You ready?"

"As ready as I'll ever be," said Gamm.

"Haha, that's the spirit."

"Come on you two, we've got to go save the world," said Letje, smiling despite herself at the sight of Arcene and Leel playing like they didn't have a care in the world.

Oh boy, thought Gamm. *Oh boy*.

The Man who Would be King

"Come on, hurry up, we haven't got all day."

"Yes Mother, sorry."

Malessa Ligertwood stared scornfully at her son. Her short red hair, cut in a tight bob like her son's, accentuated the ethereal quality of her skin. Her eyes sparkled with all the joy of death. The hem of her tight fitting green dress teased the spotlessly clean floor as she turned and walked regally towards the stables. You couldn't trust those stupid little nuns for a second if they were left unsupervised, and the horses needed to be tended to properly if they were going to be going out again the following day.

No doubt her son would end up stood outside the vast stables preening himself, holding his nose like his olfactory senses were somehow different to everyone else's. They had work to do and this lazy boy of hers had better have instructed the help right — she wouldn't stand for shoddy work. Everything had to be perfect, just perfect. No disobedience and no mess, she wouldn't stand for it, she simply wouldn't.

Her country — it was very nearly all nice and neat, there were just a few more loose ends to tie up.

It wouldn't be long now though, soon everything would be just right, in its place, her subjects finally acknowledging their ruler, even if the boy did still have a lot to learn.

But first there needed to be a cleansing, she couldn't have genetic misfits running around out there as if they had a right to do so.

Oh no, that wouldn't do at all. Not at all.

The End

Author's Note

Sign up for The Newsletter for news of the latest releases as well as flash sales at Alkline.co.uk

Book 5 in the series is Desolation. Find a full list of titles at the author's Website.

Made in the USA
Charleston, SC
20 February 2016